Through My Eyes

Through My Eyes

Women of the Bible

DONNA HERBISON

AuthorHouse™
1663 Liberty Drive
Bloomington, IN 47403
www.authorhouse.com
Phone: 1 (800) 839-8640

Published by AuthorHouse 04/14/2015

ISBN: 978-1-5049-0497-1 (sc)
ISBN: 978-1-5049-0496-4 (e)

Library of Congress Control Number: 2015905029

Print information available on the last page.

This book is printed on acid-free paper.

Table of Contents

Eve

Looking back, it was all like a dream, though I know it all really happened that way. The first thing I remember was opening my eyes and seeing the most beautiful garden in the world. The greens were greener than anything I have seen since. Flowers were everywhere in every hue imaginable. The fruiting trees had both flowers and fruit at the same time. I knew the names of every single piece of vegetation, though I certainly can't remember them now. There was a lot of vegetation that I haven't seen since that awful day we left the garden, but I'll tell of that day later. I heard the sweet song of birds singing and the murmur of the brooks. Here and there were some of the animals and I knew their names too.

I quickly became aware of the presence of the LORD God. I really can't describe what he looks like and I'm sure I didn't see him in all his glory; I just knew immediately who he was. I was able to carry on a conversation with him too.

Then he took me to Adam. He was different from the animals I had seen. He was standing upright like I was. He was the same but different, taller than I, with a slightly, but definitely, different shape. The first words out of his mouth were, "This at last is bone of my bones and flesh of my flesh; and she shall be called Woman, because she was taken out of Man."

God had caused Adam to go into a deep sleep. He took one of Adam's ribs and fashioned me from it, then filled the space in Adam's side with flesh.

We were happy in those days. Yes, there were days, alternating periods of dark and light. There was a pleasant rhythm even of the temperatures, warm during daylight, somewhat cooler, but still comfortable, at night. Food was easy to get; we just walked up to the trees and helped ourselves to the fruits and nuts that grew there. Fruits and vegetables on bushes and vines were in their places and we knew where to dig for other varieties. There were fields rich with grain ready to pluck as we liked.

The animals too found their food easily. Many grazed on the grasses. Insects frequented the flowers, as did some of the birds. Other birds fed on the grains in the fields. Sometimes we would hand feed them. At that time we could get up close to all kinds of creatures, unlike now. Can you imagine trying, or even wanting, to get close to a lion these days?

The days were pleasant, every single one of them. Time existed but it wasn't important. I don't know how long our perfect life lasted, days or years or decades. But it was perfect, until THAT day.

Adam was in another part of the garden when the serpent approached me. He was different from the snakes we see today. For starters, there was no reason to fear him; he was a snake, no more, no less. I didn't think anything of it when he spoke to me, though it would certainly freak me out if any animal talked to me today. And he had legs; he was standing right in front of me when he spoke. Little did I know that it was Satan speaking through him.

"Did God actually say, 'You shall not eat of any tree in the garden?'" he asked.

"We may eat of the fruit of the trees in the garden, but God said, 'You shall not eat of the of the fruit of the tree that is in the midst of the garden, neither shall you touch it, lest you die.'" That was my first mistake. God had said don't eat of it but he didn't say anything about not touching it.

"You will not surely die," he said. "For God knows that when you eat of it your eyes will be opened, and you will be like God, knowing good and evil". Well, more knowledge sounded good to me. And the fruit did look tasty. So I tried some. Adam had just come over so I gave him some too.

Suddenly we were aware of our nakedness. Nothing was physically different; we had just not made anything of it before. We had more knowledge alright, but it was knowledge of things which we were better off not knowing. Trying to cover our nakedness, we sewed some fig leaves together and made loin cloths of them. It wasn't very much of a cover, and we knew God would be angry for at us for disobeying him, so when we heard the LORD God walking in the garden, we tried to hide in the trees.

But there is no hiding from God. He knew where we were and what we had done. He called out, "Where are you?"

I was too nervous and ashamed to speak. Adam replied, "I heard the sound of you in the garden, and I was afraid, because I was naked, and I hid myself."

"Who told you that you were naked?" said the LORD. "Have you eaten of the tree of which I commanded you not to eat?"

Adam put the blame on me, and blamed God for bringing me to him. "The woman whom you gave to be with me, she gave me fruit of the tree, and I ate."

I was too vain to accept the blame. "The serpent deceived me, and I ate."

The LORD said to the serpent, "Because you have done this, cursed are you above all livestock and above all beasts of the field; on your belly you shall go, and dust you shall eat all the days of your life. I will put enmity between you and the woman, and between your offspring and her offspring; he shall bruise your head, and you shall bruise his heel."

To me he said, "I will surely multiply your pain in childbearing, in pain you shall bring forth children. Your desire shall be for your husband, and he shall rule over you."

Finally, he turned to Adam. "Because you listened to the voice of your wife and have eaten of the tree of which I commanded you, 'You shall not eat of it,' cursed is the ground because of you; in pain you shall eat of it all the days of your life; thorns and thistles it shall bring forth for you; and you shall eat the plants of the field. By the sweat of your face you shall eat bread, till you return to the ground, for out of it you were taken; for you are dust and to dust you shall return." Then the Lord God made us more appropriate clothing out of animal skins. That was the first time something had to die for our sake.

We didn't die right away, but we no longer had the assurance of life going on as it had been. That was the end of our time in the garden. To make sure we didn't eat of the tree of life and live forever in our misery, we were sent away. God set cherubim with a flaming sword at the entrance to the garden which prevented us, or anyone later, from ever entering the garden again. Without God doing something spectacular, our souls would die, and we would miss out on the glory of God and would be punished forever for our sin. I don't think you can quite understand what a tragedy that would be since you never had the opportunity to walk and talk with God like we did in that garden. Adam and I have lived every day remembering and longing for that closeness.

Fortunately for us, God still loved us and had a plan for us to be reunited with him after passing from this earth. That's what he was talking about when he addressed the serpent. I would have a descendent who would destroy Satan's power over us even though it would cost that descendent dearly. I didn't fully understand this, and still don't, but I do believe it and count on it.

We settled into our new life outside the garden. It was no longer so easy to get food. We had to sow and harvest. The fruit still grew on trees and bushes, but only for part of the year. Much of what was produced was destroyed by insects and disease and it got worse every year. And the weeds! It seemed like we were out there every day pulling those things. Some of them, what God had called thorns and thistles, poked at our skin and at times even caused bleeding. God had said that Adam would produce our food "by the sweat of your face" and boy did Adam sweat! What a smell!

I soon found out what God had meant when he said I would bring forth children in pain. I was sick for months, unable to keep anything down. It did get better after a while, but the real pain came at the end of the pregnancy. I labored for so long, longer than with any other of my children. When at last Cain was born, I said "I have gotten a man with the help of the Lord." I was under the mistaken idea that this was the descendent God had promised in the garden. We certainly found that wasn't the case.

Next to be born was Abel. Those boys were as different from each other as could possibly be. Cain had quite a temper while Abel was always quiet and gentle. They even looked very different from each other. As they grew, Cain was drawn to field work while Abel was more of a shepherd. We loved them equally, fervently, just differently. We went on to have many other sons and daughters. I didn't know I could hold so much love in my heart for these children. Eventually most of them paired up and had children of their own.

We had brought them up to know the LORD God, even though he was no longer appearing to us regularly. We told every child of the promise he had made to us to send that descendant who was going to save us and showed them how to honor God and that promise with sacrifices on the altar. At first they made those sacrifices with Adam, but eventually they were to bring sacrifices of their own.

Working the fields, Cain brought an offering of the fruit of the ground. Abel brought his offering from the firstborn of the flock. One day, neither one of them came home. I wasn't worried at first because they would often be gone for days at a time, tending to their fields and flocks. When some of their brothers returned a few days later, we found out what had happened.

Cain and Abel had each made their sacrifices. The smoke went straight up to heaven from Abel's offering, but just kind of floated there above Cain's. This made Cain very angry. He later complained to his brother, Jared, that God had chastised him. God had said to Cain, "Why are you angry, and why has your face fallen? If you do well, will you not be accepted? And if you do not do well, sin is crouching at the door. Its desire is for you but you must rule over it."

Despite this warning, Cain had approached Abel and got in to a fight. Things got physical and Cain had risen up against Abel and killed him. Jared told us about the conversation Cain reported having with the LORD God after that.

The Lord said to Cain, "Where is Abel your brother?" Cain replied, "I do not know; am I my brother's keeper?"

But just as the LORD God knew when we had eaten that forbidden fruit, he knew what had happened between the two brothers. "What have you done? The voice of your brother's blood is crying to me from the ground. And now you are cursed from the ground, which has opened its mouth to receive your brother's blood from your hand. When you work the ground, it shall no longer yield to you its strength. You shall be a fugitive and a wanderer on the earth."

This was too much for Cain. It appeared to Jared that Cain was not sorry for what he had done, but only worried about the consequences. Even though Jared was listening patiently to him, Cain figured some of the other brothers would be after him for revenge. He had said to the LORD, "My punishment is greater than I can bear. Behold, you have driven me today away from the ground, and from your face I shall be hidden. I shall be a fugitive and a wanderer on the earth, and whoever finds me will kill me." (By this time, many of our children had already married and had children and had spread out away from the homestead.)

Then the LORD said to him, "Not so! If anyone kills Cain, vengeance shall be taken on him sevenfold." And the LORD put a mark on Cain, lest any who found him should attack him. And Cain, my firstborn son, went from the presence of the LORD and headed east toward the land of Nod. I never saw him again.

When I had another son, I considered him a replacement of sorts for Abel, though no one would ever quite fill that hole in my heart. But I did say, "God has appointed for me another offspring instead of Abel, for Cain killed him." We named our newborn, Seth, which means "appointed". Adam and I were then 130 years old, and we continued to have sons and daughters. Childbirth became easier the more often I went through it, but it never became pain free. This was a reminder of our great disobedience many years before.

The LORD God made known to us that the promised descendent would come from Seth. He married his younger sister, Azura. When Seth was 105, he and Azura had a son they named Enosh. Enosh had a son he named Kenan, who fathered Mahalalel, who fathered Jared, who had a son he named Enoch, who fathered Methuselah, who had Lamech.

The LORD God said to be fruitful and multiply and we certainly have done that. We have so many descendants that I cannot remember all their names. I remember the names of the sons of Seth because these stayed close by, not moving far away, and because this is the line of the promised one.

And now I am old. It has been many years since our last child was born. It is getting difficult to get around. I will die soon, but I will be raised again to live with God as we were meant to do all those years ago. I pray that the children do not forget him.

Awan

My life has not been pleasant. Oh, the first years were. But then my husband did something stupid and we have been wandering ever since.

Cain was the oldest of many, many children. I came some years later. Now, after hundreds of years, people don't marry their siblings. When we were young, there wasn't any choice; except for our parents, we were all siblings. God said to be fruitful and multiply, and that is what we all did. Our parents were still having children long after we started having children and when our children were having children.

Our parents told us about their life in the garden, before they disobeyed God and were evicted from Eden. Life became harder for them after that. Mother suffered from pain when each of us was born. Father had to deal with thorns and thistles while trying to grow our food. They, and all of us who came after, were condemned to die.

God had promised to send a descendant to battle Satan so our death would only be a separation from this life as we knew it instead of eternal death. When Cain was born, Mother thought he was the one who was promised. He wasn't. Hundreds of years, and thousands of people later, we are still waiting for the rescue of our souls.

Life may have been harder than it was for our parents when they lived in the garden, but it wasn't too bad. There was a lot of love to go around. Some of us, including Cain, became farmers; some became herdsmen. We used the milk from the sheep and goats for food and their wool to make clothes. Larger animals, like the oxen, were used for tilling the soil. We also used some of the animals for sacrifices to thank God for providing for us.

Then came the day that changed everything for Cain and me. Actually, it changed the world for everybody. Cain and our brother, Abel, had brought sacrifices on the same day. Abel was a shepherd and brought a perfect sheep. Cain, being a farmer, brought some of his crop. The smoke from Abel's sacrifice ascended straight up to heaven. The smoke from Cain's just kind of drifted away. Cain returned home in a horrible mood, knowing that his sacrifice had not been accepted by God.

Cain was angry, and I could understand why. He told me that God had appeared to him on his way home and spoken to him. He asked, "Why are you angry, and why has your face fallen? If you do well, will you not be accepted? And if you do not do well, sin is crouching at the door. Its desire is for you, but you must rule over it."

How I wish Cain would have heeded this warning. When he went out in the morning, he was still angry at Abel, not admitting that the fault was his own. He had brought produce for the sacrifice that was less than perfect. Worse, he knew it and he didn't care. His sacrifice was unacceptable because he did not bring it out of love for God.

Cain looked even worse when he came home that day, earlier than usual. When he told me what had happened and told me to pack up our belongings, I was stunned. He had taken Abel out into the field on the pretext of showing him a new hybrid of barley he had been working on. He picked up a rock and hit him on the head. When Abel didn't stir, Cain knew he had done a new thing, something that had never been done before. He had murdered his brother. Cain quickly dug a hole and placed Abel's body into it, trying to hide what he had done.

There were no people around to witness any of this, but God saw. He asked Cain where Abel was. Cain, trying to cover up his deed, denied knowing and asked, "Am I my brother's keeper?" But God knew; he had seen it all.

"What have you done?" God said. "The voice of your brother's blood is crying to me from the ground, which has opened its mouth to receive your brother's blood from your hand." And then came this curse: "When you work the ground, it shall no longer yield to you its strength. You shall be a fugitive and a wanderer on the earth." Cain said the punishment was more than he could bear. He was afraid that any man he met, whether brother, nephew, whatever, would try to kill him and avenge Abel. Then Cain showed me the mark God had put on him. It was to prevent anyone from taking Cain's life.

Cain had run into Jared on his way home. The two of them had always been close and Cain told Jared what had happened. Jared seemed to be understanding, but Cain was afraid some of our other relatives would be after his blood for revenge.

So we packed up and left. Cain tried farming, but true to God's word, nothing would grow. Cain had been a farmer all his life, so he didn't know anything about raising animals. Neither did I. That left us to forage. We gleaned from the edges of the fields we passed. We picked nuts and berries and the green plants that grew on their own where no people yet lived. And when there was not enough of that, Cain would break into encampments and steal food. We were not welcome anywhere.

We eventually reached an unpopulated area east of Eden, the garden our parents had first lived in. Because we were wanderers, we came to call the place Nod, which is another word for wanderer. It was in this area that I became pregnant and bore our firstborn, a son we named Enoch. When Enoch and some of his brothers were grown, Cain built a city with their help and named it after our son, the city of Enoch.

Cain was bitter and became more so every day. After he'd killed Abel, he no longer bothered to make any sacrifices at all. And he forbade me to even speak of God in his presence. When he wasn't around, I tried to teach the children about God. Most of them ignored me as they got older, choosing instead to follow their father's example.

In the course of time, Enoch had sons and daughters. His first was Irad. Irad had a son named Mehujael and Mehujael had a son named Lamech. Lamech was more wicked than anyone before him. At least Cain knew what he had done was wrong. One woman wasn't enough for Lamech. He married two, Adah and Oholibamah. When he murdered he bragged to his wives about it. He killed people just for injuring him, even if it was done accidentally.

Children are supposed to be a blessing. Some of my children remained godly, most did not. Each generation is more evil and further away from God than the last. How long will God put up with this? How long must we wait until he sends the promised one?

Azura

I think my parents did a pretty good job of raising us. There was always a lot of love shown, despite the fact that there were so many of us. They said they were trying to show us the love that they had been shown by God. They told us about how they had lived in a garden, which was called Eden, and how they used to speak with God on a daily basis. That doesn't happen very often these days. At that time they didn't have a worry in the world.

Our parents, Adam and Eve, were understanding when we didn't follow all the rules. After all, they had only one rule in the garden and they couldn't keep that one. Of all the fruit trees in the garden, Mother just had to eat from the one that was forbidden. And she gave some of the fruit to Father too.

Other than losing their innocence and being dismissed from the garden, I think the hardest thing for them was when my brother, Cain, killed my brother, Abel. That happened before I was born, but we still heard the story. I have never seen Cain. He was banished from our part of the world.

My husband, Seth, was also born after the murder. In fact, Mother told us that she gave him that name because she saw him as a replacement for my brother, Abel. She also said that Seth was the one to be the ancestor of the promised one who was to save us from an eternal death. I was born four years after Seth, but I was certainly not the youngest. My grandchildren were fully grown before my mother stopped having children.

We have many children also. Our oldest is Enosh. When Enosh grew to manhood, he made it his mission to tell others about the promise God had made to send someone to save us from that eternal death. There were a lot of people in the world by then. Many of them had forgotten. Enosh called this promised one the Messiah, or anointed one. We didn't know exactly how that was going to work out; we just believed it because God said it. Unfortunately, not everyone else believed it.

Our first grandchild is Kenan and our first great-grandson is Mahalalel. Mahalalel named his son Jared. I have the names of all our children and grandchildren and their children written down. But there are so many and some have moved so far away that I can't keep track of all of them.

Let me tell you about my husband. I believe he was Mother's favorite child. That's not to say she didn't love all of us. There was just something special about her feelings for Seth. I asked her about it once. She said that when they lived in the garden and broke that one rule God had given them, they were condemned to death. Death would not just be dying from this life. It meant the eternal death of our souls. But God was gracious. In cursing the serpent who was the embodiment of the deceiver, he also made a promise to mankind.

He'd said to the serpent, "I will put enmity between you and the woman, and between your offspring and their offspring; he shall bruise your head and you shall bruise his heel." Our parents didn't know exactly what that meant, but they did know that God would send a descendent to deal with the deceiver and rescue us from that eternal death. He would be our Redeemer. When Cain was born, Mother thought he was that descendent. Couldn't have been further from the truth. As I said, he turned out to be a murderer, allied with the deceiver and not fulfilling God's promise.

Mother had many more children after that and not one of them was the Promised One. When Seth came along after Abel's death, Mother was told that the Promised One would come from his descendants. That means me too. I am so honored, not by anything I've done, but by the grace of God. And that is why I remember the names of the firstborns so easily. It is from them that the Redeemer will come.

I have seen many types of people. Some have very good natures, some not so good. But Seth? He is the kindest, most compassionate man you could ever hope to meet. I'm sure it is because he loves God so very much and tries to express God's love to others.

Once he came in from the pastures to find a man in the barn, trying to take away one of the new lambs and its mother. The man was ragged and apparently hadn't eaten for a while. Seth could have demanded some kind of restitution. Instead, he took that same lamb, made a thank offering to God, and shared the feast with the would-be thief. The heart of the man was turned and he praised God. Abel then offered him a position as one of his shepherds. We found out later that he was one of Cain's grandsons. Lehabim married our daughter, Abia, and is still with us today.

Not long ago we witnessed what that disobedience in the garden had cost. Father died at the age of 930. Six days later, while we were mourning his passing, Mother followed him into the afterlife. Word of their deaths spread quickly and nearly the whole world joined our mourning, even those generations down the line and living far away, many who had never even met them.

Now that Father is gone, the leadership role has fallen to Seth. Those around here know that Father named him as his heir. For those who aren't around here, it doesn't matter. Their lives don't much intersect with ours anyway.

Emzara

Few people know my name; I've been known by several. I am the daughter of Rake'el, a son of Methuselah. The sons of Methuselah were the last of the godly men before Noah. When they passed, my husband, Noah, was the head of the only family left who worshipped the LORD.

There was so much violence and corruption everywhere. The LORD God came to Noah with a warning. There would be 120 years for mankind to repent and then the end would come. Noah was told to build an ark for us and for the animals of the world. Only in this way would we be saved from the deluge which was to come and destroy the whole world. 20 years later, when Noah was 500 years old, the first of our children was born. Japheth was followed by Shem and Ham.

God had given Noah the directions for exactly how the ark should be built and how many of each animal should be taken along. So Noah started working on building the boat. When the boys were old enough, they too worked on the boat. My heart ached for them. Here they were, working hard at building a boat where there was no body of water anywhere near, being ridiculed daily. None of the neighbors believed in God. Noah tried preaching to them, warning them;

he preached every day but they would have none of it. They were still scoffing when the rain started.

I didn't know where all the water was coming from. We had never had rain like that before, only a gentle mist which watered the land. Suddenly there was water coming from the skies and from the deep. The whole earth seemed to open up to release water. It rained for 40 days and 40 nights, nonstop. And the noise! The rain hitting the top of the ark was loud, but the thunder! We had never before heard such a thing.

God had closed the door when the eight of us, and all the animals, had entered the boat. Our sons had all married by this time. Japheth married Aresisia, Shem married Zalbeth, and Ham married Nahalath. They were all lovely young women and sure to give us beautiful grandchildren someday.

But back to the rain; it was awful. We could see little out the small windows, but in between the peals of thunder we could just make out the anguished cries. As the waters rose, people suddenly understood the seriousness of the situation. At first people were walking around, questioning what was happening. Then some charged the boat, trying to get in. But God had closed the door and it wasn't to open again until the land was dry. People and animals began to drown. The whole earth was soon covered with water. When we dared to look out the windows, we could see bodies floating. Neither man nor beast could survive in that flood.

By the end of the 40 days the water covered even the highest mountains. After 150 days, God had a great wind blow over the earth and the waters began to abate. Seven and a half months after the rain started, the boat settled on a mountain top.

Almost three months later, Noah sent out a raven to scout the area. It flew back and forth until the water dried from the earth. When it didn't return, Noah knew the waters had receded enough for the scavenger to remain outside of the boat.

A week later, Noah sent a dove out the window to see if there was enough dry land for it to survive out there. But the dove returned to the boat. After another week, Noah sent her back out. This time she returned with an olive leaf in her mouth. We knew the trees were growing. Then he sent the dove out again after another week; this time she didn't return.

Finally, on the first day of the new year, Noah removed the covering of the boat and we could see that the ground appeared dry. Almost two months later, God gave Noah the go ahead for us to disembark from the boat. Most of the animals quickly went their way.

Noah took some of every clean animal and bird and offered them on the new altar he had built to the LORD God. That was when the LORD promised he would never drown all creation again. That was also when we saw the first rainbow, a symbol of this promise. It was a beautiful thing. Every time we've seen it since, we have been reminded of his promises.

Noah went back to farming, as he had done before the flood. I wished he hadn't had such a good crop of grapes that one year; it contributed to bringing a curse to some of my grandchildren.

Noah had always made excellent wine. On occasion he drank too much of it and ended up sleeping it off in his tent. One time he fell asleep with his clothes off. Ham saw this, and instead of being discrete about it, went out and told his brothers, ridiculing their father. Shem and Japheth took a blanket and, backing into the tent so they wouldn't see him, covered their father with the blanket. When Noah woke up and found out how Ham had made a mockery of him, he cursed Ham through his son, Canaan. "Cursed be Canaan; a servant of servants shall he be to his brothers."

Noah used this occasion to also speak a blessing to the others. "Blessed be the LORD, the God of Shem; and let Canaan be his servant. May God enlarge Japheth, and let him dwell in the tents of Shem, and let Canaan be his servant."

It wasn't too long before they had large families of their own. Japheth had seven sons, Ham had four, and Shem had five. They all had daughters as well. Cousin married cousin and I have been able to hold grandchildren and great- grandchildren. To be honest, I can't keep track of all of the generations. Now I am old and preparing to leave this world. Not all my descendants remember God's goodness. I can tell that already some are returning to behaviors that caused the LORD to send the flood. Yet we are still waiting for that promised descendent who will make things right again with our God.

Sitidos

What a disaster! And he just sits there, a worthless pile of worm infested matter. His friends are no help to him. They talk, and talk. But they cannot change anything. Is Job the only one suffering? I too have suffered greatly.

We had it all. Our vast holdings included 7,000 sheep, 3,000 camels, 500 yokes of oxen, and 500 female donkeys. One person could not keep up with it all, so we had many servants. We had a large, well-furnished home. Job was as a king, well respected by all. He would sit with the others at the gates, judging all who came. Now it is all a memory.

My greatest loss, however, was none of these things. I once had children, seven sons and three daughters. Oh, how I loved them. And they all got along well with each other, a mother's prayer. They would gather often. Each one, on his birthday, would give a great feast and invite his brothers and sisters.

I lost them all in one day. It was the birthday of my eldest, Esau. All ten of my children were gathered at his house for the celebration. A great wind, a sirocco, hit the house and it collapsed, killing every one of them.

Other disasters struck that very same day. Out in the fields where the oxen were plowing and the donkeys grazing, the Sabeans attacked, killed all but one of the servants with them, and stole all the animals. The sheepfold fared no better. Lightning struck the pens and started a great fire which burned up the sheep and the shepherds. Again, only one escaped death to tell of it. If that weren't enough, the Chaldeans made a raid on the camels, taking them off and killing all those servants, save the messenger of the news. Coincidence? Hardly. It had to have been an act of God.

And what did Job have to say? While he did tear his robe and shave his head in grief, he found consolation in his God. The God who had allowed all this! "Naked I came from my mother's womb, and naked shall I return. The LORD gave, and the LORD has taken away; blessed be the name of the LORD." Bless the God who had cursed us? For me, there was no consolation. My soul ached for my children.

We now had no income from the animals. Job hired himself out as a shepherd for others' sheep. Having the house servants, when Job himself was basically a servant, was an expense we could no longer bear and we had to dismiss them.

Then Job got sick. He was covered head to toe with blisters that soon became open sores. The itch was so bad that he was scraping his skin with a piece of broken pottery. Yet he remained stoic as he sat in ashes.

What was I to do? Obviously, Job could no longer work. I had been helping by trading pieces of embroidery for food, but that was no longer enough. I became a servant myself, a water carrier, bringing water from the well to the neighbors who remained wealthy. Those who had been my friends were now my employers. They started out with pity, giving me a way to earn an income. Familiarity breeds contempt; I became no more than a pack mule to them. Then they found others, younger servants who could bring more water in one trip than I could in three. I was retained only by Sarai, a woman much older than myself with a need for but a little water.

Many times there was not enough bread for both Job and me. We shared the few bites we had. When I was a young wife, I could never have imagined such hunger. Then I lost my position, not because of betterment of my circumstances, but because Sarai had died. I thought I could not be debased any more than I had been, but then there was the incident at the marketplace yesterday.

We had no bread, none whatsoever. I had gone to the marketplace to beg for a little. A bread seller agreed to give me three loaves of bread if I would give him my hair. What good is hair when my husband and I are starving? I thought I could find a place alone, cut my hair short, cover what remained and then come and trade the hair for the bread. So I agreed. But the merchant removed my head covering there in the public market and hacked off my hair in front of everyone. I took the bread and returned home in humiliation. Taking a woman's hair like that is what they did to prostitutes. I had lost any honor I had left.

As I returned home, I was thinking of my children. It had been a long time since that awful day and still their bodies lay under the rubble that had been a home. They deserved a decent burial. As I neared home, I saw that there were three men sitting near Job. I begged Job to have his friends go and retrieve the bodies. He would not be persuaded. "They are home in heaven. Let their bodies remain where they are until the resurrection."

"Curse God and die," I said. He turned and rebuked me. "You speak as a foolish woman would speak. Shall we receive good from God, and shall we not receive evil?" Could my anguish be any more complete?

I took the bread home and put it on the table. I went back to Sarai's house. Her sons were there, closing up and I still had a small amount of wages due. I was asked to wait in the cattle stall. I am so tired and forlorn. I must lie down and rest….

Sarah

Abraham finally returned from the mountain with Isaac. I hadn't thought too much of it when they left. Abraham often had business away from our main camp. After all, God had blessed us with much and it was a big responsibility to keep track of it all. I'd had plenty to keep me busy here at home as well.

I couldn't help but notice that Abraham was in a much better mood on his return than when they had set out. I knew something was bothering him when they left. When he came to my tent he finally told me.

God had ordered him to sacrifice our son! Our Isaac, for whom we had prayed and waited for for so long, was to be bound and laid upon an altar and sacrificed! Abraham had always obeyed God and saw no option but to do so with this also. But God was merciful. At the last minute he stopped Abraham. It had been a test. Praise God for returning my son to me.

We had moved from Ur with Abraham's father, Terah, and his nephew, Lot, and settled in Haran, a city named for Abraham's deceased brother. Lot was Haran's son. After Terah died, God gave a command to Abraham. He told us to leave our home and travel to some land he would show us. We didn't even know where we were headed, but because God said to go, we went. God told Abraham he would make a great nation of his descendants. I was skeptical; I was 65 years old and Abraham was 75. There were still no children.

The land God showed us was the land of Canaan. While at Shechem, God promised to give the entire land to our offspring. It was a country already inhabited by the Canaanites. We moved from Shechem to the hill country between Bethel and Ai. From there we headed toward the Negeb.

We moved again. We could not stay in Canaan, not if we wanted to eat. So we went to Egypt. Before we got there, Abraham told me to say I was his sister. He was afraid that if they knew I was his wife, someone would kill him to get to me. So I went along with the charade. I was taken as a wife to the pharaoh and Abraham prospered. Bad things started happening to the pharaoh. He was no dummy; he soon figured out he had been tricked and sent us away.

We returned to the place where Abraham had built an altar near Bethel. By then Abraham and Lot had accumulated so much livestock that the land could not support both estates; the herdsmen of the two leaders were constantly battling one another over water or pasture or some other perceived wrong. This was too much for Abraham and he suggested that Lot take his possessions and find another part of the country to live in. Lot chose the valley around the Jordon, near Zoar. Lot moved to the valley and settled in Sodom, and we moved on to the oaks of Mamre near Hebron.

Eventually, a coalition of kings attacked the kings of the valley. The kings of Zoar, Sodom, Gomorrah, and Admah, retaliated, and lost. Lot and many others were taken captive. When Abraham heard of this, he took his trained men, all of 318, and went to rescue them. All the captives were released and returned to their homes, including Lot and his family.

After this, God came again to Abraham. Still not having children, Abraham bemoaned the fact that his servant, Eleazar would be his heir. Once more God promised Abraham a son, and descendants as numerous as the stars. Abraham believed and I still had hope, faint though it was.

But I was losing hope as time went by; I came up with a plan to help things along. I would give my servant, Hagar, to Abraham. She would bear his child and I would take him as my own. But once Hagar had conceived, she began to be contemptuous to me. She would gloat about becoming pregnant, rubbing it in my face constantly. When I complained to Abraham, he reminded me that she was my servant and in my hands. I was harsh and she fled. But she returned and gave birth to a son, Ishmael. And she continued to be my nemesis.

Thirteen years later, we had three visitors who came walking in from the desert. One turned out to be the LORD God himself. It was a time of great change. The first of the changes was our names. Up to that point we had been Abram and Sarai. Abraham's new name means "father of many nations", and mine was "princess", indicating that I would be the mother of those many nations.

This was also the time the LORD commanded circumcision. This rite would separate God's people from all the others. Later, Abraham took Ishmael and all the men of the household, those born in our house and those purchased from foreigners, and all were circumcised.

I was in the tent after making bread for Abraham to feed the visitors. I listened to the men as they talked. After asking where I was, the one said to Abraham that by this time next year I would give birth to a son. I tried not to betray my eavesdropping, but I could not stifle the laughter. I would have a son? I, who was well past menopause and the ability to conceive? How absurd! But they heard me. When called on it, I denied laughing, but they knew. They left shortly after this, heading east toward Sodom.

I may not have believed them then, but I should have. A year later, I gave birth to Isaac, just as predicted. What a joyous time that was! It was still hard to believe. Who would have dared to say to Abraham that I would nurse children? But I have borne him a son for his old age.

Time sped by and too soon it was time to wean Isaac. We had a great celebration. But that woman and her son remained an annoyance. Ishmael would tease Isaac and I could hear Hagar laughing about it. I had to insist that Abraham turn them out for good. He was reluctant to do so, but Isaac was the child of the promise and we couldn't allow them to continue mocking us.

Which brings us to the present. I am so thankful to have my son back. God is true to his word. Abraham will be the father of a great nation, through our son Isaac. Praise the LORD!

Hagar

Children and grandchildren, a blessing from God. At one time I thought my son, Ishmael, would be taken from me. Now I have my son and also grandsons. Let's see if I can name them in order: Neboloth, Kedar, Adbeel, Mibsam, Mishma, Dumah, Massa, Hadad, Tema, Jetur, Naphish, and Kedemah. You are probably asking why I thought Ishmael would be taken from me. Let me tell you my story.

I was born and raised in Egypt, the daughter of a prominent man. My parents loved me and life was good. One day a man arrived from Canaan, accompanied by a beautiful woman he said was his sister. Pharaoh was smitten by this woman and put her in his harem. When Pharaoh and his household were stricken with plagues, he knew it was because of this woman, that she was the man's wife, not his sister. It was not enough to return the woman to the man, but Pharaoh gave him many gifts, including me as a servant.

At the age of 14, I was now reduced to the status of slave girl to a Hebrew woman. It was okay at first; Sarai treated me well and her husband, Abram, made no demands on me. They were good people who worshipped a God I did not know. After learning of this God, I too became a worshipper of him.

As good as they were, they were bothered by one thing. God had promised them many descendants, but Sarai was barren. According to custom, I was presented to Abram to bear a child for Sarai. Normally, in cases like this, the child would belong to my mistress. She would be there at the birth and take the child for her own as soon as he was born.

When I became pregnant, it broke my heart to know I would not be a mother to my child. I must admit that I wasn't very nice to Sarai after that. Sarai was indignant and started treating me harshly. I could not take it anymore and ran away into the wilderness.

God came to me when I was resting near a spring of water. He told me I was to go back to Sarai and submit to her. I could not disobey him who had become my God. He also gave me a promise at that time; I would bear a son and was to call him Ismael. I returned, but Sarai was no longer interested in claiming my son for her own. She continued to treat me poorly, but I had God's promise that all would be well.

Ishmael and I had our own tent, away from Sarai. Ishmael grew like a weed. When he was thirteen, Abram had a visit from God, who directed him to circumcise every male in his household. Ishmael was Abram's son, so he too was circumcised. I'll never forget that week. Every man and boy in the household was sore and half of them were limping.

God had more to say to Abram. For starters, he gave him and Sarai new names. They were now to be known as Abraham and Sarah. He also promised them that Sarah would bear a child the next year. True to his word, Sarah had a son and they named him Isaac.

About three years later, Isaac was weaned and Abraham made a great feast. It was a joyful celebration and I was laughing along with everyone else. Sarah saw me laughing and became upset. She must have thought I was laughing at her. The next thing I knew, Ishmael and I were sent away.

Abraham had provided us with food and water, but we ran out of these supplies too soon. Again I thought I would lose my son. We had both grown weak and I could no longer help Ishmael along. I settled him under a bush and went to sit a ways off, far enough that I would not have to watch him die. I could hear him calling out. God heard him too and came to me to tell me to take Ishmael by the hand. He promised to make Ishmael into a great nation. When I looked up, there was a well of water nearby. We drank and were refreshed. I filled the skin with water and we went on our way.

We lived in the Wilderness of Paran. Ishmael grew and became an excellent archer. When the time came, I found him a wife from among my family in Egypt. I became a grandmother and great grandmother. It is a rough life here in the desert, but a good one. Eventually, word came to us that Abraham had died. Ishmael had been sent away, but was still Abraham's son. He went back to Canaan and, with Isaac, buried their father. And then my son returned to me.

Pheine'

Oh, yes. I remember that day, the Day of Fire. Fire and brimstone rained down from heaven. I lost my mother and my husband in that disaster. That was the end of our good life in Sodom.

My father, Lot, was a nephew to Abraham. They came to the land of the Canaanites from Ur, a country by the great rivers. Abraham was a wealthy man, and my father became wealthy as well. Their flocks were so great that my father had to move away to keep the many shepherds from quarrelling. Father had first moved his flocks to a fertile field near Sodom, but eventually he moved into the city and became involved in their government.

My mother, Idit, was born and raised in Sodom. She was the daughter of a wealthy man and used to the finer things in life. Father was a natural draw for her and her father saw a beneficial match in my father.

We had seen troubles before that day of fire. A coalition of five kings in the east had conquered the coalition that Sodom was part of. They did not destroy us, but subjected our kings and countries to tribute. After 13 years, Bera, king of Sodom, along with the kings of Gomorrah, Admah, Zeboiim, and Zoar, rebelled against the kings of Shinar, Ellasar, Elam, and Golim. The eastern coalition attacked and took us all captive, along with all our possessions.

I thought we were doomed to a life of slavery. All our wealth did not do us any good; it now belonged to the foreigners. But someone escaped and went to Uncle Abraham. Not only did Abraham have many flocks and worldly goods, he also had 318 trained men. Unbelievably, his small army was able to overtake the eastern coalition and we were rescued. We were still almost ruined. Bera offered all our goods to Abraham. We might as well be slaves. But Abraham would not take them. He let his trained men take their shares, but the rest was returned to the people it had been stolen from.

And so we returned to our normal life. Father had found husbands for my sister, Thamma, and me. We hadn't yet actually married but were planning our weddings. Thamma was to be married first, as I was the youngest.

Father was sitting at the city gate early one evening, his usual place at that time of day. He had been making judgments in the legal cases brought before him. There hadn't been many that day and most of the people in the city had already returned to their homes for the evening meal. When two strangers arrived, Father rose to meet them. Hospitality was taken seriously. At first the men politely declined Father's offer of food and lodging. They said they would stay in the town square. The night would have been calmer for us if they had.

But Father couldn't leave well enough alone and pressured them until they accepted. When he brought them home, he told Mother to fix the guests something to eat. The trouble started when they had barely finished eating.

There was pounding at the door. When we looked out, the house was surrounded by the men of the city. They were demanding that the visitors be brought out so they could have sex with them. Father went out to talk to them. He was appalled at this breach of hospitality. What he did next appalled us. He was so concerned with saving his guests that he offered Thamma and me to be ravished by the maniacs outside.

They threatened Father, warning him to stand back, calling him a stranger who had come to judge them. They said they would do worse to him than to the visitors. They shoved him out of the way and moved to break down the door. Our two visitors pulled Father back in and shut the door behind him. I don't know what magic the visitors used, but suddenly the men outside were blinded. In vain they groped for the door and finally dispersed to their own homes.

The visitors warned us to leave the city because the LORD had sent them to destroy it. Father was to go and warn all the other family members. He went to our fiancés to warn them, but they must have thought it was a joke. Father returned home alone.

At dawn, the visitors woke us up and told us to leave to avoid the punishment of the city. It was a quiet morning and we could see no reason to go. The visitors grabbed us, my parents, my sister, and me, and dragged us out of the house and outside of the city. They told us to run for our lives and escape to the hills. They also warned us not to look back or stop in the valley.

Father was sure the hills were too far away, that disaster would overtake us before we could get there. He suggested that we go to a nearby small city instead. The men agreed to Father's request and promised that that city would not be destroyed with the others.

The sun was up when we got to Zoar. Nothing had happened yet. Then it came! The sulfur and fire rained down on Sodom, the nearby city of Gomorrah, and the entire surrounding valley which had so appealed to Father all those years ago. We didn't know the extent of it then, for we had been warned not to look back. But Mother did not heed the warning. When she looked back, she was turned into a pillar of salt! If she had not been ahead of us, we wouldn't have known what had happened because Thamma and I were too scared to turn around.

We did eventually go up into the hills as the visitors had originally told us to do. Father was afraid of the people of Zoar, that they would blame us for the destruction and perhaps kill us. We lived in a cave in the mountains, away from all society. What were Thamma and I to do for husbands? We knew no man would have us because of what happened in the valley. So Thamma came up with a plan. We would get our father drunk and have sex with him. That was the only way we could continue his line.

Father had found some wild grapes in the area and cultivated a vineyard. We'd had a bountiful crop and father had made a good quantity of wine. Thamma convinced Father that we needed to celebrate. Father got drunk and Thamma slept with him. The next day we continued the celebration and I slept with him. Then we waited to see if we had gotten pregnant.

Sure enough, nine months later Thamma and I each gave birth to boys. She called her son Moab and I named mine Ben-ammi. Father has since died and we have moved out of the caves with our sons. We have gone east, across from the Salt Sea. The boys found wives and had children. Here it is I will live out my remaining years.

Keturah

Of course I knew of Abraham. Rebekah was my best friend and I spent many hours in her tent. My older sister married her brother, Laban. Anyway, her father, Bethuel, would often tell us the stories of his Uncle Abraham and his journeys to a far off land. My own father had died when I was very young. When my mother died ten years later, Bethuel took me in. I was part of the family. Not long after that, Bethuel died and Laban became head of the household.

I was there when Eleazar came, looking for a wife for Abraham's son, Isaac. I was happy for Rebekah, she had a bright future. I was not so happy for myself. I had lost my parents and now I was going to lose my friend who was more of a sister to me than just a friend. Rebekah was sad to leave me as well. When she asked me to go with her, I was thrilled. Certainly I would go.

When we got to our destination, Isaac and Rebekah were immediately smitten with each other. Isaac had lost his own mother three years earlier; Rebekah had left hers behind. They provided solace to one another and theirs turned into a true love story. Their only sorrow was that Rebekah could not seem to get pregnant. It took 20 years, but it finally happened and she had twins.

I was not to be left behind. I knew Abraham had loved his wife, Sarah, dearly. But he was ready to remarry. I know he was considerably older than me, but he was such a kind, sweet man, totally reliant on God. He was also rather nice to look at too. He did not want a Canaanite woman for his next wife any more than he wanted one for his son. When he asked me to be his wife, how could I say no?

I knew his history. He had fathered a son by Sarah's servant and that led to a lot of friction between the two women. Sarah had made him send his firstborn, Ishmael, away with his mother after Sarah had had a son of her own. Not right away, but Ishmael was only about 17 when he was dismissed. Abraham told me later that it had distressed him greatly, but God told him to do as his wife wanted.

Isaac was Abraham's pride and joy. I knew that any children we might have would be considered second best. But second best of Abraham's would still be better than anything else.

So we were married. I had been there for Rebekah's wedding and she was there for mine. I gave Abraham six sons: Zimran, Jokshan, Medan, Midian, Ishbak, and Shuah. They were good boys, as faithful to the LORD God as their brother Isaac and their father Abraham. Abraham did send them away, as he had sent away Ishmael, but not at so young an age. And he gave them gifts enough to establish themselves wherever they would end up settling down.

Losing Abraham after 35 years was hard to bear. He was a good man and a good husband. Ishmael returned for his father's funeral and he, along with Isaac, buried their father in the cave of Machpelah, alongside Sarah, his first wife.

I am content. Children are, after all, only a loan from the LORD. Abraham provided well for me and I was not going to have to depend on them for my support. And I was still near my best friend, Rebekah.

Rebekah

How can I send off my son, Jacob? What choice do I have? If I try to keep him here with me, his brother will hunt him down and they will kill each other. Then I lose both.

I remember the circumstances that brought me from my homeland to this place. I lived in Nahor, named for my grandfather. I am the only daughter of Bethuel, the sister of Laban. I had gone out to draw water at the city well when a stranger asked for a drink of water. Naturally, I gave him some, and also watered his camels. He gave me some jewelry and asked who I was and if there was room in my father's house to host a visitor. I ran home to let Laban know about our visitor.

Seeing the jewelry, Laban questioned me, then ran to the door to welcome him. Though food was set before him, the man would not eat until he had said what he came to say. He told us he was Eleazar, Abraham's servant. Abraham was my grandfather's brother, a kinsman, and this man was on a mission to find a wife for his master's son, Isaac. Then Eleazar asked if I would go back with him. Convinced the request was from the LORD, my brother and father said I should go. At this, Eleazar brought out more gifts, both for me and for my family.

The next morning, Eleazar was ready to return with me. Laban and my mother requested a delay of at least ten days, time for them to get used to the idea and say goodbye. But Eleazar was anxious to get started. They called me to make the decision and I consented to go immediately. And so I left my home with my nurse, some of the other servants, and my best friend, Keturah, who was like a sister to me. I would not return.

When we arrived in the Negeb, I saw a man walking towards us in the field. Eleazar said it was his master, Isaac. Eleazar explained to Isaac all that had occurred on his trip and Isaac and I were married almost immediately.

Isaac was a kind and funny man. We laughed often. But after a while there was also a great sadness. I was unable to conceive. This went on for 20 years. After much prayer, I finally got pregnant. Twins, no less. We were so happy.

It was a tough pregnancy. It seemed the children were battling in my womb. I went to my father-in-law to have him inquire of the LORD as to why this was happening to me. The LORD said to me, "Two nations are in your womb, and two peoples from within you shall be divided; the one shall be stronger that the other, the older shall serve the younger."

The first to be born came out covered in red hair. We named him Esau. When the second came out, he was holding on to the heel of the first, so we called him Jacob. There was no mixing up the two of them. In addition to looking very different, they behaved very differently. Esau became a hunter while Jacob stayed close to home and tended the crops. I hate to admit it, but Jacob was my favorite. Esau was the favorite of Isaac.

As happened often, there was a famine in the land of Canaan. We thought of going down to Egypt, but were hindered by the LORD and settled in Gerar in the land of the Philistines. Maybe I should be flattered that Isaac still thought me beautiful. He told Abimlech, the king in Gerer, that I was his sister, thinking someone might otherwise kill him on my account. We had been there quite a while when the king saw us flirting in the courtyard and figured out that we were married. He was furious, afraid of the wrath of God if someone else had tried to take me as his wife.

We stayed on in Gerar and Isaac planted crops there. The harvest was plentiful and Isaac became even richer. He had so much livestock, so many servants, that the Philistines became jealous and we were sent away and settled in Beersheba, where the boys were born.

When Isaac became old, he lost most of his vision. He could see forms but could not make out the face of those standing in front of him. Being certain he was to die soon, he called for Esau. He asked Esau to hunt some game and prepare a meal for him the way he liked it. After eating, he would bless Esau.

I heard this conversation and acted quickly. I knew that Jacob was to be the blessed one. I called him and told him what I had heard. Then I sent him for a couple goats from the flock and prepared the meal Isaac had requested from Esau. Jacob was afraid that Isaac would know he wasn't Esau and would curse instead of bless him, but I had a plan.

I took Esau's garments, with his smell on them, and put them on Jacob. I put the goat skins on his hands and the smooth part of his neck so that if Isaac felt him he would think he was Esau. It worked. Before Esau could return with his game and fix a meal, Jacob had procured the blessing.

As would be expected, Esau was furious with this outcome and out for blood. I heard that he said he would wait until Isaac died and then kill Jacob. I had to find a way to send Jacob away quickly. When enough time had elapsed, surely Esau would calm down and I could send for Jacob to return.

Esau had married a couple of Hittite women. Their ways were not the ways of our God and that caused me grief. I pointed this out to Isaac, along with my concern that Jacob would also marry a local woman and my life would be ruined.

Isaac took the hint and sent Jacob back to my homeland to find a wife from my brother's family. Now Jacob is safely on his way to Paddan-aram. I may never see him again. May God go with him.

Leah

It was so long ago that I first set eyes on Jacob. My sister, Rachel, was the first to see him. The son of our father's sister, he had come from Canaan after a dispute with his own brother. My father, Laban, welcomed him into our home.

It soon became evident that Jacob and Rachel were taken with each other. It was really no surprise to me; Rachel had always been the pretty one. After staying with us for about a month, Jacob and my father made a deal. Jacob would work for my father for seven years in exchange for receiving Rachel as his wife.

The seven years went by and I, the elder, still had no prospects for marriage. When the time for their wedding arrived, my father substituted me for the intended bride. He said it wasn't right that the younger sister be married first. An obedient daughter, I went along with the ruse. I kept quiet and, in the dim light of our wedding night, Jacob seemed to have no idea he had been tricked into marrying me.

With the light of day, Jacob discovered the deception. He was furious with my father. He was given the same story about the younger daughter not marrying before the elder. To his credit, Jacob gave me my wedding week. Then he broke my heart by marrying my sister just seven days after he married me. He had worked out a deal with my father to take Rachel as a wife also in exchange for seven more years of labor. Then I knew that my father had not been looking out for my interest in getting a husband; he had merely discovered a way to keep Jacob around to work for him.

Jacob was a dutiful husband, but the LORD knew as well as I that I was unloved. So he gave me someone to love. I was blessed with a son whom I named Rueben. And the LORD blessed me with three more sons, Simeon, Levi, and Judah.

In all this time, Rachel did not have any children. Wanting desperately to have a child, she gave her servant, Bilhah, to Jacob to have a son by her. Bilhah gave birth to two sons, first to Dan and then to Naphtali. Rachel took them as her own.

Meanwhile, I had ceased having children. If Rachel could give her servant to Jacob, I could do the same. I presented Zilpah to Jacob. Through her I had two more sons, Gad and Asher.

There was a day during the wheat harvest when Reuben found some mandrakes in the field and brought them to me. I thought that eating their fruit would make me fertile once again. But Rachel heard about the mandrakes and implored me to give them to her; she had still not given birth to a child. First she takes my husband and then she wants my mandrakes? But we made a deal. In exchange for the mandrakes, I would have Jacob in my bed. I agreed because, after all, what good is a mandrake if there is no husband to get you pregnant?

I was to have Jacob more than just that one night. I became pregnant several times more and gave birth to two more sons, Issachar and Zebulun. I thought that since I had given Jacob six sons, and Rachel still had given him none, surely my husband would love me now, but it still wasn't enough to earn his love. No matter what, Rachel would always be the one to have his love. I settled for the solace of my children, including my daughter, my youngest, Dinah.

Rachel did eventually get pregnant and gave birth to a son, Joseph. Shortly after that, Jacob decided it was time to go to his own home and country, but my father convinced him to stay longer by promising him a share of the livestock. Jacob's share increased to the point that my brothers felt he was taking away their inheritance. Jacob could tell he was unwelcome.

When the Lord told him it was time to return to the land of his fathers, Jacob called Rachel and me to him. He told us how our father had changed his wages ten times over, trying to get more from him. He was no longer favored in our father's eyes. Besides all this, his God had told him to return to the land he came from. What did we wives have to gain by begging to stay? Nothing! Our father had sold us and regarded us as foreigners; we had no inheritance to look forward to. We, the both of us, told Jacob to do whatever God had said for him to do.

We women and children mounted camels and headed out to the land of Canaan. Jacob drove all the livestock he had acquired away from Paddan-aram toward Canaan. Father had gone out to shear his sheep. He and his men were shearing and feasting and would not notice we were gone for several days.

But the day soon came when our father found out we had left and set off after us. After a week he caught up to us with his men. They could move much faster than our group with women and children. When they found us, Father accused Jacob of tricking him and sneaking away with his daughters and grandchildren. He said he would have thrown us a goodbye party. Right!

Then he threatened Jacob. He didn't follow through on that only because God had appeared to him and warned him not to. But he did accuse us of stealing the statues of his gods. Jacob knew none of us would do that and allowed Father to search, promising that if they were found, the one who took them would not live. Father searched, but could not find them.

Then Jacob became angry. He pointed out how he had been a faithful worker and protected my father's flocks from harm, how God had blessed my father through him. What had he done to incur my father's wrath that he should be sent away empty handed?

Father knew there was nothing he could do. He still felt that everything Jacob was leaving with, his wives and children, his livestock, still belonged to him. But what could he do about it? So he made a covenant of peace with Jacob.

We reached Canaan and were met by Jacob's brother, Esau. Jacob had expected trouble, but there was none. Esau went his way and we went ours. We moved from place to place as many in the land did. When my daughter was raped and her brothers sought revenge, we were forced to move again. Rachel died in childbirth on the way to Bethel, but her son, Benjamin, survived and, along with Joseph, became one of Jacob's favorites. Still no love for me. When Joseph was killed by a wild animal, or so we thought, Benjamin became Jacob's whole world.

There was a great famine in the land and we ended up moving the entire family to Egypt. Turns out that Joseph had not been killed, but was now a great leader in Egypt. Jacob was overjoyed to find out his favorite son was still alive and didn't think twice about moving us all to a foreign land to be near him.

It's ok though. We were given the land of Goshen to settle in and no longer have to move around all the time. I really cannot complain. Jacob may not love me like he did Rachel, but he has always been good to me. I have made friends with the wives of our children. There are certainly enough of them. Our sons and daughters-in –law have given us many grandchildren. The love I have from them almost makes up for the lack of a husband's love. I am content.

Rachel

My father said it was because Leah was older and should be married first. I had no choice in the matter because I was his daughter. So, even though Jacob had been working the last seven years so we could be married, when it came time for the wedding it wasn't me under the veil.

Leah and I had always been close, even for sisters. I admired her because she was gentle and kind. That all changed when she married the man I loved. I suppose she had no more choice than I, but she should have at least tried to tell Father it was wrong and talk him out of making the switch. No, she seemed quite happy to go along with the ruse.

Jacob told me that he had no idea it was Leah under that veil during the wedding. By the time he knew it was her, the deed had been done; she was his wife. I know Jacob loved me, so I have no reason to doubt his word. When he found out that he was married to Leah, he agreed to work for Father for another seven years in exchange for marrying me as well. Jacob's name means "trickster". He had tricked his father into giving him the birthright instead of to his older brother, Esau, but now the trick was on him.

A week later, after Leah's bridal week, Jacob and I were married. It is not easy sharing one's husband with one's sister. The nights I shared with Jacob were wonderful. The nights he spent with Leah tortured me. To make matters worse, Leah quickly became pregnant while I remained barren. Not long after Rueben was born she became pregnant again and gave birth to a second son, Simeon. And still again she got pregnant and gave Jacob a third son, Levi. He was soon followed by a fourth, Judah.

By this time I was more than a little depressed and, I admit, jealous. I had to do something. I had to have a child. I decided to follow the custom of claiming my servant's child for my own, so I gave Bilhah to Jacob. I would be there when the child was born. I would be the first to hold him. He would be my own. Bilhah did become pregnant and bore us a son. I felt vindicated and named him Dan. Bilhah became pregnant again and gave birth to Naphtali.

I guess that Leah figured that if I could have children by my maidservant, she could do the same with hers. She gave her servant, Zilpah, to Jacob for a wife. It wasn't enough that she had twice the sons I had. Zilpah became pregnant and gave birth to Gad; she became pregnant again and gave birth to Asher.

One day, Rueben was out in the fields and found some mandrakes and brought them to Leah. Because these plants are known to increase fertility, I begged Leah for some of them for me. I still wanted a child from my own body. In exchange, I promised Leah that Jacob could sleep with her that night (he had been spending most nights with me). Wouldn't you know? She became pregnant and had still another son, Issachar. And yet again, and another boy, Zebulun.

The next time she got pregnant, it was a girl. She named her Dinah.

Finally, after all of that, God had mercy on me and I became pregnant myself. I presented Jacob with a son, and we named him Joseph. After Joseph was born, Jacob thought it was time to go back to his home in Canaan. But Father talked him out of it. Jacob amassed so many sheep and goats under this new agreement with my father that my brothers soon became jealous. They thought those animals should belong to them. Father's attitude about Jacob also changed.

One day Jacob called Leah and me out to the field where he had his flocks. This time God had spoken to him about going back to Canaan. He told us that, and also about how our father had changed his wages ten times, trying to get the best of him. He asked us about leaving. What could we say? Leah and I finally agreed about something. Because of Father's attitude about Jacob, his attitude about us had also changed. We felt we had no stake in our father's household, no inheritance. Jacob should do whatever God had told him.

The right time came when Father and his men were out in the pastures, shearing his sheep. Jacob packed up his goods, put us and the children on camels, and sent us on our way while he drove the livestock ahead of him. Over a week later, Father and the others caught up to us in Gilead. Father laid into Jacob about stealing his daughters and grandchildren. He said he would have held a celebratory farewell had he known we were leaving. Then the chiller; he accused Jacob of stealing his household gods. Jacob said that if he found them on any of our party, the person responsible would be put to death.

Jacob did not know it, but I was responsible for that. We were going on a journey far away, never to see our homeland again. I thought that if I took the small statues of the gods I had grown up with we would be guarded by those gods. Now I was more frightened than ever. I took the statues and put them under my camel's saddle and sat on it. When Father came into my tent looking for the gods, I begged his pardon for not rising. I told him I was having my period. Mine was the last tent he checked, having already been through all the others.

Now it was Jacob's turn to lash into Father. "What crime did I do?" He recounted how he had worked for Father for twenty years and brought him prosperity. It was only because the God of Abraham and Isaac had been with him that Father hadn't sent him away empty-handed.

Father responded that we were his daughters and that all Jacob's goods were really his own. He could do nothing about it, so he proposed a covenant between them. They made a monument of stones to mark the boundary and shared a meal to seal the covenant. Jacob called the place Galeed but Father called it Sahadutha. It was also called Mizpah. There they called upon the LORD to watch between them and theirs and to judge if either went past the boundary to cause harm.

Jacob offered a sacrifice and, after the meal, we all spent the night there. The next morning Father kissed Leah and the children and me and blessed us. When he turned to go home, that was the last we ever saw of him.

Trying to avoid trouble, Jacob sent a message to his brother, Esau, to let him know we were coming. The messengers returned saying that Esau was on his way with four hundred men to meet us. Jacob feared for what could happen when they met up, so he divided us up into groups to go ahead of him. He figured that if Esau attacked one group, the group remaining could escape. He also sent ahead gifts of many cattle to pacify Esau, hoping he would be mellow by the time he met up with the people.

The next morning Leah and I, along with Bilhah, Zilpah, and the children, crossed the ford of the Jabok river while Jacob stayed behind one more night. He rejoined us the next day. When Jacob saw Esau in the distance, he split us up into four groups. Bilhah and her children went first, then Zilpah and hers. Leah and her children followed them. Joseph and I brought up the rear.

What a shock when Esau met up with us. Not only was he not angry, he was happy to see us all. Jacob had a hard time convincing Esau to accept the gifts he had sent, but finally prevailed. Esau was ready to accompany us the rest of the way. When Jacob declined, Esau wanted to leave some of his men with us, but Jacob declined that too. Esau started on his way back to Seir, but Jacob took us to Succoth, and later to Shechem where he bought land for our tents.

Because of problems with the people in Shechem, we moved on toward Bethel. From Bethel, we headed toward Ephrath. Because I was again pregnant, we moved slowly. We are still some distance away and I have gone into labor. But something is wrong. I have given birth to a boy. Because of my trouble, I name him Ben-Oni……

Bilhah

Ben-Oni, son of my trouble. With those last words, Rachel died. Jacob would not have that reminder. He named the child Benjamin, son of my right hand. Rachel was buried there in Ephrath. And we journeyed on.

Who am I? I am a concubine, the daughter of a concubine. I am a wife, yet not a wife. I am a servant, yet more than a servant. I have a younger sister, Zilpah who is also a concubine. Our father's name is Laban. We grew up with Leah and Rachel, Laban's daughters by his wife who is a wife.

There was little difference in the lives of Zilpah, Leah, Rachel and me until well after Jacob arrived on the scene. The four of us played together, learned together, worked together. The one difference was that my mother died when I was very young. Rachel's mother tended to ignore Zilpah and me, still resentful that our father had taken our mother as a concubine.

As I said, things changed after Jacob arrived. He was our cousin, come to us after a fight with his brother. He and Rachel fell for each when he showed up at our city's well. Jacob and Laban entered a pact that Jacob would work for seven years in order to marry Rachel. Laban benefited from this deal greatly. He had been moderately well off, but with Jacob as his main shepherd, Laban became quite prosperous.

He even had more children, sons who took the place of his daughters. I'm sure that is why Laban made the switch.

When it came time for the wedding, Laban substituted Leah for Rachel. In order to support his charade, he gave Zilpah, the younger, to Leah as a servant, implying that it was the younger daughter, Rachel, under the bridal veil. Jacob was furious. Laban gave him the excuse that the elder daughter should marry first, but he could still marry Rachel if he agreed to work for Laban another seven years. A week later, Jacob wed Rachel and I was given to her as a servant.

We had been almost equals, now Zilpah and I were merely servants. But when Leah had children and Rachel didn't, we became almost equals once more. That was when I became a concubine. Rachel sent me to Jacob so she could have children through me. Being a servant, my children by Jacob would be her children. I had two boys, Dan and Naphtali.

Leah was not going to be bested. She gave Zilpah to Jacob to have more children for her. That's how Gad and Asher were born. Then Leah had more children herself: Issachar, Zebulum, and Dinah.

Finally, Rachel was able to conceive a child of her own. Joseph was a handsome child. Rachel doted on him, leaving me to be a mother to the sons I had given birth to. We had all settled into a pattern of cooperation. Unlike Abraham's wife, Sarah, did with his concubine, Hagar, Leah and Rachel did not make our lives miserable nor did we irritate them. Each of us dwelt in our own tents with the children we had born. All Jacob's children were considered equal, although he obviously favored Joseph as he favored Rachel.

Jacob continued to work for Laban. (I no longer could call him Father since he had given us away as servants.) And Laban continued to prosper, as did Jacob. But the time came to go back to Jacob's homeland. Leah and Rachel agreed with this as Laban had pretty much written them off. Zilpah and I were not consulted, but we certainly did not feel we were any concern of Laban's. We headed east while Laban and his men were off with the sheep.

Laban caught up to us a week later. He asked Jacob, "What have you done, that you have tricked me and driven away my daughters like captives of the sword?" But we knew that he was only concerned with his prosperity, not his children and grandchildren. Harsh words were spoken, but eventually a truce was achieved and Laban returned home while we moved on toward Gilead.

As we got closed to Canaan, Jacob became worried about how his brother would greet him, especially when he heard that Esau was coming with 400 men. He sent gifts ahead and split us up into four groups, each with our own children. If one or two groups were attacked, maybe the others would survive.

After the heavy apprehension, we were all surprised. Esau greeted Jacob warmly. He even tried to decline the gifts Jacob had sent. The brothers were on good terms when we parted ways. Esau returned to Seir and we moved on to a place which would be called Succoth. From there we crossed the Jordan to the city of Shechem.

We ran into trouble in Shechem. Dinah was attacked by the son of the prince of the land. After raping her, he wanted to marry her. Bottom line, Dinah's brothers ended up killing all the men and boys of the city. We had to move again.

One of the saddest moments of my life came as we were traveling to Ephrath. Rachel had once more become pregnant. She went into labor while we were on the road. She died giving birth to her son.

We moved beyond the tower of Eder. There I was disgraced. Jacob's eldest son, Reuben, came to my tent and lay with me. He deceived me; it was dark and I thought he was Jacob. I did not realize who he was until he got up and left instead of staying the night. Jacob heard of it and would not even speak to me afterwards. Because I had not cried out, he thought I had enticed Reuben.

Our next move was to Kiriath-arba where Jacob's father, Isaac lived. We had not been there long when Isaac died. Esau came and he and Jacob buried their father. That was the last time we saw Esau. He took his entire family, his three wives and five sons, his daughters and all he possessed and moved to the hill country of Seir.

As I said earlier, Jacob doted on Joseph. Not surprisingly, his brothers, except for Benjamin, resented this. One day Joseph did not return home.

The brothers brought back his bloody coat. Jacob mourned for a long time. He never did get over the loss, but he turned all his attention to Rachel's remaining son, Benjamin. It wasn't until many years later that we found out Joseph was still alive.

It was because Joseph was alive in Egypt that we all avoided starvation. Because of him, there was food in Egypt and we eventually moved there to join him. His country gave us the land of Goshen to live in.

Leah died not that long after we got here. I miss her; she was my sister and my friend. Jacob died about five years ago. We all miss him. God gave him the name Israel and we now call ourselves Israelites. Joseph and the others took Jacob back to Canaan for burial. Now it is Zilpah and me and the children and grandchildren and their children and their children. I am an old woman and get confused about how many generations there are now. Someday we too will all return to Canaan. God has promised us.

Zilpah

I am the last of my generation. My husband is dead, buried in the land promised to our people. My sisters, co-wives of Jacob, have all passed. Rachel died in childbirth long before we came to Egypt. Leah became sick soon after we settled in Goshen and died a week later. I have just returned from burying Bilhah. I miss them all. We four are sisters, all daughters of Laban. But Bilhah and I have a mother other than Leah and Rachel's mother. Like Bilhah and me, our mother was a concubine.

The difference between the four of us became more obvious when Leah, and then Rachel, were married to Jacob. Bilhah and I were given to them by Laban as servants. Leah and Rachel in turn gave us to Jacob as concubines. Wives, but not wives. Rachel was by far Jacob's favorite.

The wonder of it all was that we got along as well as we did. I guess it helped that the four of us had grown up together, not only sisters but friends. Oh, there was jealousy, especially between Leah and Rachel. Leah knew Jacob only married her because he was tricked into it. Rachel was the one Jacob loved. Leah had children right away and Rachel couldn't get pregnant. That is why Rachel gave Bilhah to Jacob, to have children for her. Then, of course, Leah gave me to Jacob to have more children for her.

Eventually, Rachel did have children of her own, two boys, Joseph and Benjamin. Joseph was Jacob's favorite. One day the older brothers came home with Joseph's bloody coat and we were all convinced Joseph had been killed by wild animals. After that, Jacob became overly protective of Benjamin, Rachel's sole surviving son.

Bilhah and I knew we would never be loved by a husband. But we did have the love of our children. Because Leah had given birth to six children, and Rachel had her precious Joseph, Bilhah and I were allowed to be mothers to those we gave birth to. We were not shut out of their lives. As mothers of his children, we were treated well by Jacob.

We have been through a lot in the passing years. We have moved frequently. That is to be expected when you have many flocks and herds to care for. Jacob worked for Laban for many years until the resentment built up. We left there on unpleasant terms, but Laban did reach a peace with Jacob instead of hauling us all back to Paddan-aram.

We'd had a scare when we met up with Esau, Jacob's brother, on our way to Canaan. It was because of a disagreement with Esau that Jacob had left in the first place. Esau had threatened to kill him, he was so angry. We thought he might still be intending to do that. However, Esau was pleased to see Jacob and Jacob had a difficult time getting Esau to accept the gifts he had sent. Years later, Esau returned when their father, Isaac, died and the two of them together buried Isaac.

Then there was the rape of Dinah, Leah's daughter. Leah's sons, Simeon and Levi, were hot tempered and killed all the men and boys of the city. We had to move on. We were on the road to Ephrath when Rachel died in childbirth.

Some time later there was the incident of Bilhah and Reuben, another one of Leah's children. He snuck into her tent and raped her. Leah may have had the most children, but they were also the most trouble.

When the crops didn't grow, we thought it would be a short term problem. We didn't grow grain ourselves, but traded meat, vegetables and crafted items for what we needed. There was no rain for a season, and then another season. We didn't have enough grain for bread or to feed our flocks and herds. Jacob heard there was plenty of grain available in Egypt, so he sent his ten oldest sons there to buy some. When they returned, Simeon was not with them. The loss of another son reminded Jacob of Joseph and he was despondent for months.

The famine continued and we were about to run out of grain again. Jacob sent his sons back to Egypt. This time, Benjamin went along. Jacob did not want to let him go, but Judah reminded him that the vizier in Egypt had told them that if the younger brother did not come along, they would not be able to buy food. After balking, Jacob realized that he really didn't have any choice in the matter.

When all eleven returned with food and in good spirits, the rest of us found out that the vizier was actually Joseph. God had not just rescued him but had elevated him to the highest position in the land, next to the pharaoh himself. God had worked through Joseph to stockpile enough grain to save Egypt, and us, from starving.

Judah told us all the wonderful things that had happened on this latest trip to Egypt and showed us all the gifts that they had brought back. He also said that the pharaoh himself had invited the family, all 70 of us, to move to Egypt where we would not have to face hunger for the remaining years of the famine. Jacob was so excited to hear that Joseph was alive and that he would see him again that he could not contain himself. We left as soon as we could pack up.

Jacob had not forgotten to thank God. We made camp at Beersheba, a place where Abraham and Isaac had previously worshipped. There Jacob made sacrifices and there God spoke to him. Jacob was not to be afraid to go to Egypt. God promised to make a great nation of him there and when the time was right to bring the people back to Canaan.

We went straight to Goshen as we had been directed. Judah went ahead to notify Joseph that we would be there. Joseph came to Goshen where he was reunited with his father. Then Joseph took him to meet Pharaoh.

We had lived here in Egypt for 17 years when Jacob called all his sons together. He blessed them and made them promise to bury him with his father in the cave of Machpelah, east of Mamre. Even Joseph came with his sons, Ephraim and Manasseh. Jacob died at the age of 147.

Joseph had Jacob embalmed in the manner of the Egyptians. The entire country mourned for 70 days, just two days short of the time they would mourn for a pharaoh. Then Joseph, his brothers and their wives, and all the elders of Egypt took the body back to Canaan where they buried Jacob.

I am now an old woman, one with an old woman's shortcomings. I will soon join Jacob, Leah, Rachel, Bilhah, and all of our people who have gone before, in the afterlife as promised by the LORD God. May he be gracious to his people, Israel, and bring them back to the land as he promised Jacob years ago.

Tamar bat Aaron

I never thought it would be so difficult to have a family. I never thought I would end up living in Egypt. Isn't it funny how things work out?

I grew up in Canaan, just like the rest of my family. I married when I was fourteen. My husband, Er, was not the best of men. He was always getting into trouble of one kind or another. He treated me decently, but not particularly what I would call well. I remember the day he didn't come home. I was in shock, left a widow at the age of sixteen.

My father-in-law's family has a tradition of levirate marriage. When I married Er, I married into that tradition. In order to maintain a family line, a widow is married to her husband's brother. Their first child is considered the child of the original husband and entitled to all rights of inheritance of that man. So I was married to Er's brother, Onan. Our first child would be Er's child. Apparently, Onan did not like the idea of Er having a son, and refused to know me in a way that could produce a child. He spilled his semen onto the floor, leaving me childless. In his way, Onan was even more evil than Er. God knew it too, and soon, Onan followed his brother Er into death.

My father-in-law, Judah, sent me back to live with my own father until his third son, Shula, would be of marriageable age. Years went by; Shula reached his majority; yet Judah would not have me marry him. It seems Judah thought I was a curse and would cause the death of his last remaining son.

What was I to do? Judah would not have me married and he would not release me to find another. He expected me to live as a childless widow in my father's house the rest of my life. Did you know he could have served as the levir himself? He was unwilling to do that either.

So I took things into my own hands. Judah's wife had died over a year ago. When Judah ended his grieving period, he went up to Timnah for the sheep shearing. I covered myself with a veil so as not to be recognized and sat down at the entrance to Enaim, which is on the way to Timnah, giving the impression that I was a prostitute. As I expected, I got Judah's attention. He promised a young goat in payment for sex. I demanded a surety; he did not have the goat with him and would have to pay later. He gave me his seal, its cord, and his staff as a pledge. After he left, I took of the veil, put my widow's clothes back on, and went home. I had succeeded in my mission; two weeks later I knew that I had indeed become pregnant. When Judah sent his friend to redeem his pledge with the goat, the prostitute was nowhere to be found.

Five months after that, when it became obvious to others that I was pregnant, Judah heard of it. He assumed I had broken my vows and demanded I be brought out and be burned to death for being a prostitute. As they were bringing me out, I sent a message to Judah, along with his pledge, saying I was pregnant by the owner of those items. He recognized them as his own and acknowledged that I was righteous in doing as I did since he did not give me to Shelah as a wife. Then Judah took me into his own home as his wife, though we did not have marital relations. When the time came, I delivered two sons for him. We named them Perez and Zerah.

So, after all of the turmoil, I was a part of Judah's household when the time came for us to move to Egypt because of the famine. I have my family, including Hezron and Hamul, my grandsons. God has richly blessed me.

Dinah

Being a daughter with twelve brothers is an interesting way to grow up. Big brothers are supposed to be protective, but mine went too far.

We were living in Shechem. I had had enough of being around so many men. When my mother, Leah, and the rest of the women were busy I would go out to visit some of the women of the land with whom I had made friends. On one of those visits I ran into Shechem. He was named after the city, or the city was named for him, I'm not sure which came first. Shechem was the son of Hamor the Hivite, who ruled the area. Shechem was used to taking what he wanted and he raped me. It was strange that after he had violated me he started to sweet talk me. He later told his father he wanted to marry me.

My father, Jacob, had heard about the rape but didn't do anything in response. When my brothers heard about it they came in from the fields and discussed it with my father. They were quite angry, but I was humiliated. A few days later, Shechem and his father came to my father to ask for me as a wife for Shechem. Hamor proposed that Father and the rest of the family settle down in the area. Shechem told Father to name the bride price; he would pay anything.

My brothers acted as if this would be ok except that they couldn't let me marry a man who wasn't circumcised. They said that I could marry Shechem if all their men were circumcised. Shechem and Hamor were agreeable to this and all the men in their city were soon circumcised. I was sent to Shechem's house.

Three days later, while they were still in some pain from the circumcisions, my brothers Simeon and Levi took their swords and attacked the city. They killed all the men, including Shechem and his father. Now, in addition to having been raped, I was widowed. Because I had been shamed, no other man would have me. What was I to do?

I told Simeon that since he had caused me to be a widow, he was responsible to take me in and take away my shame. It was not a marriage, but at least I had a home and my child would have a father figure.

What Simeon and Levi did was so bad that we had to move. Father said we had become a stench to the surrounding people. He was afraid they might attack us. So we soon headed to Bethel. While there, I gave birth to a daughter.

I did not even have a chance to name her. My brothers did not want what they saw as an an illegitimate child to be part of the family and were talking about killing her even before she was born. They thought she would bring disgrace on the family. Father intervened. He put a talisman around her neck and laid her under a thorn bush, trusting her fate to

God. I was heartbroken. I snuck off to rescue her the next day, but she was gone.

We moved a lot through the years. Now we are living in Goshen, in Egypt. I have been reunited with my daughter in a very strange manner after all these years. When Father was presented to Pharaoh, he was also presented to the wife of my brother, Joseph, who was viceroy in Egypt. Father recognized the talisman she was wearing. Trusting her fate to God had been the best for her. The story is that an angel carried her to Egypt. She was found by Poti-phera and raised by him and his wife who had no children of their own. They named her Asenath I don't know if that is really how she got to Egypt, but it filled me with joy to know that she was not only alive and well, but had married back into the family.

There have been a lot of trials and tribulations along the way. We had left Bethel and were on our way to Ephrath when my father's wife, Rachel (his second wife, not my mother, Leah), went into labor. She died giving birth to my youngest brother. Benjamin survived to become a favorite of my father.

My brothers were still rash after what had happened in Shechem. They were jealous of Rachel's other son, Joseph. And he made it worse by telling them about his dreams of ruling over them all. They came in from the fields one day, telling Father that the wild animals had attacked Joseph and bringing Joseph's bloody coat as evidence. It wasn't until much later that we found out he was still alive and that our brothers had sold him as a slave to a caravan of Ishmaelites.

We also lost my cousins, sons of Judah. Er married a woman named Tamar. When Er died, Tamar was given to his brother, Onan, according to the Levirate custom. Soon, Onan also died. The other brother, Shelah, wasn't old enough to marry, so Tamar returned to her father's house to wait for Shelah to become of marriageable age. But Judah did not have him marry Tamar as expected. Sometime after Judah's wife died, Tamar tricked Judah into marrying her. She ended up having twins, Perez and Zerah, a very short time later.

Then came the famine in Canaan. We were well off, so it didn't affect us much at first. Eventually, we were running out of food as well. We had heard there was food that could be purchased in Egypt. Father sent the brothers, except for Benjamin, to Egypt to get food. When they had to go back a about a year later, they were forced to take Benjamin as well. We found out when they returned that time that the person responsible for stockpiling the food in Egypt was none other than our brother, Joseph. After spending time as a slave and then in prison, he had come to be the second most powerful man in Egypt.

When the brothers came back the second time, they came with an invitation to move the whole family to Egypt. So here we are. The Egyptians don't particularly like shepherds but, out of respect for Joseph, they gave us some good land in Goshen and we have settled in.

Many others from neighboring countries also moved here to Egypt because of the famine. I was blessed to meet, and marry, a good man from Edom. Like me, he had gone through some hard times. Job had been a wealthy man, blessed with sons and daughters. Tragedy struck hard. He lost his children and his wealth. His health was taken from him. His wife died of misery in a fire in a neighbor's cattle barn. He had been healed and was getting back on his feet when the famine came.

Because he was family, a descendant of our father Abraham, Job settled near Goshen. I had thought that after the incident with Shechem no decent man would have me and I would never have another child. When I met Job, I started to hope. We have been married twenty years now. We have seven sons and three daughters. Job is once more a very wealthy man. He tells me that God has given him twice what was taken away.

After Father died, the whole country mourned. Joseph and the other brothers took Father's body back to Canaan, as he had made them promise. Job went too. They were accompanied by Pharaoh's officials. Father was buried in the field of Machpelah, near Mamre, which was bought by my great grandfather, Abraham.

God had blessed my father, Jacob. He has blessed Job. He has blessed me. He has blessed all his people. Blessed be the name of the LORD.

Asenath

I was raised in the house of Potiphera, priest of On. It was a good thing that my father was a man of importance. I always looked out of place and I'm certain that if it weren't for his status I would have been ridiculed to no end. You see, while most people resembled at least one parent in some way, I did not look at all like either my mother or my father, or anyone else for that matter. My skin was relatively pale. My nose seemed out of proportion to my face. My eyes were blue whereas everyone around me had dark eyes.

As I got older, my differences seemed to work in my favor. Apparently, people thought I was beautiful, or so it was said. I think they were just attracted to the prestige of my family. I had many suitors, but none seemed sincere to me.

One day my father came home to tell me he had found a suitor for me. It was someone I had never met, though I had certainly heard of him: Zaphenath-paneah, who held the second highest position in the land. Father hadn't made a marriage contract yet and I was not interested. Father, on the other hand, thought this would be a perfect match, the only one that was good enough for his daughter. He had set up a meeting; we were invited to eat with Zaphenath-paneah and the pharaoh that evening.

We stood when Zaphenath-paneah and Pharaoh came into the room with their attendants. I was surprised to see that Zaphenath-paneah had blue eyes. I felt a kinship with him and was beginning to think maybe this could be a marriage for me. Imagine Father's surprise when Zaphenath-paneah said he would not marry a woman who did not worship his LORD God. But something had been kindled in me.

The next day I sent a message to Zaphenath-paneah, telling him I wanted to learn more about his God. He arranged to have Ahmose, one of his attendants, meet with me to instruct me in the ways of Yahweh, which was the name of his God. My heart was stirred; I wanted to hear more about this God of love. I was changed; I could no longer worship at On. Ahmose carried this news to Zaphenath-paneah. My father was greatly disappointed when I would not go to the temple with him. He threatened to disown me, but when Zaphenath-paneah sent Ahmose to talk marriage terms, he was more than agreeable.

As soon as we were married, Zaphenath-paneah told me his birth name was Joseph and asked me to call him that. The name Zaphenath-paneah was given to him by the pharaoh. It means "a peaceful settlement between us". He told me that Pharaoh had some dreams and God had told Joseph what those dreams meant. Joseph then told Pharaoh the meaning, that there would be seven years of plenty followed by seven years of famine. We were married in the midst of the plentiful years.

Joseph had not been born in Egypt. He was a teenager when he was brought here as a slave from the north. That explained the blue eyes. He had been in jail when Pharaoh had his dreams. He advised Pharaoh to appoint overseers to collect the grain and keep it for the years of famine. Pharaoh appointed Joseph, and so he became an important man to the entire nation.

Worshipping his God brought Joseph and me closer together. Father recognized Joseph's God as a great God, although he never went as far as saying he was the only God. We were blessed and knew that the blessings stemmed from his God whom we knew to be the only true God. Two of those blessings were our sons, Manasseh and Ephraim.

The famine was the impetus of Joseph being reunited with his family. His brothers came to Egypt to buy grain. When they came the second time, Joseph revealed himself to be their brother. After that, his entire family came down to Egypt and settled in the area of Goshen. That was when I found out who I really was.

Joseph had gone to Goshen to meet his father, Jacob. After the reunion, he came home to update Pharaoh. His brothers and Jacob were to follow to be presented to Pharaoh. When they were admitted to the room where Joseph and I were waiting, Jacob seemed to be staring at me. When they returned after meeting with the Pharaoh, he spoke to me, quite contrary to protocol. Joseph translated when he asked where I had gotten the necklace I was wearing. It had a large medallion on it with some writing I could not read on one side and a thorn bush etched into the other. Since I couldn't read the writing, I wore it with the picture showing. I told him I had no idea where it came from. I had possessed it all my life.

When Jacob asked to see it, I placed it in his hands. As he read the writing, tears came into his eyes. Now Joseph was looking at me intently. Then Jacob explained. I was his granddaughter. I had been born as the result of the rape of his daughter, Dinah. Knowing my life was in danger, Jacob had taken me and laid me under a thorn bush, praying that God would protect me. Before he left me there, he had engraved the circumstances on the medallion and placed it around my neck. That explained my blue eyes.

It did not explain how I ended up in Egypt. My Egyptian father had died two years ago, so I could not ask him. I asked my mother when I next saw her, but she did not know either. She said my father just brought me home one day and said I was a gift from the gods.

It was no wonder my heart was moved when I heard about Joseph's God. Yahweh was my God too, the God of my fathers. Joseph's people were my people. I was still an Egyptian, as Joseph had become, but I was also an Israelite. As soon as we could prepare for the journey, I accompanied Jacob back to Goshen to meet my birth mother. I had to take a translator, but later learned to speak Hebrew and have some real conversations with her before she died.

I also got to meet my half-siblings, though they weren't born yet when I first met Dinah. (I have to call her Dinah. My mother is the woman who raised me.) Though I was raised an only child, I now have three sisters and seven brothers. After living in Egypt for a few years Dinah had married another of Abraham's descendants, though not of Jacob's line. Job had been through some hardships of his own and that apparently bonded them.

If you will excuse me, I am setting out to Goshen in one hour. Dinah's youngest just had a baby and I can't wait to see him.

Jochebed

I am of the people of Israel. My husband, Aram, and I are of the house of Levi. Once we Hebrews were welcome in the land of Egypt. A great man of Israel saved Egypt, and the world, by overseeing the stockpiling of grain in the seven good years so there was plenty during the seven years of famine. Joseph was elevated to the second highest position in the land, second only to Pharaoh. Joseph had sent for his father, Jacob, and his entire family, to come to Egypt and they settled in the area of Goshen. Those 70 people have grown to millions during the 430 years of captivity.

Joseph was much loved by the people and his family greatly respected. When Jacob, also known as Israel, died, there was national mourning. After the mourning period, all the members of his household, accompanied by officials of state, journeyed to Canaan to bury him. When Joseph died, all the people in Egypt mourned his passing as well. He was embalmed and his body is with us to this day, waiting for our return to the Promised Land.

Through the years, the Egyptians forgot about Joseph and grew afraid of us, though we had no thoughts of taking over or interfering in their government. They enslaved our people, putting them to hard labor, trying to limit our population.

Our people slaved, building the cities of Pithom and Rameses. Our numbers still increased. When hard labor didn't reduce that number, or even keep it level, the Pharaoh decided all our male children should be put to death as soon as they were born. It was during this murderous time that I gave birth to my second son.

I had hidden my pregnancy and was able to hide my child for three months. When he could no longer be hidden, I took a chance on the river. I got a papyrus basket and coated it with tar and pitch to make it waterproof. I put the child in it and placed the basket among the reeds at the bank of the Nile. My daughter, Miriam, stood in the reeds nearby to see what would happen to him. I returned home to await the outcome with a heavy heart, barely seeing my way through the tears in my eyes. All I could do was pray. The child was now in God's hands.

God was watching over my son to spare his life. Pharaoh's daughter came to the Nile with her attendants to bathe. Walking along the bank, she found the basket and was moved with compassion, even though it was clear the child was a Hebrew boy. Miriam walked over and asked if she would like a Hebrew woman to nurse and care for the child. And that is how I got my son, whom she named Moses, back for a time.

I was able to keep Moses with me for about three years, until he was weaned. I made the most of that time, teaching him about his people, the Hebrews, and more importantly, about the God of our fathers. I could only hope and pray that he would remember this when he lived in the palace as an Egyptian prince.

Moses must have remembered his people. When he was a grown man of 40, he was out watching our people labor. Seeing an Egyptian beating a fellow Hebrew, he defended him, killing the Egyptian and hiding him in the sand. Moses' actions were not hidden. The next day he went out again. That time he saw two Hebrews quarrelling and spoke up, asking the one why he was fighting with his brother. The man responded, asking Moses who made him judge. When he asked Moses if he was going to kill him as he had killed the Egyptian the day before, Moses became afraid, knowing that what he had done was not a secret.

So I lost my son again. Fearing for his life, he fled from Egypt. That was the last I heard of him. I don't even know if he is dead or alive. Aram died shortly after Moses went to live in the palace, leaving me a widow. I thank God daily for my other children, Aaron and Miriam. Still, there is a hole in my heart. I pray for Moses too, as well as the people of Israel. Our people remain in bondage, laboring under the whips of the Egyptians. We still pray, waiting for our deliverance.

Zipporah

I married a simple man, a shepherd. But that is not who my husband is now. Let me explain.

I had gone to the village well with my six sisters to draw water for the flocks. This was usually a man's job, but my father did not have any sons, so the task was left to us girls. It was always a challenge because the other shepherds would come and drive us away. Many times we would have to wait for hours at a distance until all the others had had their fill. While we waited, we were subject to much verbal abuse. It was only the fact that our father was a priest of Midian that we were not physically assaulted as well.

We had been pushed away once again when a stranger came to our rescue. He not only made the other shepherds give way, but he watered our flocks for us. Father was surprised when we returned home much earlier than usual. When we explained that an Egyptian had rescued us from the other shepherds, he asked why we did not bring him home with us. So a couple of us went back to ask the man to our home to share a meal and let Father thank him appropriately. The man ate like he hadn't had a meal in days. And he hadn't.

Moses was his name. He told us how he had been raised by an Egyptian princess in the house of Pharaoh but had been born a Hebrew. He had killed an Egyptian for beating a fellow Hebrew and when it became known to the Pharaoh, he fled for his life. After weeks of wandering in the desert, he had come to the well where we met him. Father invited him to live among us and eventually he and I were wed. Soon we had a son whom Moses named Gershom, and then another he named Eleazar.

We lived in peace and prosperity for many years. Moses became our shepherd and we never again had a problem with the other shepherds. Some forty years after Moses had first appeared at that well, he came home with an amazing story.

While he was tending the flock across the desert at Mount Horeb, he was drawn to a fire. It looked like the bush was burning, but it was not being consumed. Then he heard a voice calling his name. When he answered, he was told to take off his shoes as he was standing on holy ground. It was his God and his God was asking him to do something unbelievable. He was to go back to Egypt, a place where his very life was in danger, and lead his people out of Egypt to the land of the Canaanites.

Moses told us that he had questioned his own ability to do that and had asked God to find someone else. But God was firm. When Moses asked what he should tell the people when they asked who sent him, God said to him, "I AM WHO I AM. Tell them I AM has sent me." He was the God of their fathers, Abraham, Isaac, and Jacob. So Moses asked what he should do if they didn't believe him or listen to him. As a sign, God told Moses to throw his staff on the ground and it changed into a snake. When Moses picked up the snake by the tail it became a staff again. Moses was not yet convinced, so he was directed to put his hand in his cloak. When he removed it, the hand was white with leprosy. When he put it in the cloak and withdrew it again it had returned to normal.

Moses still was not ready to take on this enormous task that was presented to him. He pointed out his lack of eloquence in speaking and his stuttering. He asked the LORD God to please find someone else to do it. The LORD became angry. He told him he would send Moses' brother, Aaron, to speak for him. Finally convinced, Moses returned home and told us what had happened. Father gave his blessing, and we headed back to Egypt with our sons.

We stopped at a lodging place along the way. God was about to take Moses' life. I knew it was because our son had not been circumcised, so I took a flint knife and did the circumcision myself. It was a task I detested, but it needed to be done. I then took the bloody knife and laid it at Moses' feet.

We met up with Aaron at Mount Horeb. Moses told Aaron everything that had happened to this point, especially about his meeting with God and the mission they were on. We all went on to Egypt. When we got there, the children and I stayed with Moses' sister, Miriam, and her family. But Moses had a big job to do, so after a couple months our sons and I returned home.

After quite some time, word came to us that Moses and his people were traveling through the desert toward our part of the country. We had heard what God had done for Moses and his people Israel. My father went with us out into the desert to meet Moses where he was camped at the mountain of God. It was good to be reunited with him. Our sons were happy to be with their father again. After too short a visit, Father returned home while we three stayed with the Israelites.

While Israel was camped at the foot of the mountain, Moses went up to the mountain to meet with God. It had been three months since they left Egypt. Moses came down and told the people to consecrate themselves and prepare to gather near the mountain, but not go all the way up to it. On the third day there was thunder and lightning, but no rain. As a thick cloud covered the mountain, a loud trumpet blasted and Moses led us out of camp to the base of the mountain. It was covered in smoke and shook violently. We could not remain and listen to the voice of God. Moses went back up the mountain.

Moses was gone for so long that the people became restless. It was over a month and we did not know if Moses was ever coming back. The people needed leadership, so they convinced Aaron to make a god for them. Aaron collected gold jewelry from all the people and made a golden calf, fashioned after the gods of Egypt. This was something concrete that the people could see. The leaders announced that this was their god. Trying to mitigate the idolatry, Aaron announced a festival to the LORD the next day and so all came to make offerings, eat and drink, and indulge in revelry.

It was while they were feasting that Moses came down from the mountain. When he saw the golden calf and the dancing, he broke the tablets of stone he had been carrying. He burned the calf and ground it into powder, then made the people drink it. Moses called out for those who sided with the LORD. The tribe of Levi responded and Moses directed them to go through the camp, killing about three thousand of those who had turned against the LORD. It was an awful day. This was followed by a plague and many more died.

Soon after, Moses went back up the mountain. He stayed away for 40 days again, only this time there was no rebellion in his absence. When he returned, the stone tablets with the law remained intact. This was not, however, the last of the uprisings. The Hebrews are a most ungrateful people.

As I said earlier, my husband is no longer a simple shepherd. He is the leader of a great number of people, guided by his God. There are ups and downs, but we are getting closer to the promised land.

Miriam

What I remember most about my childhood was the abundance of love. Don't get me wrong, life was harsh. Mother was always busy, and so was everyone else. We learned early on that everyone had to pitch in. We had plenty to eat, and some to share, but only because the women and girls not only cooked our food every day, but also grew most of it. Because of the Egyptians, the men and older boys were not home very much. They were off building cities for the Pharaoh. When they were home in Goshen, the taskmasters kept them busy working in the fields for the Egyptians. But at least then they got home long enough to eat and sleep.

There was always love. My parents showed their love to each other whenever Father had a chance to be home. It was obvious in the way they spoke to each other and touched each other. We children would usually fall asleep trying to wait up for Father when we knew he would be returning. The minute he walked through the door, we were wide awake. We would practically knock him over rushing into his arms. He would always spend a little time with us, despite the fact that he was exhausted. He'd tell us stories about our ancestors and what God had done for them before shooing us off to bed.

We Israelites, Hebrews as the Egyptians know us, have always been very close, especially within our larger family groups. I am a Levite, a descendent of Levi, who was one of twelve brothers. Hundreds of years ago, our fathers came to Egypt because it was the only place to get food during the famine. It was due to one of our own people, Joseph, that there was any food for anyone. He invited his father, Jacob, and the entire family to move here. (Jacob's other name was Israel, that is why we are called Israelites.) They were given the land of Goshen to settle in because they were sheep herders. It was a good area of Egypt, but away from the greater part of the population. You see, the Egyptians love to eat meat but they hate the odor and sounds of the flocks.

Through the years, those 70 people had grown into millions. The Egyptians had forgotten Joseph and what he did for them. They had forgotten the reverence they held for him and his father. All they saw in our people was a group whose numbers were so great that they feared a rebellion. And so they tried to work us to death.

When hard labor didn't reduce the Israelite population, Pharaoh decreed that all the male children were to be put to death at birth. The midwives wouldn't do it. When questioned by Pharaoh they said it was because the births were over by the time they got to the mothers' houses. Then Pharaoh ordered that all baby boys were to be thrown into the river. When his soldiers came, it didn't matter if the baby was a newborn or had not been found for a year. They were all tossed into the Nile to be drowned.

It was at this time that my mother became pregnant again. I already had one brother, Aaron, who was born before the decree. But if this child were a boy, he would not live long. It was a boy. Mother hid him for three months, as she had hidden her pregnancy. When he could no longer be hidden, Mother put him in the basket and put the basket in the reeds along the river. I hid in the reeds a ways off to see what would happen.

Pharaoh's daughter was the one to find him and she wanted to keep him. I was able to get her to let me find a Hebrew nurse for him, my mother. So Moses, as the princess named him, was able to be home with us for three years before moving to the palace.

It wasn't long after that when Father died. Pharaoh had succeeded in working another man to death, though it had taken 80 years. That, on top of Moses leaving the house, was a terrible burden on Mother. Aaron and I did what we could to help. Eventually we married and had children. I think Mother's greatest joy in those days was seeing her grandchildren. She lived with Aaron until the day came when she joined Father in the afterlife.

We saw Moses once in a great while during those years. He lived the life of a prince, until he was 40. At that time he killed an Egyptian for beating a Hebrew. It was found out and Moses fled.

We didn't hear a word about him for another 40 years. Then Aaron was told by God to go and meet up with Moses in the desert. He brought Moses home with him. That is when our lives started to change drastically.

Moses and Aaron met with the elders of the community, told them what God had said about the Israelites leaving Egypt, and showed them the signs God had given them. After that, Moses and Aaron went to Pharaoh. The pharaoh who had been after Moses' life had since died. This was the pharaoh Moses had grown up with.

Pharaoh may have been agreeable to hearing them out, but he was not agreeable to granting their request to allow the Israelites to go out to the desert to worship. Instead he gave an order to make their work even harder. While they had been provided straw to make the bricks before, the Israelites were now to gather their own straw, and still make the same number of bricks each day. The taskmasters became more severe and the people became angry with Moses and Aaron, blaming them for making their lives even more miserable.

That is when trouble really started. Now we call them the ten plagues of Egypt. First, God turned all the water in the land into blood. Fish died in the river and there was a horrible stench throughout the land. Even the water we had in jugs in our homes turned into blood.

Then came the frogs. They were everywhere; you had to watch where you were stepping and still you were apt to step on a frog. Pharaoh told Moses that if he prayed to God to take away the frogs, he would let the people go. But when the frogs were gone, so was Pharaoh's permission to leave.

Next came the gnats. Everywhere, all over the people, the animals, everything. I heard that Pharaoh's magicians told him it was the hand of the Hebrews' god, but he would still not let us leave.

With the fourth plague we Israelites got some relief. God kept the flies away from the Hebrews when he infested the Egyptians with them. Their houses were filled with flies, the people were covered, and the land was ruined with them. Pharaoh called for Moses and told him to take the people to make their sacrifices. Moses pointed out that shepherds were offensive to the Egyptians and the sacrifices would be detestable to them. The sacrifices must follow a three day journey into the desert to be far enough away to not upset the Egyptian people. Pharaoh finally consented, but as soon as the flies were gone, he withdrew his consent.

The next plague hit the livestock. All the livestock of the Egyptians died, but those of Israel were spared. The men Pharaoh sent out found that not one of the Hebrews' livestock was affected. And still he would not let the people go. This was followed by boils on man and beast. All the Egyptians were affected. The boils on Pharaoh's magicians were so bad that they could not stand when Moses and Aaron came to them. Still Pharaoh would not relent.

Next came a hailstorm, the likes of which had never been seen before. The only place not affected was Goshen, the area where we Israelites lived. Those

Egyptians who had heard Moses say this was going to happen, and believed him, brought in their servants and livestock. Those who didn't lost them all to the hailstorm. The hail stripped the trees and beat down the crops in the fields. This got Pharaoh's attention. He called for Moses and told him to take the people and go. But when the storm passed, he changed his mind once again.

When Moses told Pharaoh that the land would be infested with locusts which would destroy what little vegetation remained, Pharaoh would grant permission for only the men to go. The next day there were so many locusts that the land, except for Goshen, was blackened with them. Nothing green remained. Pharaoh panicked and begged Moses to pray to God to remove the locusts. True to form, when the locusts were gone, Pharaoh would not let the Hebrews leave.

Another plague came upon the Egyptians, this time total darkness in the land. It was so dark that, except in Goshen, a person could not see his hand in front of his face. After three days of this, Pharaoh gave permission for the men, women, and children to leave, but they would not be allowed to take their flocks and herds. When Moses told him the animals must also go, Pharaoh became so angry he threatened Moses with death if he ever showed his face again.

The final plague was the grimmest of all, death to the firstborn in every household. It would affect man and beast alike. Moses told our people to prepare for it by having a special meal and painting the blood of the lambs we would be roasting onto the doorways of our houses. We were also to go to our neighbors and ask for silver and gold. I wouldn't have thought the Egyptians would give us anything, but God, and fear, moved them to do just that.

The deaths started at midnight. Loud crying went throughout the land. Every Egyptian family had a loss. When Pharaoh's firstborn son died, Pharaoh summoned Moses and told him to take the people and animals and leave the country. He had had enough; so had all the people. They urged the Israelites to leave quickly. Some of them even came along with us from Rameses to Succoth.

We moved on from Succoth to Etham at the edge of the desert. It was an amazing journey. During the day we followed a pillar of cloud and by night a pillar of fire. Moses said it was the LORD God leading us to the Promised Land. It seemed odd to us when Moses had us turn around and encamp near Pi Hahiroth, between Migdol and the sea. We were stunned when we saw the Egyptians coming at us with their horses and chariots. Pharaoh had changed his mind again. The Egyptians were behind us and the sea stretched out in front of us. There was no way to turn. We felt doomed. The people were severely frightened and badgered Moses about taking them out in the desert to die. It was with forlorn disbelief that we moved toward the sea as directed.

Then an even more stunning event occurred. The pillar of cloud moved behind us, blocking the Egyptian army from view. At night it again became a pillar of fire, giving us light. Moses stretched out his hand over the water and it dried up. The waters had piled up on the left and the right and we crossed over on dry land. Panic again when we saw that the army was following us onto the path in the midst of the sea. But then we watched as the wheels fell off their chariots and they seemed totally confused. Moses again stretched his hand over the sea and the walls of water collapsed over the Egyptians, drowning them all.

I will never forget how we celebrated. Moses and the people of Israel sang this song to the LORD, saying,

> "You have led in your steadfast love the people
> whom you have redeemed;
> you have guided them by your strength to your
> holy abode.
> The peoples have heard; they tremble;
> pangs have seized the inhabitants of Philistia.
> Now are the chiefs of Edom dismayed;
> trembling seizes the leaders of Moab;
> all the inhabitants of Canaan have melted away.
> Terror and dread fall upon them;
> because of the greatness of your arm, they are
> still as a stone,
> till your people, O LORD, pass by,
> till the people pass by whom you have
> purchased.
> You will bring them in and plant them on your
> own mountain,
> the place, O LORD, which you have made for
> your abode,

the sanctuary, O Lord, which your hands have established.
The LORD will reign forever and ever."

Then I took a tambourine and led the women singing and dancing in celebration, echoing "Sing to the LORD, for he has triumphed gloriously; the horse and his rider he has thrown into the sea." We would never be bothered by the Egyptians again.

The people were moved to fear the LORD and to put their trust in him and in Moses. But that was short lived. Now and then there is an uprising and the people must be taught a lesson. Moses has had to bring water out of rocks and put down revolts. Still he presses on. When there was no food to be found, God sent manna. It is kind of like a grain and is found covering the ground every morning except the Sabbath. Quail come in the evenings. We are sick of the same thing, but at least we are not hungry.

Three months after we left Egypt, we reached the Sinai desert and the mountain. The first time Moses went up the mountain, the people totally lost faith. He was gone for so long we didn't know if he would ever return. Here we were, stuck out in the middle of the desert with no one to lead us. I don't remember whose idea it was at first, but soon just about all the people were clamoring for a god they could see. Aaron took all their gold jewelry and gilded a wooden bull calf with it. I think he may have regretted it almost as soon as it was done. He declared the next day to be a feast to the LORD. Almost everybody forgot what that meant. Not only was there feasting, but there was all manner of dancing and wantonness.

When Moses came down from the mountain, that is what he saw. He was so angry, he threw down the stone tablets he was carrying and broke them. Then he burned the golden calf, ground it up and made the people drink the ashes in water. He called for defenders of the LORD God to rally and to slay the evil doers. People of my own tribe, the Levites, took up swords and destroyed thousands of people that day. That was just the start. God sent a plague upon the people that took part in the revelry. Many more died in the days that followed.

Moses again went up onto the mountain. With all those deaths in their minds, this time the people were patient. When Moses returned after another 40 days, he had a fresh set of stone tablets with him. Not only did he have the laws which were engraved on them, he had God's instructions for many other laws as well as directions for building a tabernacle for worship. We were to use that tabernacle many, many years.

Moses gave us several types of laws. There were the moral laws, some of which were engraved on the stone tablets. Basically they came down to the theme of love, love for God and love for our neighbors. Things like not murdering, stealing, coveting, or committing adultery. There were laws of sanitation. We were to avoid certain foods and practices. We were given laws for government. There were ceremonial laws, covering different types of offerings and certain feasts and customs we are to observe.

Some of these ceremonial laws included the consecration of my brother, Aaron, and his sons as priests. Their line was to continue to provide our priests forever. Aaron had four sons: Nadab, Abihu, Eleazar, and Ithamar. Abihu and Ithamar were destroyed by fire when they ignored the instructions of the LORD and offered unauthorized incense. Only Nadab and Eleazar would continue the line of Aaron.

The rest of the tribe of Levi was to support the work of the tabernacle. They would be responsible for putting up, taking down, and transporting the tabernacle whenever we moved. When we were in camp, they took care of everything that needed taking care of which related to the tabernacle.

We spent over a year camped at Sinai. I think this was to establish us as a nation. Though we had no land to call our own at the time, we were a people set apart from those around us.

Our group had many people with us who were not of the children of Israel. Most of them came with us from Egypt, but some joined us along the way. One of those who joined us was Zipporah, Moses' wife. She was a Cushite he had met during his exile. Her father was a priest of Midian. She had come with Moses when he returned to Egypt, but went back to her father before the plagues and the exodus. Her father returned her to Moses before we camped at Sinai. As she grew more comfortable with us, she forgot her place. I thought she was preparing her sons to take over from Moses.

Did the two of them think Moses was the only one God spoke with? God had also spoken with Aaron. And I myself was a prophetess. I was even more upset than Aaron. I must admit, neither I nor Aaron handled things well. We were upset with Zipporah and also with Moses. We forgot, for the moment, that it is only God who decides who is to lead. Aaron and I were summoned to the tent of the meeting with Moses. A cloud descended and a voice called out to us. The LORD was angry about our grumbling, especially mine. When the cloud lifted, I had become leprous, white as snow. Aaron and Moses prayed to God that I would not die. I would be healed, but not before I was vanquished to an area outside the camp for seven days. I did not complain against Moses again.

When I was whole again, the camp moved on to the wilderness of Paran. We were getting close to the Promised Land. Moses sent out 12 men, one from each of the tribes. They were to scout out the land and bring back a full report. They returned after 40 days, bringing with them some of the fruit of the land. One single cluster of grapes was so big that they had to carry it on a pole between two men. They brought pomegranates and figs. They reported that the land was rich in produce and other resources.

It wasn't all good news. They also told of the giants who lived in the well-fortified cities whom they thought would overpower us. Joshua and Caleb still had confidence that God would help us to overcome, but the people shouted over them, grumbling against Moses and Aaron. They were certain it would have been better to die in the wilderness or go back to Egypt than to try to enter Canaan.

When Joshua and Caleb tried to convince them that it was a good land and the LORD could bring us into that land and give it to us, the people would have stoned them. Only the glory of the LORD appearing at the tent of meeting stopped them. Angry at the crowd, God himself was ready to wipe us off the face of the earth and start over, making a people for himself from Moses.

Moses intervened and the LORD relented. But there were to be consequence. None of the people who had seen what God did in Egypt and the desert up to this point, save Joshua and Caleb, would enter the Promised Land. All the others over the age of 20 would die in the desert. We were to wander in the wilderness for 40 years until this had all come to pass. The ten spies who brought back the frightening reports died of a great illness soon after that announcement.

After being told this, the people repented of their reluctance to rely on God and were ready to charge into the land and take it over. Moses told them it was too late. God would not be with them and they would be slain. But many tried anyway and were defeated by the Amalekites and the Canaanites.

Some people never learn. Having forgotten the lessons of that failure, some of the men, led by Korah, another Levite, gathered up 250 chiefs of Israel to confront Moses and Aaron. The crowd charged them with elevating themselves above all others, and claimed a share of the leadership for themselves. Moses said to them that God would show who is his own the next day. They had gone too far. The Levites should have been content that God had set them apart to do service in the tabernacle and to minister to the congregation.

Dathan and Abiram, of the tribe of Rueben, were also part of the rebellion. They refused to come to Moses when he called for them. They accused Moses of making himself a prince and failing to take them into the land of milk and honey.

The next morning the rebels, Moses, and Aaron, met at the tent of the meeting. By God's command, Moses had all the other people get away from the tents of Korah, Dathan, and Abiram. Moses declared, "If these men die as all men die, or if they are visited by the fate of all mankind, then the LORD has not sent me. But if the LORD create something new, and the ground opens its mouth and swallows them up with all that belongs to them, and they go down alive into Sheol, then you shall know that these men have despised the LORD."

Immediately, the ground opened up and swallowed the three trouble makers, along with their entire households. Their families, their goods, everything went into the deep. Then fire came from the LORD and burned up the 250 men who had conspired with them. People still missed the point. The next day they complained that Moses and Aaron had caused all those deaths. 14,700 people died in the plague that followed.

It has been nearly 40 years that we have been wandering in the desert. There have been more rebellions and punishments, but God continues with us. I am an old woman now, one of the few old people left. My generation is almost gone; the LORD said we would not enter the Promised Land. I expect to pass from this world soon. I may never see Canaan, but I will soon enter the afterlife. God has been good to me. I am not afraid.

Rahab

The wars are pretty much over and we are settled in the land. I have lived here in Canaan all my life. My new family was born and raised in the desert. God did marvelous things for them on their journey from Egypt to my homeland. We had heard of these wonders and the people in my hometown of Jericho were frightened of the tribes of Israel who were making their way toward us. Their God had dried up the waters of the Red Sea to allow them to pass through, bringing the waters down on the Egyptians when they tried to follow. He fed them and kept them alive for the 40 years they roamed the desert. Most recently, before they came to Jericho, their God had led them to victory over Sihon and Og, the two kings of the Amorites on the other side of the Jordan.

I ran an inn on the wall of Jericho. In the name of hospitality, and to supplement my income, I also would sleep with some of the guests. It was expected and my father encouraged it. Though my job was primarily that of an innkeeper, you could also say I was a prostitute.

One night, two men came to the door. They were two of the Israelites whom we feared. They had come to spy out our city in preparation for attacking us. I did not know their names at the time but they were Salmon and Abner. I laid a meal before them and while they were eating they told me about their LORD God and his plan of salvation. My heart was stirred and I knew their God was the only true God.

Someone had seen them come to my inn and had told the king. He sent men to take the aliens into custody but I had taken the men to the roof top and hidden them under the flax that was spread out and drying there. I told the king's envoys that the men had been there but had already left before the city gates were about to be closed. I told them I didn't know where the men had gone and advised them to go after the spies. They left and the city gates closed behind them.

When I took Salmon and Abner up to the roof I told them how frightened we were of them and that I knew the LORD had given them the land. I requested that they swear to me by their LORD that they would show mercy to me and my family. They were grateful that I had saved their lives and promised they would spare ours. If I would keep their secret, they would honor the promise. If not, they would be released from that promise.

They gave me a scarlet cord to put in the window. They told me that all members of my family who would be in my house at the time of the attack would be spared. If they were not there with me their lives would be forfeited. I agreed to the terms and put the cord in the window.

I let them down through that very window. Because my house was built into the wall, this got them outside of the walls and they avoided the gates and the people in the city. I knew that the king's men were searching between Jericho and the fords of the Jordon River, so I told Abner they should go to the hills. They were to wait three days until the searchers gave up and then go on their way.

The morning after Salmon and Abner returned to their camp on the far side of the Jordon, their company started to move. When they reached the Jordan, another miracle occurred. The waters were parted as when the Israelites had crossed the Red Sea. 40,000 armed men, their women and children, and all their property crossed the Jordan on dry land. When the kings and peoples of the land heard about this, all were more frightened and disheartened. From king to wash maiden, we knew their God would defeat us. Jericho was closed up. No one came in or went out of the city.

We thought the attack would come immediately, but the Israelites made camp at Gilgal. There was no sign of them moving on. After a week, the strangest thing happened.

The armed men approached the city but made no attempt to enter. They did not speak or shout, just walked around the city. The only sound was the continuous blowing of the trumpets. They repeated this action for six days. Once around the city and then they were gone. The seventh day they didn't leave after circling Jericho as they had done before. They went around again and again, seven times in all. We heard the loud blast of the rams' horns and then all the assembly shouted. I didn't know men could make such a racket.

Before the shouting died down we heard a different sound. The walls of the city were collapsing. The only part that didn't fall flat was my house. With the walls down, the Israelite army just walked into the city. Salmon and Abner came to my house, led us out, and had us stay just outside their camp. Meanwhile the Israelites destroyed every living being in Jericho, both man and beast. Then they burned the city down.

Thus started the conquest of the land of Canaan. There were many battles after that. Most battles were won easily by the army of God. Sometimes the people defied God and things did not go so well. After they took Jericho, they went up against the city of Ai. When Jericho was destroyed, the Israelites were not to take anything as spoils. But someone did. As a result, God allowed the people of Ai to rout the people of Israel. It was found out that a man named Achan had taken a cloak from Shinar, some gold, and some silver, and buried them beneath his tent.

God's vengeance for this disobedience was frightful. They took Achan, his whole family, the stolen goods and everything Achan possessed up to the valley. The people stoned them and burned everything with fire. After that, the army went against Ai a second time and defeated them.

Eventually, much of Canaan was defeated and occupied. The exceptions were the lands of the Philistines near the Great Sea, the land of the Geshurites, and some other specific areas. Enough was conquered that the land could now be allotted to the tribes of Israel. The Reubenites, Gadites, and half the tribe of Manasseh had already been given land on the eastern side of the Jordan. The other nine and a half tribes were to receive their inheritance on the western side, the land of the Canaanites.

There are still skirmishes, but we have pretty much settled in. I have been accepted as one of the people of God. Remember the spies? I married Salmon. We have a five year old son we named Boaz. He keeps us running. His name means "quick" and he lives up to it every day. And I have to run. I wonder what he is up to now. He is much too quiet.

Mahlah

My name is Mahlah. I am the eldest of my father, Zelophehad, a man of the tribe of Manasseh. My sisters are Noah, Hoglah, Milcah, and Tirzah. We would have passed unknown into history if we had even one brother. But that was not to be.

Our people had been roaming the desert for 40 years. We had come from Egypt where our people had been enslaved. When the group neared Canaan, the Promised Land, spies went out to survey the land. They came back with glowing reports of the land, and dreadful reports of the people in it. Although two of them, Caleb and Joshua, said we could defeat the natives with God's help, the people by and large rebelled. Thus we were condemned to stay in the desert until all that generation, excepting Caleb and Joshua, had died.

It was nearing the end of the 40 years when God directed Moses and Eleazar, the priest, to take a census. When the census was completed, God told Moses that the inheritance of the Promised Land was to be allotted according to those numbers.

We sisters had been born during the years in the desert, so we were not barred from entering Canaan. Had our father been of our generation he would have received an allotment in the new land. But he had died years before, leaving no sons to continue his line.

Being daughters rather than sons, it looked like we were not to receive any inheritance.

Why should the name of our father be taken away from his tribe because he had no sons? We took this question to Moses and boldly asked for a share. I say boldly, because it is uncommon for women to leave their tents without an escort. We approached Moses at the entrance of the tent of meeting in front of Eleazar, the chiefs, and the entire congregation. Congregation being the men that is. We were nervous, never having stepped out of custom like this before.

We reminded Moses that our father had not died as a result of being involved in the rebellion of Korah, but had died for his own sin. Then we asked the question. Moses would not give us an answer without bringing it to the LORD for a decision. The LORD agreed with us. We were to be given a share of his inheritance.

I was to be very glad that Moses had given us this answer in the presence of many people. Years later, when the land had been conquered and Joshua was dividing up the land, we reminded him of what Moses had told us. We received our portion north of the Yarmuk River, east of the sea of Chinnereth. It is an area that has proven good for growing grapes and various other fruits. There is also good pasture for our sheep.

Before we even got to this land there was a minor bump in the road to our getting the inheritance. The heads of the clan of Gilead, of the tribe of Manasseh to which we belong, came to Moses with concerns.

They were afraid that if we took our inheritance and married outside the tribe of Manasseh, the inheritance would be lost to that tribe. Moses saw how this could be and added to the rule of inheritance.

Any daughter, not just we daughters of Zelophehad, holding an inheritance was to marry within her own tribe. We could marry whomever we liked, but it must be within our own tribes. No inheritance was to be transferred from one tribe to another; each tribe was to hold on to its own territory.

This seemed good to us and we married accordingly. Our father had no sons but he did have brothers. We each married a son of our father's brothers. To honor our father, Shem and I named our son Zelophehad. He and the sons of my sisters will inherit the land in my father's place. Father would be pleased.

Deborah

Since Joshua's death, this nation has been alternately at war and at peace. It's our own fault, really. God told us to conquer the land of Canaan and we have done a poor job of it. We took over enough land so that we could settle here, but we failed to drive out the heathen inhabitants as we were supposed to do. With such examples around us, many of our own people have turned to idols. It's like they've forgotten both what God has done for us and what God expects from us.

Many of the Israelites have bowed down to the false gods in the land. They've served the Ashtaroth and the Baals. We've had no formal government; each man does as he pleases. We are often oppressed by the surrounding peoples. When we were badly oppressed, the LORD showed us pity and provided us with judges to save us. Israel would repent of her sin and put away the false gods…until that judge died. Then the people would begin to again whore after the false gods.

We fell first to the king of Mesopotamia, Cushan-rishathaim. Eight years he enslaved us! The people cried out in distress and God sent us Othniel, the son of Kenan, Caleb's younger brother. He led our people against Cushan-rishathaim and freed us from the grasp of the foreigners. We lived in peace for 40 years. Then Othniel died. Israel returned to her evil ways.

Next, the Moabites came against us, allied with the Ammonites and the Amalekites. They took possession of Jericho which gave them a foothold on our people. Israel served Eglon, the king of the Moabites, for 18 years.

When the Israelites again cried out in despair, God raised up Ehud. He was a Benjaminite with a unique trait. He was left handed. Because of that, he was able to approach Eglon with a concealed weapon. When Ehud took the tribute to Eglon, no one suspected that a sword was bound to his right thigh. Ehud managed to get a private audience with Eglon, telling him that he had a secret message for him. The message was from God. Ehud reached under his cloak with his left hand, grabbed the sword from his thigh and pushed it into Eglon. The man was so fat, the sword went entirely into his belly.

Ehud escaped to Seirah. He sounded the trumpet, calling the people of Israel to battle. They took on the Moabites at the fords of the Jordon and defeated them, killing about 10,000 men. None escaped. Ehud led the Israelites for 80 years. Then he died and the people returned to their idol worship.

The LORD sold us into the hand of Jabin, king of Canaan, from the city of Hazor. Sisera was the commander of Jabin's army. They ruled over us for 20 years. This is when my story begins.

My name is Deborah. I am a prophetess and the wife of Lappidoth. The LORD had chosen me to be a judge in Israel. I would sit under the palm between Ramah and Bethel and the people would bring their legal issues to me for a decision. The LORD led me to call the people to rebel against Jabin and his army.

At God's direction, I summoned Barak, the son of Abinoam from Kedesh-naphtali. God wanted him to go against Sisera and promised to give Israel the victory, but Barak hesitated. He said he would only go if I went with him. Guided by God, I told him I would go along, but because of his reluctance, the glory of victory would not go to him but to a woman. We returned to his home in Kedesh and he mustered an army of 10,000 men.

When Sisera heard about the Israelites forming an army and going up to Mount Tabor, he called up his 900 chariots and all his men. I told Barak that this was the day the LORD had given them into his hand. The Israelites defeated the Canaanites and destroyed most of them. Except for Sisera, who had escaped.

As Barak was pursuing Sisera, Sisera came to the tent of Jael. She was the wife of Heber the Kenite. Now it is important to know that there was peace between the people of Jabin and the people of Heber, so Sisera figured this was a safe place. Jael went out to meet him when he came into their camp and convinced him to come to her tent. But it wasn't a safe haven. Jael ran a peg through his temple and killed him. The people of Israel pressed on against the army of Jabin, which was now without their commander, until it was destroyed and Israel was again free.

Barak and I were moved to poetry to praise God. We sang:

"That the leaders took the lead in Israel,
that the people offered themselves willingly,
bless the LORD!
"Hear, O kings; give ear, O princes;
to the LORD I will sing;
I will make melody to the LORD, the God of Israel.
"LORD, when you went out from Seir,
when you marched from the region of Edom,
the earth trembled
and the heavens dropped,
yes, the clouds dropped water.
The mountains quaked before the LORD,
even Sinai before the LORD, the God of Israel.
"In the days of Shamgar, son of Anath,
in the days of Jael, the highways were abandoned,
and travelers kept to the byways.
The villagers ceased in Israel;
they ceased to be until I arose;
I, Deborah, arose as a mother in Israel.
When new gods were chosen,
then war was in the gates.
Was shield or spear to be seen
among forty thousand in Israel?
My heart goes out to the commanders of Israel
who offered themselves willingly among the

people.
Bless the LORD.
"Tell of it, you who ride on white donkeys,
you who sit on rich carpets
and you who walk by the way.
To the sound of musician at the watering places,
there they repeat the righteous triumphs of the LORD,
the righteous triumphs of his villagers in Israel.
"Then down to the gates marched the people of the LORD.
"Awake, awake, Deborah!
Awake, awake, break out in a song!
Arise, Barak, lead away your captives,
O son of Abinoam.
Then down marched the remnant of the noble;
the people of the LORD marched down for me against the mighty.
From Ephraim their root they marched down into the valley,
following you, Benjamin, with your kinsmen;
from Machir marched down the commanders,
and from Zebulun those who bear the lieutenant's staff;
the princes of Issachar came with Deborah,
and Issachar faithful to Barak;
into the valley they rushed at his heels.
Among the clans of Reuben
there were great searchings of heart.
Why did you sit still among the sheepfolds,
to hear the whistling for the flocks?

Among the clans of Reuben
  there were great searchings of heart.
Gilead stayed beyond the Jordan;
  and Dan, why did he stay with the ships?
Asher sat still at the coast of the sea,
  staying by his landings.
Zebulun is a people who risked their lives to the
  death;
  Naphtali, too, on the heights of the field.
"The kings came, they fought;
  then fought the kings of Canaan,
at Taanach, by the waters of Megiddo;
  they got no spoils of silver.
From heaven the stars fought,
  from their courses they fought against Sisera.
The torrent Kishon swept them away,
  the ancient torrent, the torrent Kishon.
March on, my soul, with might!
"Then loud beat the horses' hoofs
  with the galloping, galloping of his steeds.
"Curse Meroz, says the angel of the LORD,
  curse its inhabitants thoroughly,
because they did not come to the help of the LORD,
  to the help of the LORD against the mighty.
"Most blessed of women be Jael,
  the wife of Heber the Kenite,
  of tent-dwelling women most blessed.
He asked for water and she gave him milk;
  she brought him curds in a noble's bowl.
She sent her hand to the tent peg
  and her right hand to the workmen's mallet;

she struck Sisera;
  she crushed his head;
  she shattered and pierced his temple.
Between her feet
  he sank, he fell, he lay still;
between her feet
  he sank, he fell;
where he sank,
  there he fell—dead.
"Out of the window she peered,
  the mother of Sisera wailed through the lattice:
'Why is his chariot so long in coming?
  Why tarry the hoofbeats of his chariots?'
Her wisest princesses answer,
  indeed, she answers herself,
'Have they not found and divided the spoil?—
  A womb or two for every man;
spoil of dyed materials for Sisera,
  spoil of dyed materials embroidered,
  two pieces of dyed work embroidered for the neck as spoil?'
"So may all your enemies perish, O LORD!
  But your friends be like the sun as he rises in his might."

Jael

I knew he was coming. The LORD spoke to me and gave me direction. When Sisera came into our camp I was ready. He was going past my tent, but stopped when I called his name. He hesitated when I invited him into my tent. Hospitality could be expected; my people were at peace with his people. Still, going into a woman's tent was something not normally done. I assured him it was ok, that he would be safe. My husband, Heber, was busy with tribal business and would greet him later.

He had been running since his army faced defeat by the Israelites. Tired and cold, he eagerly took the rug I gave him for a covering when he lay down. When he asked for a drink of water, I offered him warm milk. It made him more sleepy. Sisera told me to watch at the door and if anyone asked, to tell them no one was in the tent.

When he was sleeping, I picked up a tent peg and a hammer. Going slowly with a prayer on my lips to where he lay, I drove the peg into his temple, pinning him to the ground. He never even opened his eyes as he passed into death. Perhaps I had betrayed my husband and his peace treaty with Jabin, king of the Canaanites, but I had been loyal to God, following in the footsteps of our father, Hobab, father-in-law of Moses.

Barak, the leader of the Israelite army, arrived at our tent with the dawn. I went out to meet him and said I would show him the man he was seeking. Sisera was where I left him, pegged to the ground. I understand Barak was hesitant to go up against the Canaanites, but he was no less thankful to see the demise of Sisera than any other Israelite and praised God for his help.

My life was forfeit if I was in camp when Heber returned from his business in the south. When Barak left, I went with him. I was well received in the house of Deborah in the hill country of Ephraim. As Zipporah joined with the Israelites in the days of Moses, I now make my home with them. Under Deborah's leadership, we are at peace.

Zeleponith

I live in the village of Zorah in the land of the Danites. It has been a hard life. Manoah and I have a farm, but we get to keep little of the produce. When the crop comes in, the Philistines are right there to claim their share as taxes. They have ruled over us for the last 40 years. We cry out to the LORD for deliverance of our people.

And I have cried out for my own sake as well. Like our mother, Sarah, I was barren and unable to have a child. My prayer was answered in a most astonishing manner.

I almost dropped my bucket of water when I saw the man standing there. He seemed to appear from nowhere. The prophet had the appearance of an angel and I was so shocked, I never asked him his name or where he had come from. Then, even more surprisingly, he told me I would have a son. He was to be a Nazarite, starting in the womb. I was not to drink wine or any strong drink and to abstain from anything unclean. My son was to continue with those restrictions and never cut his hair. He was to begin to save us from the dreaded Philistines.

I went and told Manoah what had happened and what the man had said. Manoah wasn't sure what to make of it, so he prayed that the man would come again and teach us what we were to do with this child.

Manoah was in a different area of the field when the man appeared to me again. I quickly went to get Manoah and brought him to the man. Manoah asked him what I had already been told. He repeated the Nazarite restrictions and admonished Manoah, "All that I commanded her, let her observe."

Manoah asked the man to stay, saying we would prepare a young goat for him. The man said he would not eat, but we should prepare a burnt offering for the LORD. Manoah said to the angel of the LORD, "What is your name, so that, when your words come true, we may honor you?" And the man said to him, "Why do you ask my name, seeing it is wonderful?"

Manoah made the offering. As we were watching, the man went up to heaven in the flame of the offering. Only now we knew he was no man, but the angel of the LORD. We fell to the ground on our faces. Manoah said, "We shall surely die, for we have seen God." But I told him that if God had meant to kill us he would not have accepted the offering or given us this wonderful news of a child.

At first life went on as it always had. I returned to weaving my cloth and selling it in the marketplace. When the child was born, we named him Samson. I continued with my weaving, but it was broken up caring for Samson. He was a wild and strong willed boy, but we doted on him. Maybe too much.

When Samson was grown, I had him take my cloth to the market. One day he came back from Timnah with some disappointing news. He had fallen in love with a Philistine woman named Sari. He told us to get her for him as a wife. We pleaded with him. "Isn't there a woman among our people that you could take for a wife? Do you need to choose someone from the uncircumcised Philistines?" As I said, he was strong willed. He demanded that Manoah get this Philistine woman for him.

So we traveled to Timnah. Samson went on ahead of us because we were getting old and moving more slowly. When we got to Timnah, Manoah met with the girl's parents and arranged the marriage. Too soon we were going there again for the wedding.

There was a huge feast which lasted a week, done according to the Philistine style. Samson had no friends who were willing to go into the Philistine territory, so when we got there 30 young men of the land were brought to be his attendants. Only much later were we to find out what trouble that caused.

Samson had given them a riddle. "Out of the eater came something to eat. Out of the strong came something sweet." If they could solve it by the end of the feast, he would give them 30 changes of clothes. If not, they would give the 30 outfits to him.

When they could not answer by the third day, they came up with a plan. On the fourth day the men went to Samson's wife and threatened her. If she did not get the answer for them from Samson, they would burn her and her father's house to the ground. It took Sari three days of crying before Samson gave in. Sari told the men and on the last day of the feast, the men answered him, "What is sweeter than honey? What is stronger than a lion?"

Samson knew where they had gotten the answer because he had told no one else, not even us. Apparently, when we went down the first time, Samson had come across a lion. He had torn the lion apart with his bare hands. When we went down for the wedding, he had seen bees in the lion's carcass and scooped out the honey. He had given some of it to us without saying where it came from. He knew we would not have accepted it because it came from a dead body, which by the way, he never should have touched in the first place.

Samson was infuriated, but a bet was a bet. He went down to Ashkelon and killed 30 men there, taking their belongings and giving their clothes to the 30 men at the wedding. After that he remained so angry that he went home with us instead of returning to his wife.

After a while, he went to see his Sari. Her father would not let him in. He said he thought Samson hated her so he gave her to Samson's best man. He tried to talk Samson into taking her younger sister, but he would not.

Samson had to get his revenge. He went and caught 300 foxes, tied them tail to tail, and placed torches between each pair. Then he turned them loose, some into the Philistines' grain fields which were ready for harvest and the others into the olive orchards. When the Philistines found who had done that and why, they burned down Sari's father's house with the entire family in it. Samson went to the group of men and threatened them. With his great strength he was able to give them all a beating. Then he went and stayed in cave of Etam, near Lehi.

Soon after that, the Philistines made a raid on Lehi. The inhabitants asked the raiders why they had attacked them. They were after Samson. So 3000 men of Lehi went to Etam to collect Samson and turn him over to the Philistines. Samson said that if they swore not to attack him themselves he would allow them to take him. They tied him with sturdy new ropes and took him back to Lehi, to the Philistines.

The Philistines came to meet them, shouting, thinking they would now get their revenge. But the Spirit of the LORD came on Samson. He flexed his muscles and the ropes just fell off. He grabbed an ass's jawbone for a weapon and killed 1000 men with it.

For a while Samson stayed in Zorah, working with his father, taking my cloth to market. I guess he really did love Sari; her death had hit him hard. We so wanted him to find a good woman among us and settle down. But, once again, a Philistine woman got him in trouble.

Samson had gone to Gaza. The Gazites found out he was spending the night there with a prostitute. They surrounded the house and set an ambush at the city gate. They were going to attack him in the morning. But Samson got up at midnight. He went to the gate, pulled up the gate with the two posts and pulled them up, bar and all. He put them on his shoulders and carried them all the way to the hill near

Hebron. He had made a mockery of the Philistines once again.

Sometime after this, Samson moved in with a woman named Delilah, in the Valley of Sorek. He said he loved her and he was finally able to get past all that had happened with Sari. Manoah had died eight months earlier. I missed him but I was happy that he did not have to see this latest escapade with still another Philistine woman. It was because of Delilah that the Philistines were able to capture Samson, put his eyes out, and take him to prison.

I frequently made the journey to where Samson was imprisoned, bringing him food. He seemed a changed man. His strength was gone but his faith had strengthened. He told me how all his problems with the Philistines were the result of God working through him against them. They were being punished, not for what they had done to Samson, but for what they had been doing to God's people. My nephew, Aaron, also visited Samson, and often stayed with him.

A week after I had returned to Zorah the last time, Aaron brought word that Samson was dead. They had taken Samson to the temple of Dagon to show him off during one of their feasts. They were bragging that their god had given their enemy into their hands. Then they called on Samson to entertain them and placed him between the pillars of their temple.

Aaron said that Samson told him to put his hands on the pillars for him so he could lean against them. He heard Samson pray, "O Lord GOD, please remember me and please strengthen me only this once, O God, that I may be avenged on the Philistines for my two eyes." Samson grasped the two middle pillars on which the house rested. He leaned his weight against them, his right hand on the one and his left hand on the other. And Samson said, "Let me die with the Philistines." Then he told Aaron to leave.

Watching from outside the temple, Aaron saw Samson grab the pillars and pull them down. The house fell on all those inside the temple, killing more people than Samson had already killed in his lifetime.

The men of Zorah went to dig Samson's body out from under the rubble. They brought him up and buried him beside Manoah in the Sorek valley. The time of mourning is almost over. But I shall never stop mourning. My son, my son. God have mercy on your soul.

Delilah

I remember the first time I saw him. Samson was taller than the average Israelite, about the same height as the average Philistine, but he was much larger than one, being very muscular. His hair was long, divided into seven braids. I had heard about some of the things he had done to others in my country and was actually a bit frightened of him.

He was sitting in the corner of the inn. I served him his meal and he asked me to sit and talk. After our conversation, I still didn't know why he was here, only that he had come from Zorah.

After he had left, my brother, Heth, and some of the leading men here in the Valley of Sorek pulled me aside and said, "Seduce him, and see where his great strength lies, and by what means we may overpower him, that we may bind him to humble him. And we will each give you 1,100 pieces of silver." Although I could always use more silver, it wasn't that which convinced me to do so. I was more frightened of what they would do to me if I didn't do what they wanted than I was frightened of Samson.

So the next time Samson came in for a meal, I flirted with him. He was a pushover, actually. It wasn't long before we moved in together. I think he even loved me. I asked him where his great strength came from. At first he just laughed and wouldn't tell me anything.

Again I asked how he could be bound so that one could subdue him. When he stopped laughing, he said, "If they bind me with seven fresh bowstrings that have not been dried, then I shall become weak and be like any other man."

I told this to Heth and the next day the men brought me seven fresh bowstrings. While Samson was sleeping, I tied him with all seven ropes and the men hid in an inner chamber, waiting. I shouted, "The Philistines are upon you, Samson!" When he jumped up he snapped the bowstrings as if they were threads of flax in a fire. The men who were waiting in the other room snuck out without Samson seeing them.

He had made a mockery of me. I asked him again how he could be bound, telling him not to lie to me again. This time he said, "If they bind me with new ropes that have not been used, then I shall become weak and be like any other man." I passed this on to Heth and they brought me the new ropes. Again I bound Samson while he was sleeping and for the second time I called out, "The Philistines are upon you, Samson!" Again the men who waited to ambush him ended up sneaking off when the ropes gave way like thin threads.

I asked Samson for the third time how he might be bound. He sounded sincere when he said, "If you weave the seven locks of my head with the web and fasten it tight with the pin, then I shall become weak and be like any other man." After I passed this on to Heth, he and his friends came to the house in the middle of the night to wait. During the night I took Samson's seven locks of hair and wove them into the web. I pulled them tight and fastened them with the pin. When I said the Philistines were upon him, he sat up and pulled away the pin, the loom, and the web. And he laughed at me.

Heth came to me with a message that night. His friends didn't believe I was trying to get the truth and threatened to burn down my father's house if they didn't get the answer they were looking for. I was getting desperate. I asked Samson, "How can you say, 'I love you,' when your heart is not with me? You have mocked me these three times, and you have not told me where your great strength lies." I kept pleading with him, day after day. Finally, he gave in.

I think he was so worn down by then that he wanted to tell me. He opened up and told me how his parents had wanted a child but did not have one for many years. An angel came to his mother and told her she would have a son. The son must be a Nazarite. Part of that meant never cutting his hair. If that was done, he would be no stronger than any other man.

I knew that he was finally telling me the truth. I rushed to my brother's house to tell him. Many of his friends were there and I told them all, "Come up again, for he has told me all his heart."

Even though abstaining from wine was supposed to be one of the conditions of being a Nazarite, I knew that Samson liked to imbibe and would sleep like a log when he'd had his fill. I brought him some new wine and encouraged him to lie in my lap. When he had fallen asleep there, I motioned to one of the men who came and cut off Samson's hair.

When the man had left the room, I woke Samson. "The Philistines are upon you, Samson!" As he woke up he laughed saying, "I will go out as at other times and shake myself free." He didn't realize that his strength had left him. The Philistines jumped him and put out his eyes. They threw the pieces of silver at me. The money landed on the floor and I just looked at it. The scene in front of me was just too brutal. And I was responsible.

When the shock wore off, I picked up the money. I could not stay in that house, so I returned to my mother's home. Years later I heard that Samson had gotten his revenge. His hair had grown back and his strength had returned one last time. He'd brought the house down, literally, on his enemies, killing thousands.

Naomi

God has renewed me. I had wanted to die back then. When I returned from Moab, I told the women of Bethlehem not to call me by my given name of Naomi but Mara. Though I went away a woman rich in blessings, I had returned with pain and disappointment. They should call me Mara, I said, for the LORD has dealt bitterly with me.

When I was young, I married Elimelech, a prominent man in the small town of Bethlehem. We prospered and were blessed with two boys, Mahlon and Chilion. Everything was going well. Then the famine hit. It was ironic. Bethlehem means house of bread, but it had become very difficult to find bread there. Many of the villagers headed northeast to the more fertile plains of the Jordon. Elimelech thought the best move for us would be to Moab, across the Jordon and somewhat south, into the area that had been assigned to the tribe of Reuben when the land was first conquered by our ancestors.

While in Moab, the boys reached marriageable age. They took wives for themselves from the Moabites, Orpah and Ruth. I was unhappy about it at first. I wanted them to marry fellow Israelites. I learned to care deeply for the women; they were lovely young ladies who learned to know and accept our God, Yahweh. But alas, there were no grandchildren.

I was terribly sad when Elimelech died, but at least I had my sons. When Mahlon and Chilion died within the year, I was devastated. We were three widows; we did the best we could. When I heard that there was again food in Bethlehem, it seemed prudent to return.

Orpah and Ruth wanted to go with me. I guess I was a reminder of their husbands and that provided them a measure of comfort. I tried to send them back to their own mothers. Perhaps the LORD would be with them and they could find new husbands among their own people. I kissed them each good-bye, but instead of leaving they just cried and said they wanted to go with me. "Why?" I asked them. Did they think I would have more sons? Even if I did, it would be a long time before they would be old enough to marry. I had little chance of even finding another husband at this point in my life. Again I urged them to return to their childhood homes. I explained how difficult, how bitter, it was for me for their sakes that the hand of the LORD had gone out against me. They should go and be happy. I would never be happy again.

They continued weeping, but Orpah was finally convinced to go back. She kissed me and walked away. But Ruth clung to me. I told her she should follow Orpah, but Ruth just said, "Do not urge me to leave you or to return from following you. For where you go I will go and where you lodge I will lodge. Your people shall be my people, and your God my

God. Where you die I will die, and there will I be buried. May the LORD do so to me and more also if anything but death parts me from you." The girl was not to be dissuaded, and so we continued on our way. We came into Bethlehem when the barley was ready for harvest.

It is the custom that when the reapers go through the fields they leave some grain ungleaned for the poor among us. We certainly qualified for that now. Ruth asked me if she could go and glean among the grain. Boaz, the landowner, noticed her there and asked about her. The man in charge of the reapers told him that she had returned with me from Moab. She had asked permission to gather after them in that field and he had granted it. The hired hand also told Boaz that Ruth had been there since early morning, taking just one short rest.

Boaz must have been impressed. He approached Ruth and told her to keep coming to his fields and not go elsewhere. He also told her to keep close to the young women who were working there. He had warned the young men not to touch her. She was to go to the water vessels whenever she felt a need and to drink what she desired.

This was far more kindness than custom dictated. Ruth asked him why she, a foreigner, had found such favor in his sight. He said he had heard of the kindness she had shown to me. He said, "The LORD repay you for what you have done, and a full reward be given you by the LORD, the God of Israel, under whose wings you have come to take refuge." His kindness continued throughout the day and the days to follow.

When she returned from the field that first day, she brought more barley than would be expected in a day, and also some other food. She told me what had happened and the kindness she had encountered. I said, "May he be blessed by the LORD whose kindness has not forsaken the living or the dead." Boaz was a man of excellent repute. Further, he was a close relative, in a position to redeem Elimelech's property. I encouraged her to do as Boaz said, to stay with the young women in his field. She may not be so fortunate in another's field. Fieldworkers have been known to assault young women in her circumstances.

Ruth continued in the fields that Boaz owned, through the barley season and the wheat season as well. One thing led to another. Boaz did redeem Elimelech's property and he married Ruth. When Ruth's son was born, the women who had pitied me when I returned from Moab, now rejoiced for me. They said, "Blessed be the LORD, who has not left you this day without a redeemer, and may his name be renowned in Israel! He shall be to you a restorer of life and a nourisher of your old age, for your daughter-in-law who loves you, who is more to you than seven sons, has given birth to him."

I took the child, who had been named Obed, and I cared for him. It is wonderful being a grandmother. I no longer wish to be called Mara. My name is Naomi, "Pleasant". It is a good description once again.

Orpah

Tomorrow is my wedding day. This time I will be married according to the Moabite customs of my homeland. Mesha is a fine man, well respected in the village. His wife died recently and he was looking for someone to be a mother to his three young children. Perhaps we shall have one of our own, I don't know. I don't love him yet, but he will be a good provider.

I have known love. Chilion was truly a good man. He came from Israel to Moab with his parents and brother when there was a famine in their city of Bethlehem. My father welcomed them and sold them a piece of his land. There were not many decent young men in our village and I think Father had his eye on the older of the two newcomers for his daughter. His brother would take the younger for his daughter.

My cousin, Ruth, and I came to know their mother first. Naomi was kind and pleasant, but seemed a little sad. She missed her homeland. The first time I saw Chilion, my heart skipped a beat. Fortunately, Ruth's did not. She was taken with his brother, Mahlon. Their mother, Naomi, didn't seem too happy when our fathers arranged our marriages. I think it bothered her that her sons were marrying women who did not know their God.

Through the years, we learned about their God and all the wonderful things he had done for his people. We learned how the land they lived in had been promised to their ancestors hundreds of years earlier. And we learned about the promised life after we depart from this one.

We were happy except for one thing. Neither Ruth nor I was able to have a child. Year after year, and nothing. We kept hoping and praying. Naomi told us about Sarah and Rebekah, their ancestors, who did not have children until much later in life. Rebekah had been married 20 years before she had her twins. Sarah was 90 years old, way past menopause, when she had Isaac.

Elimelech died a few short years after the weddings. Ruth and I tried to console Naomi, but within the year we were bereft of our husbands also. There was a horrible accident making us widows. So much for hopes and prayers.

The three of us continued to live together. We subsisted on gifts from our parents and by working on my father's land. After ten years in our country, Naomi heard that the famine was over in Bethlehem. She missed her homeland and wanted to return. Ruth and I had become so close to her we wanted to go with her.

We packed up our belongings and headed back to Israel. We walked in silence the entire day. Little was said when we made camp for the night. In the morning Naomi spoke to us. "Go, return each of you to her mother's house. May the LORD deal kindly with you, as you have dealt with the dead and with me. The LORD grant that you may find rest, each of you in the house of her husband!" She kissed us and we all cried. We loved Naomi and did not want her to leave us. We told her no, we would go back with her to her people.

She insisted. "Turn back, my daughters, why will you go with me?" She said she was too old to have more sons for us to marry, but we should go back to our fathers and find new husbands here in Moab. We continued to weep and pleaded to go with her. She was filled with sorrow and wanted better for us.

I finally gave in and kissed her goodbye. Ruth still would not turn aside, so I took my leave of the two of them and returned alone to my mother's house.

A month after that, Father came home with Mesha. What good is a widowed daughter? The marriage was arranged for two weeks later. Did I make the right decision coming back? Only the gods know and time will tell.

Ruth

We laugh ourselves silly watching Obed run around the way he does. It seems my little one went from crawling to running without learning how to walk. What a joy he is to Boaz and me, and especially to Grandma Naomi.

Things weren't always this pleasant for us. I first met Naomi when her family moved to Moab because of the famine here in Bethlehem. There were Naomi, her husband, Elimelech, and their sons Chilion and Mahlon. Mahlon was to become my husband. My cousin, Orpah, married Chilion.

When Elimelech died, we all tried to comfort Naomi. But within a year, Chilion and Mahlon died in a horrible accident. All three of us missed the three of them terribly. When Naomi heard the famine was over, Orpah and I set out with Naomi to return to Bethlehem. Naomi was headed home, but Orpah and I were going to a place that was as foreign to us as Moab had been to her.

Not much was said the first day of travel. The next morning, Naomi told us to go back to our mothers. She was concerned that we would not find husbands in her country, but perhaps we could in our own. Neither of us wanted to leave her. Orpah was finally convinced to go back, but I would not. I clung to her and begged Naomi not to send me away. When she saw she could not change my mind, she consented to have me stay with her.

As we came into Bethlehem, the whole town took notice. Naomi had changed so much in her sorrow that the women weren't sure it was her. Naomi didn't think she was the same person either and told the women to call her Mara, an indication of the bitterness God had dealt her.

Naomi's people have a custom, a rule given by God, that when the fields are harvested, the poor are allowed to follow the reapers and collect what they missed, especially around the edges of the field which were to be "missed" on purpose. Naomi was too old to go out and do this so I asked her to let me take care of it. I went to the field early in the morning and asked the servant in charge to let me glean in that field.

The field I went to belonged to Boaz, a kinsman of Elimelech. Late in the afternoon he came to me and said, "Now listen, my daughter, do not go to glean in another field or leave this one, but keep close to my young women. Let your eyes be on the field that they are reaping, and go after them. Have I not charged the young men not to touch you? And when you are thirsty, go to the vessels and drink what the young men have drawn."

I had done nothing to deserve such kindness, and asked why he was being so good to me. He said it was because he had heard how good I had been to my mother-in-law. I still didn't think I had done anything extraordinary but I was grateful for the benevolence shown me. When it was time for the evening meal, Boaz had me join the reapers and share their food and drink. I had my fill and still there was more.

When I went back to glean again, I found that Boaz had told his young men to let me glean after them and before the young women came to bundle the sheaves. They were also to pull some grain from the bundles and leave them for me to pick up.

I showed Naomi the barley I collected, a full ephah of grain, which Naomi told me was far more than expected for a day's work. I also gave her the food left over from the evening meal and told her what the owner of the field had said to me. Astonished, she asked where I had been. When I told her I was in Boaz' field, she told me about the kinship, how Boaz was what they called a redeemer.

Encouraged by Naomi to go only to the field of Boaz, as he had said, I worked every day throughout the barley harvest and then the wheat harvest. When the end of the wheat harvest had come, Naomi said she wanted things to go well for me and told me what to do that night. I was to clean up, put on perfume, and go to the threshing floor where Boaz would be. I was not to let him know I was there until he had finished eating and drinking and had lain down to sleep.

Nervous, I did as she had instructed. Boaz lay down near the heap of grain, to protect it from would be thieves. When he was sleeping soundly, I quietly went over and uncovered his feet. Then I lay down and waited. At midnight he awoke with a start and saw me there. The light was dim and he asked who I was. I told him and asked that he spread his wings over me, his servant, because he was a redeemer.

Let me explain what a redeemer is. There are different things a redeemer will do for a close relative. The duty that applied here was to buy back the property of the deceased, thereby keeping it in the extended family. It also included taking the immediate family of the deceased into his own by marrying the widow, especially if there were no children. The first child born of that union would continue the line of the deceased.

So I was in effect asking Boaz to marry me. That is why I had been so nervous. What if he rejected me? What would happen to my reputation if it became known that I had been with him at night? What Naomi had directed me to do was a gamble.

Boaz thought I was being kind in seeking him rather than some young man. He said to me, "Do not fear. I will do for you all that you ask, for all my fellow townsmen know that you are a worthy woman." But he told me that there was someone more closely related who had priority as a redeemer. If that person wanted to be the redeemer, it was his right. If not, Boaz promised to redeem us himself.

I did not need to worry about someone seeing me return home that night. Boaz knew there would be talk, and he also knew it could be dangerous for me to be out in the middle of the night. So he told me to lie down and sleep. I got up to leave before dawn's light would let someone recognize me. Before I left, Boaz filled my cloak with six measures of barley to take back to Naomi.

Naomi was more interested in what had transpired than in the barley. She was sure that Boaz would take care of the matter quickly, that very day. It was hard to sit and wait, but it was settled that day as she had surmised.

The nearer relative was at first willing to redeem the land that Naomi was selling. But when he found the deal included taking me as a wife, he was no longer interested. Had he done so, he would be putting his own inheritance in jeopardy. He would lose the property rights of the first son. Boaz had the freedom to redeem the land and to marry me.

The women in town called down a blessing on us, that we would have children who would build up the house of Israel. Mahlon's name would be carried on through the first son.

We soon had that son, Obed, and happiness was restored. While he brought his parents great joy, Naomi may have been even happier. She had a grandson to carry on the family name and, more immediately, to make her laugh again. Any day now we will have another child. Maybe another son to carry on the name of Boaz. Or maybe a daughter, whom I think we shall name Naomi.

Peninnah

Everybody talks about the women who were unable to have children in their prime but were gifted with children later in life, like Sarah, Rebekah, and Rachel. But I identify with Leah. Like her, I am the wife that is unloved. Like Hagar, Bilhah, and Zilpah, my purpose was only to have children. I should have known what I was in for when I married Elkanah and became a secondary wife. But Elkanah was a nice, well-respected man, and well enough off that supporting two wives and many children was well within his means. And there was no one else in Ramah who seemed interested in marrying me.

Praise God, I was easily able to have children. I had ten, six boys and four girls. Elkanah loved them. But Hannah, Elkanah's first wife, became moodier and moodier with each child I had. She cried all the time. What was her problem? Elkanah loved her; he only used me. Don't get me wrong, he didn't treat me badly. He just didn't love me. I have to admit that I wasn't very nice to her. After my third child, I told Hannah she must be cursed. It had to be her; Elkanah wasn't having any difficulty fathering children.

The balance changed one year after we had gone up to Shiloh for the feast. Elkanah had made the sacrifice and divided up the food. He gave Hannah twice the portion he gave to the rest of us. But if you add my children's portions to mine (they are MY children after all), my portion could be said to have been more than double hers. Not that it mattered much. Hannah would not eat what she was given.

Anyway, after we had eaten, Hannah disappeared. When she returned something was different. She had wiped away her tears and washed her face. She was smiling. She never told us why. It became obvious a couple months later when I noticed that Hannah was pregnant. Ten months after her change of mood, Hannah gave birth to a baby boy and named him Samuel. To Elkanah's credit, he never treated my children any differently when Samuel was born. But I felt more unloved that ever.

One year, when I had just given birth to my first daughter, I did not go to Shiloh with the others. I was shocked when they came back without three year old Samuel. It was then that Hannah told me about promising to return him to God and why she had made him a Nazarite. She also told me that she was pregnant again. If Hannah was having more children, I knew I could never win Elkanah's love.

So I poured all my love into my children. It has served me well. My son was the firstborn and when Elkanah died, Juda was the son to inherit the double portion. He has taken over as head of the household and I am able to remain in my home of many years. I no longer have to contend with Hannah and her children; they live elsewhere. My younger children have moved out on their own, yet they live close enough for me to see frequently. I also have grandchildren surrounding me. I am no longer jealous, but at peace. God may have blessed Hannah, but he has certainly blessed me also.

Hannah

For the first couple years we were gloriously happy, Elkanah and I. The only thing marking the lack of perfection was that I could not have a child. When Elkanah's mother pushed him to take another, younger wife so he could have children, I could not object. Children were important in carrying on the family name.

When Peninnah had her first child, I was happy for Elkanah. I was even happy for Peninnah. But as more children were born to them, Peninnah became a thorn in my side. She constantly held it over me that I was barren, said I must have been cursed by God. I felt cursed, but I did not need her rubbing it in.

We went to Shiloh for the feast each year and Elkanah distributed the food after the sacrifice. He always gave me a double portion. Peninnah would always point out how the portions given to her children was her portion and it added up to far more than a double portion. I had no problem with the children getting their shares and would have given them mine. But the way Peninnah put it was very hurtful. She took every chance she could find to put me down.

It was so bad that one year all I could do was weep. I didn't touch my food. Elkanah asked me why, even though he knew what was in my heart. He added, "Am I not more to you than ten sons?" What could I say? He meant well, but I desperately wanted a child.

While Elkanah was finishing up his Levitical duties and Peninnah was busy with the children, I went to the temple and pleaded with God. "O Lord of hosts, if you will indeed look on the affliction of your servant and remember me and not forget your servant, but will give to your servant a son, then I will give him to the Lord all the days of his life, and no razor shall touch his head." I poured out my heart for half an hour.

A priest had been watching me. I must have been a sight with my mouth moving and no words being audible. Finally, the priest came up to me and chastised me. He thought I was drunk and told me to quit drinking the wine. I said, "No, my lord, I am a woman troubled in spirit. I have drunk neither wine nor strong drink, but I have been pouring out my soul before the LORD. Do not regard your servant as a worthless woman, for all along I have been speaking out of my great anxiety and vexation." The priest, Eli, answered, "Go in peace, and the God of Israel grant your petition that you have made to him." A promise from God? I said, "Let your servant find favor in your eyes." I dried my eyes and returned to where Peninnah and the children were. The food was still set out and I ate.

After worship the next morning, we returned home to Ramah. Peninnah's words could no longer hurt me. I was to have a child. A month later, I knew I was pregnant. The time came and my son was born. I named him Samuel, because God had heard me.

Soon it was time to go up to offer at the feast. I didn't go that year. Instead, I told Elkanah that I would go when Samuel had been weaned and then present him to the LORD in fulfillment of my vow. He said to do what seemed best.

After Samuel was weaned, we went up to Shiloh. Elkanah presented a sacrifice of a three-year-old bull, some flour and wine. When we presented the child to Eli, I reminded him of what transpired four years earlier. "Oh, my lord! As you live, my lord, I am the woman who was standing here in your presence, praying to the LORD. For this child I prayed, and the LORD has granted me my petition that I made to him. Therefore I have lent him to the LORD. As long as he lives, he is lent to the LORD."

So we returned to Ramah without Samuel. It was hard leaving my son behind, but I did it with a willing heart. He would be serving the LORD. It was what I had promised God. But God had not only blessed me with Samuel. As we walked back to Ramah, I couldn't keep the smile off my face; I was pregnant again.

That was not to be my last pregnancy either. Since the time I had given Samuel back to the LORD, I have been given three more sons and three daughters. And it wasn't the last I saw of Samuel. Each year, when we went up to the feast, I would bring him a change of clothes and we would sit and talk a while. He was doing well, assisting Eli and learning the duties of a priest.

Yes, the LORD God has richly blessed me.

Sedecla

Saul thought he had put one over on me. When he became king, he tried to rid the land of my kind. I am a necromancer, one who raises the spirits of the dead. Some of the mediums in the land were killed or put into prison. The rest, and the speakers to the dead, were chased out of the Jewish cities into those still controlled by the people the Israelites had stolen the land from years ago. If we were found out, our lives would be forfeit.

Now I live in En-dor. I am the daughter of Ado, a Midianite diviner. He taught me his trade. I turned out to be very good at summoning the spirits and so I specialize in necromancy. Many people don't realize it, but we who speak to them know the spirits of the departed don't really leave until a year has passed from their death.

The Philistines are a people who have hung on to the area by the great sea, despite attempts by the Israelites to wipe them out. Every so often, fights would break out between the nations. It was happening again. The Philistines had gathered their army and camped at Shunem. The Israelite army was camped at Gilboa. When King Saul had seen the size of the Philistine army he became frightened.

I'm no fool. I suspected from the start that it was Saul who came to me that day, even though he had tried to disguise himself with ragged clothes. At first he didn't say whose spirit he wanted me to conjure, just "whomever I shall name to you." I played along, saying to him, "Surely you know what Saul has done, how he has cut off the mediums and the necromancers from the land. Why then are you laying a trap for my life to bring about my death?" It was only after he swore to me that no punishment would come to me that I asked whom he wanted. He was looking for Samuel, to get his advice on fighting the Philistines.

Samuel had been a great prophet. Samuel had himself led an army against the Philistines after calling the Israelites together at Mizpah. He would travel around the country, serving as a judge and giving advice. When he got older, he delegated that work to his sons, but they were corrupt and so the people asked for a king. Samuel was the one who anointed Saul to be Israel's first king. At first Samuel was an advisor to Saul. But Saul became more interested in his own good than that of his God and they had a falling out.

Everyone knew that Samuel had died not long ago; there was a great deal of mourning in the land. As I said, it was not difficult to bring up the spirit when less than a year had passed since his death. But the spirit came so fast, before I'd had a chance to call for him, that I let out a yell. This was when I knew for sure that the visitor was the king himself. I asked Saul why he had deceived me. He told me to not be afraid but to tell him what I saw.

When a necromancer brings up a spirit, she can usually see it. The person seeking the spirit can usually hear but not see. What I saw was a god coming up out of the earth, an old man wrapped in a robe. Saul fell to the ground.

Samuel was angry with Saul for disturbing him and asked why he had done so. Saul told him he had not been able to get an answer from God regarding the upcoming battle. Samuel said, "Why then do you ask me, since the LORD has turned from you and become your enemy? The LORD has done to you as he spoke by me, for the LORD has torn the kingdom out of your hand and given it to your neighbor, David. Because you did not obey the voice of the LORD and did not carry out his fierce wrath against Amalek, therefore the LORD has done this thing to you this day. Moreover, the LORD will give Israel also with you into the hand of the Philistines, and tomorrow you and your sons shall be with me. The LORD will give the army of Israel also into the hand of the Philistines.

This was not what Saul wanted to hear. He rose from the ground, trembling. He was terrified. Since he obviously hadn't eaten recently and I try to be a good host, I offered him some food. At first he refused it. His servants pressed upon him and he finally consented. They left right after they had eaten.

All of Samuel's words came true. The Philistines routed the Israelites. Saul and all his sons died, though I heard that Saul had fallen on his own sword and not waited for the Philistines to kill him. The Philistines took over the cities in the area that had been occupied by the Israelites.

As for me, I gave up my practice. I did not bring up Samuel; I never had a chance to try. It had to have been the work of Israel's God. I would not go up against him again. I learned of this God and came to accept that he is the one true God. He does not permit contacting the spirits and I shall not cross him.

Nitzevet

I certainly didn't realize how much our lives would be affected that day Samuel showed up in Bethlehem. We all knew who Samuel was; I think Jesse had even had some business with him in the past. The elders were a little fearful when he came because they thought he might have come to judge them. But Samuel said he came in peace, to offer a sacrifice to God.

Ordinarily, I wouldn't have known any of this. I was busy at home and didn't get involved in what was going on at the city gates. But Jesse was invited to the sacrifice. I heard about it all when he returned.

Samuel had our sons presented to him, oldest to youngest. Apparently none of them were who, or what, Samuel was looking for. He said, "The LORD has not chosen these", and asked if there were any others. Our youngest had been in the field with the sheep. Jesse hadn't thought the man of God would want someone that young for whatever it was he was looking for.

When David arrived, Samuel took a horn of oil and poured it on him. Jesse said he had no idea what that was supposed to mean. After anointing David, Samuel just got up and left. Meanwhile, something had come over David, something more than just the oil. We didn't know it at the time. It wasn't until later that we realized it was the Spirit of the LORD.

War had broken out again with the Philistines. Our three oldest sons, Eliab, Abinadab, and Shammah, had joined King Saul's army. David would go between home and the battlefields, alternating between caring for the sheep and bringing food for his brothers. I think Jesse was more concerned about how the older boys were faring in the war than that they get the fresh food from home.

On one trip, David was gone longer than usual. He had arrived at the battlefield as the lines were drawn for battle. David left the supplies with the food in the charge of the baggage keeper and went to find his brothers. As he was talking to them, he heard one of the Philistines taunting the Israelites. It was Goliath, a giant of a man, even compared to the other Philistines who were on average at least a foot taller than the average son of Abraham. He had been coming out and challenging our army every day saying. "Why have you come out to draw up for battle? Am I not a Philistine, and are you not servants of Saul? Choose a man for yourselves, and let him come down to me. If he is able to fight with me and kill me, then we will be your servants. But if I prevail against him and kill him, then you shall be our servants and serve us. I defy the ranks of Israel this day. Give me a man, that we may fight together."

Saul was also taller than the average of our men, though not nearly as tall as Goliath. He should have been taking care of this, but he was just as frightened as everyone else. When Goliath showed up, they panicked. David questioned what was going on and was told, "Have you seen this man who has come up? Surely he has come up to defy Israel. And the king will enrich the man who kills him with great riches and will give him his daughter and make his father's house free in Israel."

David was enraged. "Who is this uncircumcised Philistine, that he should defy the armies of the living God?" Eliab heard David and accused him of coming to the battlefield to satisfy his youthful curiosity. Others heard what David had said and work got back to Saul, who sent for him. David said no one should fear Goliath, that he would go up against him. Saul was skeptical. After all, David was still a youth and Goliath was an experienced soldier. David told Saul of the times that he had saved sheep from the mouths of lions and bears. He said the Philistine would be like one of them. Furthermore, David had confidence that the LORD would help him.

Saul was not much of a man and agreed to let this youth go up against a giant. He did try to protect David with his own armor, but it was too much for David. He could hardly move in the heavy protection. Instead, David took his staff in his hand, picked up five smooth stones, and took his sling out to meet Goliath.

The Philistine was scornful. He said to David, "Am I a dog, that you come to me with sticks?" The Philistine cursed David by his gods and threatened to feed David to the birds and beasts. Then David said to the Philistine, "You come to me with a sword and with a spear and with a javelin, but I come to you in the name of the LORD of hosts, the God of the armies of Israel, whom you have defied. This day the LORD will deliver you into my hand, and I will strike you down and cut off your head. And I will give the dead bodies of the host of the Philistines this day to the birds of the air and to the wild beasts of the earth, that all the earth may know that there is a God in Israel, and that all this assembly may know that the LORD saves not with sword and spear. For the battle is the LORD's, and he will give you into our hand."

Goliath started coming at David, but instead of running as the others had done, David went up to Goliath. He put a stone in his sling and flung it, hitting Goliath square in the middle of his forehead. The giant went down. David ran over, took Goliath's own sword, and cut off his head. When the Philistines saw their champion was down, the fled. Emboldened, the Israelite army pursued and defeated the Philistines.

Sometime later, men came from the king's palace and took David back with them. It seems Saul had been seized by a tormenting spirit. His servants said to him, "Behold now, a harmful spirit from God is tormenting you. Let our lord now command your servants who are before you to seek out a man who is skillful in playing the lyre, and when the harmful spirit from God is upon you, he will play it, and you will be well." David played the lyre beautifully, and he sang too. Saul's men had heard of David and soon he was playing for the king. Because of the incident with Goliath, David was also put in charge of part of the army.

Saul had been enamored of David's skills, but that was not to last. Multiple times Saul tried to kill David. Saul tried to get David to marry his oldest daughter, Merab. All David would have to do would be to be valiant for the king and fight the LORD's battles. David knew that was just a political move and politely declined, claiming unworthiness to be the king's son-in-law. He told me later that he suspected it was an attempt to have him go to battle and be killed by the Philistines.

David was to become the king's son-in-law however. He would not be married to Merab though. When the time came that they were to be married, Saul gave her to someone else as a wife. He was again angry with David and did this in an attempt to humiliate him. But David had fallen in love with Saul's other daughter, Michal. When Saul's men told him of their attraction to each other, Saul thought he could use it to his advantage.

Saul summoned David and told him again that he would be his son-in-law. Saul had his servants say the same thing to David. When David protested that he was a poor man, without fame, Saul sent another message to David. Saul would ask for no money as a bride price, only the foreskins of a hundred Philistines. He thought David would surely die in any attempt to get them.

But get them he did. When David brought the foreskins to the king, Saul had no choice but to give his daughter to David. We, David's whole family, attended the wedding. It was a wonderful feast. Michal seemed like a wonderful girl and David was so happy. They were very much in love.

David became a well-respected soldier. But, as with other men of renown, he took other wives. Eventually, everything fell apart between David and Michal. I love my son, but you can't blame Michal for becoming bitter.

Through the years, Saul's feelings for David ran hot and cold. At times Saul depended on David and David still played for him. But at other times, the demons got the best of Saul and he would again try to kill David. While they were still together, Michal helped to save David from her father. Sometimes it was David's close friendship with Saul's son, Jonathan, that spared him. Eventually, David had to run for his life. There were times when David could have killed Saul and ended the threat, but David would not raise his hand against the man God had appointed king.

Eventually, there was no kindness left at all. David was expected at Saul's table for the new moon observance. Jonathan had a plan which would let David know if Saul was angry at him. Of course, he was. He had even thrown a spear at Jonathan, he was that mad.

David hid out in Gath, of the Philistines, for a while. When he left there, he went to the Cave of

Adullam. When we heard he was there, his brothers went down and joined him, along with about 400 other men.

Now that his family was involved, David was more worried for his father and me than for himself. He came to Bethlehem to get us and took us to Moab. Jesse's grandmother was from Moab, so David figured that might be a good place for us to stay until things cooled down with Saul. David went straight to the king of Moab and asked his protection for us. Things never did settle down with Saul.

Jesse and I stayed in Moab until Saul fell in battle. I was anxious to return to Bethlehem. I had not seen my daughters, Zeruiah and Abigail, in all the time we were hiding out in Moab. And I wanted to see my grandchildren. Fortunately, Saul did not know about David's sisters and their families, so they were safe.

David is such a good, forgiving person. After all the grief Saul caused him, David was distraught when Saul died. He even had the Amalekite who brought him the news killed because of his part in the king's death. Soon after that, David was again anointed king over Judah.

The other tribes, however, did not acknowledge his kingship. Abner, Saul's commander, took Saul's son, Ish-bosheth, and made him king over the rest of Israel. But Abner and Ish-bosheth had a falling out and Abner came over to David's side. Ish-bosheth was disheartened and sued for peace. Even though David had two other wives by this time, Abigail and Ahinoam, he wanted Michal back and made her return a condition of the peace. Her new husband had followed after her. Abner was able to bring her to David after sending the husband home.

Not everyone accepted Abner's change of allegiance. Joab, my grandson, was now the commander of David's army. He went after Abner again and killed him. David, being the kind-hearted man he is, mourned the loss of Abner.

Not long after that, David was mourning the murder of Ish-bosheth. Again, those who had killed David's adversary were rewarded with their own death. Rechab and Baanah had brought Ish-bosheth's head to David after killing him in his bed. David buried the head where he had buried Abner in Hebron.

Eventually, the elders of Israel came to David at Hebron and made him king over them. They rejoined with Judah and now my son is king over all the tribes of Israel. Will peace reign? Only time will tell.

Michal

It was love at first sight, at least on my part. David had the most beautiful eyes I had ever seen. He wasn't especially tall, but neither was I. My father, Saul, is very tall but I took after my mother, Ahinoam. I saw David frequently when he came to the palace to play and sing for my father.

David was also a military hero. He had killed the Philistine giant, Goliath, when the army was afraid. My father had promised his daughter to the man who could do that. But it was my sister, Merab, who was promised, not me. I thought I was fortunate when David turned her down. But father arranged the marriage anyway. My father can be something else though. When the time for the marriage came, he gave her to Adriel. I think he was trying to humiliate David that way. David seemed to bring out the worst in him. At any rate, there was still hope for me.

I took every chance I had to talk with David. When word got back to my father, he wanted me to marry David. Again David declined. But when Father told him that the only bride price was proof of killing 100 Philistines, David changed his mind. Apparently Father thought David would be killed going after the Philistines. When David returned with 100 foreskins taken from the Philistines, Father had no choice but to let us marry. David had fulfilled the requirement.

I was not the only one in the family who loved David. My brother, Jonathan, was his best friend. It wasn't the same kind of love I had for David, but Jonathan and David became very close. Jonathan even saved David's life. More than once.

Father had announced to all the men of the household, sons and servants alike, that they should kill David. Jonathan warned David to hide until further notice. Jonathan went to Father and somehow convinced him not to kill the man who had done so much for him and for the kingdom. Father relented, at least for the time being. David went out and led the troops against the Philistines again.

After this round of fighting, David was back and playing the lyre for Father. Suddenly, Father grabbed his spear and threw it at David, trying to pin him to the wall. David dodged him and the spear stuck into the wall without its victim. David escaped to our home. But Father sent people after him, planning to kill him in the morning. I heard about it and warned David, then let him out through the window. Meanwhile, I took an image and laid it in David's bed with a pillow of goats' hair at the head. When the messengers arrived with orders to kill David I had no choice but to let them into David's room. I told them David was ill, hoping they would not look closely. But they pulled off the covers and discovered my ruse. When Father was told about this, he demanded my presence and asked why I had deceived him and let his enemy go. I told him David had threatened me with death if I did not go along with his plan.

I didn't see David again for a long while. David was running from my father from that point on. It was difficult being the wife of a fugitive. Then I heard he had taken other wives while he was away. I could not object when my father gave me to Palti, the son of Laish, to be his wife. Palti would never be royalty, but he showed his love for me more than David ever did.

After my father and three of my brothers were killed fighting the Philistines, David was made king over Judah. The other tribes of Israel recognized my last remaining brother, Ish-bosheth, as king. There was war between the two of them. When Ish-bosheth's commander, Abner, came over to David's side, Ish-bosheth lost hope and sued for peace. David would not consider it unless I was returned to him. My brother agreed. Palti would not give me up but went with me, weeping all the way to Bahurim. It wasn't until Abner demanded he go back that he abandoned me.

After Ish-bosheth was murdered, David became king over all Israel. Even though David had other wives, he must have had some respect for me as his first wife because I became queen. My only sadness was that I was the only one of the wives who did not have children. But then David embarrassed himself and me.

David had finally conquered the city of Jerusalem and we had made our home there. David again went to war with the Philistines, soundly defeating them and retaking possession of the Ark of the Covenant. He arranged to bring it into the city and had a cart built especially for it. But that was not the way God had said to transport it. When Uzzah put forth his hand to keep the ark from falling, God struck him down for touching it. Now David was afraid to take the ark into the city.

The ark was taken to the house of Obed-edom and kept there for three months. When David was ready to try again to take it to Jerusalem, he had the Levites carry it there, according the word of God. I was watching the procession from my window. David had taken off his outer clothes and was wearing only an ephod. There he was, leaping and dancing around like a common fool. How I despised him then.

When the people had dispersed to their homes, I went to meet David as he came home. I said to him, "How the king of Israel honored himself today, uncovering himself today before the eyes of his servants' female servants, as one of the vulgar fellows shamelessly uncovers himself!" David tried to justify it. "It was before the Lord, who chose me above your father and above all his house, to appoint me as prince over Israel, the people of the Lord—and I will celebrate before the Lord. I will make myself yet more contemptible than this, and I will be abased in your eyes. But by the female servants of whom you have spoken, by them I shall be held in honor."

That is how I lost my position as the queen of the kingdom and became queen of the king's harem. I have spent my days in the company of the king's concubines. I have no children, nor shall I ever. David lost out too. He may be loved by many of his people, but certainly not all. Even his own children have caused him misery. I guess he got what he deserved. You can only expect problems when you have that many wives and put away the wife of your youth.

Abigail bath Caleb

When I was young, my father arranged my marriage to Nabal. My father was a man of moderate means and I was his only daughter. The marriage was quite an achievement for him. Nabal was a very wealthy man. What my father didn't know was that Nabal was also a hard hearted, self-centered man with no compassion. I tried to be a good wife anyway. Trying to protect my husband is how I first encountered David.

Nabal owned a lot of the land around Maon where we lived. It was the time of the year for sheering sheep and holding festivals. Nabal was with the shepherds in Carmel. One of the young men came to me with disturbing news. David was on the run from King Saul and had sent ten of his men to Nabal with a request. They greeted Nabal with peace. They had been watching over the shearers and protected them. Now they were coming on a feast day and asking for some food. They didn't demand, only requested what he could spare for David and his men.

Being the harsh man that he is, Nabal refused. "Who is David?" he asked them. "Who is the son of Jesse?" He said there are many servants who are breaking away from their masters; he considered David as just one more. "Shall I take my bread and my water and my meat that I have killed for my shearers and give it to men who come from I do not know where?"

The young man told me, "They are coming after our master and his house. David had said, 'Surely in vain have I guarded all that this fellow has in the wilderness, so that nothing was missed of all that belonged to him, and he has returned me evil for good. God do so to the enemies of David and more also, if by morning I leave so much as one male of all who belong to him.' Nabal is such a harsh man, we cannot even speak to him. You have to do something."

So I did. I hurriedly gathered some supplies, bread, wine, meat, grain, figs, and raisins, and loaded up some donkeys. I did not say anything to Nabal; I would give him no opportunity to try to stop me. I sent the young men ahead and came after them riding my donkey. I met up with David and his men in the valley. When I saw David, I dismounted and fell on the ground before him.

I pleaded with David to not destroy the men. I would take the guilt. Nabal is foolish, as his name would indicate. But I had not been there when the request was made of him. I told David that so far he was not guilty of spilling blood; he should not start killing now. I asked that he accept the goods I brought and give them to his followers. I begged forgiveness for the inhospitality.

"For the LORD will certainly make my lord a sure house, because my lord is fighting the battles of the LORD, and evil shall not be found in you so long as you live. If men rise up to pursue you and to seek your life, the life of my lord shall be bound in the bundle of the living in the care of the LORD your God. And the lives of your enemies he shall sling out as from the hollow of a sling." David should stay his hand and have no cause for pangs of conscience for shedding blood without cause. I asked that he remember me when the LORD has done all this good for him and made him ruler of the land.

David saw the wisdom in my request. He said he surely would have destroyed Nabal and all the males in his house had I not stopped him. He accepted what I had brought him and sent me off in peace.

When I returned home to Nabal, he was holding a great feast. He was too drunk to hear anything I had to say. I waited until morning when he was sober and then told him of his fault and all I had done. He was shocked and the LORD caused his heart to die within him. We gave him a proper burial, but because of the kind of man he was, no one really mourned.

Soon after, David's servants came to me. He had sent them to bring me back as his wife. I welcomed them and washed their feet. Then I gathered some belongings and mounted a donkey for the journey. I took along five of my handmaids.

I became a wife to David and, eventually, the mother of his son, Daniel Chileab. In the course of time, David took another wife, Ahinoam. It was she who gave David his firstborn, Amnon. David would one day become king, but meanwhile he continued to be pursued by Saul.

We had a time of respite when David took us to Achish, the king of Gath in the land of the Philistines. We were surprised that we were accepted there after all the fighting David had done against the Philistines. But they gave us the city of Ziklag. They must have thought David would continue his fight against Saul and in that way be on the side of the Philistines. Saul was happy to have us out of Israel and quit coming after us. We stayed in Ziklag for over a year.

David fed into the notion Achish had that David had turned his back on Israel. He would take his men and make raids against the Geshurites, the Girzites, and the Amalekites. They would kill all the people but bring back the animals and personal items. David would tell Achish he had attacked some place in Israel. That was one of the reasons he killed everybody where he had actually attacked, so that there would be no survivors to contradict his story. Achish believed David and trusted him. He figured David had been so bad to his people Israel that he would always be loyal to him.

The people of Achish weren't so trusting however. One time when they were preparing to go to war against the Israelites, the Philistine commanders objected to David and his men being there. Achish wanted to keep David at his side, but gave in to the commanders when they expressed fear that David would change allegiance and go against them. David put up a protest but was glad to have an excuse not to go against the Israelites.

We did not find out about this at the time because something had happened while David and his men were away. The Amalekites had attacked us in Ziklag. They had taken all of us captive and burned the city behind them. But David found out what had happened and came after us. The Amalekites were spread out drinking and dancing, rejoicing over all the great spoil they had taken from the land of the Philistines and from the Israelites. David and his men attacked and the battle went from one evening to the next. 400 Amalekites escaped on their camels, but all the others were killed. David took back what the Amalekites had taken and rescued all of us. David sent part of the spoils of that battle as gifts to the elders of Judah, securing allies for himself for the future.

Meanwhile, the Philistines were at war with the Israelites and were winning. Three days after we had returned to Ziklag, an Amalekite came from Saul's camp and told David that Saul and his son Jonathan were killed in battle. Saul had been wounded and asked this man to finish the job so that the Philistines could not. Because he felt sure that Saul would not recover, he granted that request. When Saul was dead, the man took his crown and armlet and brought them to David.

Imagine that man's surprise when David did not reward him for killing Saul. Instead, David tore his clothes in grief. So did all the men who were with him. They mourned and wept and fasted until evening for Saul and Jonathan and all the people of Israel who had died in the battle. Then David asked the Amalekite how he dared to destroy the LORD's anointed. The man could say nothing. David ordered his execution.

With Saul's death, the country needed a new king. Abner, Saul's commander, had made Saul's one remaining son king. His name was Ish-bosheth. Due to the gifts David had sent to the elders in Judah, and the fact that David's men were for the most part also from Judah, David was made king there. War continued between the two kings until Ish-bosheth was murdered. Then the elders from the other tribes came to make David their king also. Now David rules over all the tribes of Israel.

He is king, but I am not queen. Neither is Ahinoam. We are not fools. We know our marriages were politically expedient. Shortly before Ish-bosheth was killed, David demanded the return of his first wife, Saul's daughter, Michal. She would be his queen. By the time David's kingdom was united and he moved his capital to Jerusalem, he had taken four more wives and fathered four more sons.

It's ok though. I can't say that all the wives get along. Michal was haughty but has been deposed, moved to live in the harem with the concubines. Somehow Ahinoam and I have become good friends. Perhaps it is because of our shared experiences in Ziklag and having been captured by the Amalekites. Maybe it is because our sons are so close in age and have also shared the Amalekite experience. What I am certain of is that God is good, and I am content.

Maacah bat Talmai

I am the daughter of a king and the wife of a king. My father, Talmai, was king of Geshur. I was the only daughter, doted on by both my mother and my father, as well as being protected by my brothers. I'm sure my father believed he was doing what was in my best interest when he married me to the king of Judah, even though it was a political marriage and not one of love. I had high hopes, but am now brought low. My children, who should have been my joy, have brought me tears.

Life was full of promise when my son, Absalom was born. I was not David's first wife, nor was Absalom his first son. But I was the first wife of royal lineage to give birth to a son. I just knew Absalom would become king. He was such a darling little boy; everybody loved Absalom. I know David had a special place in his heart for him. I also had a beautiful daughter. Tamar would be married to royalty. David started searching out a husband for her before she could walk.

The early years with my precious children were joyous. Absalom was a charmer and grew up expecting to get just about anything he wanted. And he wanted more and more. But he made sure there was plenty for Tamar too. He was always looking out for her. Tamar stayed sweet and unassuming. I don't think she had any idea how beautiful she was. I missed Absalom when he was old enough to move out of my apartments and into the care of his teachers. But then I had another son, Hanan, and my hands were full with him.

I blame Amnon for the start of the trouble. He was David's firstborn, the son of Ahinoam. I could see him looking over the walls into the women's quarters. He would just laugh when the eunuchs chased him away. He would always return in a day or two. A week went by, and then another, and we thought he was done bothering us. Then we got word that Amnon was ill. He had requested that Tamar come and prepare a meal for him. It was just a ruse. Amnon raped my daughter and then he scorned her.

Absalom found her with her clothes torn and ashes on her head. She had been disgraced and could not be married to a prince as we had planned. Absalom, still looking out for her, took her into his own house. He and I went together to tell David what had happened. But Amnon was the heir apparent and David loved him. He would not be disciplined. Nothing at all happened for two full years.

Then Absalom gave a feast and invited all his brothers. All, including Amnon whom he had not spoken to in those two years. While at the feast, Absalom's servants killed Amnon. David got word that all his sons were killed, but it was only Amnon, and it was ordered by Absalom in restitution for what Amnon had done to Tamar. Absalom fled to my homeland of Geshur, to his cousin, Talmai, son of my brother Ammihud who was now the king. With Absalom gone, Tamar returned to the women's quarters.

After three years, Joab, the commander of David's army, advised David to have Absalom return. David granted Joab permission to go to Geshur and bring Absalom home, and he did so. But all was not yet forgiven. David ordered that Absalom not come into his presence. At least I got to see my son again.

Absalom lived in Jerusalem for two full years without seeing his father. By now Absalom had had four children, three boys and a girl. He named his daughter Tamar, after his sister. Little Tamar was just as beautiful as her namesake. But the boys were sickly and none had made it past his fifth birthday. Absalom wanted Tamar to meet her grandfather.

Absalom sent for Joab to take a message to David, but Joab would not come. He sent again and Joab would still not come. Trying to get his attention, Absalom sent his servants to set Joab's barley field on fire. Now Joab came to Absalom. He wanted Joab to go to David and get him to see Absalom. David had mellowed and allowed it. He and Absalom were finally reconciled.

Or so it seemed. Absalom got himself a chariot and horses and had 50 men who would run ahead of him announcing his presence. He would get up early and go to the city gates where he would intercept people going to see the king for judgments. He would take the side of whomever he was talking to and tell them that they had a good claim but there was no one in the city to hear it. Then he would say how he would serve and give fair decisions. Absalom was just as charming as ever and soon had quite a following.

After four years of this, Absalom asked David for his blessing to go to Hebron to honor his vow. But he had sent out messengers to all the tribes saying that when they heard the trumpet, they were to shout, "Absalom is king in Hebron." He gathered 100 men from Jerusalem to take with him for the sacrifice. They were not in on the plot but their presence would give credence to his claims and also keep them out of Jerusalem where they might support David.

When David heard of the rebellion, he gathered up his household, including us wives and the children, along with his servants and fled from Jerusalem. He was sure Absalom and his people would come and overtake us if we stayed. The only ones who stayed behind were ten of the concubines who were left to take care of the houses. We didn't rest until we reached the Jordon.

Absalom did take his people into Jerusalem. To establish himself as the new king, he slept with the concubines David had left behind. And he did it in full sight of everyone, in a tent on the roof of the house. Absalom made himself a stench to his father.

Of course there was war. David had not fled Jerusalem because he was a coward. He left so that he could choose the time and place for the battle and so that the women and children could be put somewhere safe. He was ready to go with the army to fight, but Joab convinced him to stay behind, that he was too valuable to risk losing. He agreed but, still favoring my son, he gave orders that Absalom was not to be harmed.

The battle was fought in the forest of Ephraim. David's men were victorious, but Absalom's rebellion had cost the lives of 20,000 men. What a waste! Most of Absalom's men died due to the dense forest and its rocks. Despite David's instructions to his men, I lost my son that day.

I later learned from David that Absalom had been close to escaping. He was riding his mule out of the area when his hair, that beautiful long hair, got caught in the branches of an oak tree. The man that saw him there reported it to Joab, who berated him for not finishing off Absalom. The man protested that David had ordered no one to harm the king's son. Joab went out to find Absalom and put three javelins into his heart. Then Joab had his armor-bearers finish the murder.

When David received the news of Absalom's death he was overtaken with grief. For the sake of his men, he returned to his place at the gate. It was a good while before the people who had backed Absalom again supported David, but David was once again king over all Israel.

My grief could not be abated. I lie here in my own misery, unable to stop crying, unable to eat. The depths of Sheol await me.

Bathsheba

Though I am the Queen Mother, I suppose I am defined by the men in my life just like any other woman. My father was Eliam and his father was Ahithophel. My grandfather was one of King David's chief advisors. That is why we moved to Jerusalem from Giloh. And that is why I was married to Uriah, the Hittite, who was one of the captains in David's army. Yes, I said "was". Later I became a wife of King David and the mother of King Solomon.

Uriah was a fine man, and a fine looking one too. He treated me well. We had no children yet, probably because he was gone so much, but I had hopes of a large family.

It was springtime and Uriah was at Rabbah, fighting against the Ammonites. For some reason, the king had not gone out with them. I was in our courtyard, bathing. This may seem immodest, but there were screens around me, hiding me from prying eyes. Suddenly, a large bird appeared and flew into the screen, knocking it over. I grabbed at the towel my servant held out for me and went back into the house.

I don't know if it would have been possible for me to grab the towel fast enough. I was seen. Within the hour, the king's servants came for me. I was frightened, but what could I do? The king had summoned me and I had to obey.

David was very sweet. I was very lonely. I could not resist when he took me in his arms. It wasn't really my fault, I rationalized, when he took me to his bed. He was the king. When I found out I was pregnant, I panicked. The penalty for adultery was stoning.

I didn't dare to approach the king without being asked for, so I sent word to him. "I'm pregnant." Now it was up to him.

Soon after, I heard that Uriah had returned to Jerusalem. I think David wanted to set things up so it would look like Uriah was the father of my child. But Uriah would not come home; I did not see him. Two days later, I learned from the servants that Uriah had returned to the field. He was concerned for his troops. The next thing I knew, Uriah had been killed in battle. I didn't find out until much later that the king had orchestrated it. At his direction, Joab had put Uriah in the front line where he knew Uriah would probably be killed. Now no one would ever know my child was not his. No one except for his true father and me.

Of course I mourned. I had loved Uriah. After the initial period of mourning, the king brought me to his house and made me his wife. In due time our son was born. Soon after, David was visited by the prophet. He must have cursed us because the next day our son became ill. I sat with my child, praying for his recovery. David pleaded with God, fasting and laying on the ground. This went on for a week.

When the child died, the servants were afraid to tell David for fear of his reaction. But he saw them whispering and knew what had transpired. To be certain, he asked bluntly if the child was dead and they had to tell him the truth. David did not yell at them or complain to the LORD. To everyone's amazement, he got up from the ground, washed and anointed himself, and changed his clothes. Then he went to the house of the LORD and worshipped. After that he came home and asked for food.

While he was eating, the servants asked about what they saw as his strange behavior. He had fasted and wept while the child was alive, but now that our son was dead, David cleaned himself up and took a meal. David replied, "While the child was still alive, I fasted and wept, for I said, 'Who knows whether the LORD will be gracious to me, that the child may live?' But now he is dead. Why should I fast? Can I bring him back again?" Fasting would do no good.

I was grief stricken with the loss. David tried his best to console me and I became pregnant again. When Solomon was born, I was afraid that he too would be taken from us. But he was a healthy child. I had three more children after that, but Solomon was special.

We faced a lot of other problems through the years. The death of our infant son was not the only result of what David had done to Uriah. Nathan had pronounced other consequences even though David was forgiven. Because David had used the sword of the Amorites to kill Uriah, the sword would never depart from the house of David. God would raise up evil from within. His wives would be violated by another, in public for all to witness.

David had a lot of wives; I was neither his first nor his last, but I believe I was his favorite. Most of them were taken for political alliances. David also had many children. God used their greed to cause dissention and fulfill Nathan's prophesies.

Amnon, the son of Ahinoam, was his oldest son. Absalom and Tamar were children of Maacah. Amnon lusted after Tamar and raped her. Absalom killed Amnon. Absalom was the one to sleep with David's wives. They were actually the concubines David had left in Jerusalem when we fled because of Absalom's rebellion. Absalom was killed by Joab, David's army commander. After David death, Solomon had Haggith's son Adonijah killed. Such were David's children.

David had promised me that Solomon would become king after him. Some of David's other sons were dead. Some were born of common women. Solomon was the favorite son of the favorite wife. He was smart too.

It was not easy living with a king. In addition to matters of state, David tried to keep his wives happy, or at least contented. The women's quarters were huge. Each of us wives had our own apartments. We cared for our own children, but we also had servants. When old enough, sons went to the palace where they had tutors. Daughters were married off. Eventually, it was just a bunch of old women, vying for a night with their shared husband. I was fortunate. My apartment was also in the palace, separate from David's, but closer.

As David became older, he called for his wives less and less until he just stopped. He was frail and cold all the time. His servants piled blankets on him but it didn't seem to help. I tried to warm him, but I too was older and my body could not give him warmth. They searched for a beautiful young woman to sleep with him and to wait on him. Abishag, a Shunammite, kept him warm, but David wasn't interested in, or could not do, more than that.

This was about when Adonijah decided he should be king. As Absalom had done years earlier, Adonijah gathered chariots and horsemen. He had 50 men who would run ahead of him, announcing his arrival. Unlike Absalom, Adonijah was able to recruit Joab to his side, along with Abiathar the priest. Adonijah made many sacrifices and held a huge feast. He invited all his brothers, except Solomon, and the royal officials of Judah. He strategically did not invite Nathan the prophet, Zadok the priest, or David's mighty men. There, amongst his own followers, Adonijah announced that he was king.

When Nathan told me about this, we planned how to bring this up to David. I went in to him first. I reminded David that he had sworn to me that Solomon would reign after him. Then I told him what Adonijah had done, wooing David's men and declaring himself king. All of Israel was waiting to see what David would say and do. Without David's intervention, Solomon and I would be seen as offenders when David died.

While I was still speaking to him, Nathan came in and told him the same news, asking if he had declared that Adonijah should be king. Was this what David wanted?

I had backed away when Nathan arrived. David told him to bring me to him. He then said to me, "As the LORD lives, who has redeemed my soul out of every adversity, as I swore to you by the LORD, the God of Israel, saying, 'Solomon your son shall reign after me, and he shall sit on my throne in my place,' even so will I do this day."

Next he called for Zadok, Nathan, and Benaiah. He told them, "Take with you the servants of your lord and have Solomon my son ride on my own mule, and bring him down to Gihon. And let Zadok the priest and Nathan the prophet there anoint him king over Israel. Then blow the trumpet and say, 'Long live King Solomon!'"

This they did. When they blew the trumpet, all the people gathered there with them joined in saying, "Long live King Solomon". They made such a noise with their shouting and music that Adonijah and all the guests who were with him heard it at their feast. When Joab heard the sound of the trumpet, he asked what it meant. At that time, Jonathan the son of Abiathar the priest arrived and told them what Zadok, Nathan and the others had done, that Solomon was now sitting on the royal throne.

Adonijah's invited guests must have been filled with fear because they immediately got up and left. Adonijah was afraid of what Solomon might do to him and fled to the holy altar. He would not let go until Solomon promised not to kill him. My son was far more gracious than he needed to be. He said that if Adonijah would show himself a worthy man, he would not be harmed, but if he was found to be wicked he would die. So Solomon sent his men and they brought Adonijah down from the altar. Adonijah came and paid homage to King Solomon, and Solomon said to him, "Go to your house."

It wasn't long after that that David died and was buried in Jerusalem. Adonijah was not done scheming for the kingdom, though I did not understand his actions. He came to me with what I thought was a simple request. He wanted me to ask Solomon if he, Adonijah, could marry Abishag, the Shunammite. Not understanding his motive, I said I would.

I was welcomed by my son and made my request. Solomon became very upset. He said I might as well ask for the kingdom for Adonijah. Then I understood that marrying a woman that had been with the former king would be saying that he was the rightful successor. Solomon swore by the LORD, saying, "God do so to me and more also if this word does not cost Adonijah his life!" He sent Benaiah the son of Jehoiada, to strike him down and another brother was dead.

Solomon also sent Benaiah after Joab. David had made Solomon promise to not let Joab die in peace. Joab had killed Absalom and two army officers, Abner and Amasa, strictly against David's wishes. Joab fled to the altar for refuge. When Benaiah told

Joab to come out, Joab refused to go. He said that he would die there. When Benaiah told this to Solomon, Solomon said to let him do just that. Benaiah went and slew him at the altar. Joab was buried in his own house in the wilderness.

Remember that I said Solomon was smart? It was more than that. God had blessed him with true wisdom. One day two women came to him for a judgment. They were prostitutes, living in the same household. Each had given birth to a son just three days apart. One woman said the other had lain on her child and it died and that the second woman switched her dead baby for the first woman's live one. The one with the dead child in her bed said she knew it was not her son. The second one denied the entire story, claiming that the child that remained alive was her son. They continued their arguing, each getting louder than the other.

Solomon called for a sword and directed his servant to cut the living child in two and give half to each mother. One of the women said to give the child to the other, but not to put him to death. The other woman said the child should be divided. Solomon knew then that the child's true mother was the one that wanted him spared, even if she had to lose him to the other. He then ordered the child be given to the woman who wanted the child to live. Who else would have thought of such a solution? Word spread of Solomon's wisdom and the people stood in awe of him.

As wise as Solomon may be, he hadn't learned the lesson from his father's multiple wives. He took many wives and concubines, even more than David had. One of his prizes was the daughter of Egypt's Pharaoh. His wives led him astray; each wife he took had her own gods and he started building temples for them all. Solomon never quit worshiping the LORD, but he also went with his wives to worship their gods.

To his credit, he first built a temple to the LORD God of his father. David had wanted to build the temple, but God had let him know that the job was for Solomon to do, not him. David was a man of war and God wanted his temple to be built by a man of peace. David had started stockpiling supplies, but it was up to Solomon to direct the building.

Solomon imported cedars from Lebanon and paid the Sidonians to lead the cutting. He drafted thousands upon thousands to help with that and with stone quarrying. All the stone was dressed outside of Jerusalem. No tools were to be heard being used near the house of God. When it was built, all the stones were covered with carved cedar. The entire structure was overlaid with gold. It took seven years to complete and it was magnificent.

Solomon then turned to building his own palace, and one for his wife from Egypt. They too were magnificent. He embarked on more and more large building projects, building up entire cities.

I must say, my own apartment in Solomon's palace is not shabby at all. It is good to be close to my son. I'd like to say I am enjoying my grandchildren, but there are so many I can't keep track of who belongs to whom. And I don't have the energy to keep up with any of them. I don't think Solomon can keep track of his wives and children either.

I do think Rehoboam will be king someday. His mother is Naamah, an Amorite. She was one of Solomon's early wives. I like her.

Tamar bath David

Unlike most of my siblings, I was royalty on my mother's side as well as my father's. My mother is the daughter of the king of Geshur. My father is the king of Israel. I have come to learn that royalty does not prevent tragedy. In fact, I believe it contributes to it. There has been so much in my father's family. This is my part.

I lived in the women's quarters with my mother, Maacah. My brother Absalom was old enough that he had moved to his own place. I had just turned 14. My father had arranged my marriage, though it wasn't to take place for a few years. My future was set. Or so I thought.

My half-brother, Amnon, had been ill for a week. My father was worried about him because he wouldn't eat and sent word that I should go to Amnon's house and fix him some food. I was happy to do so. He watched while I made him fresh bread. But when I took it over to him, he would not eat it. He dismissed everyone else from the apartment, my servant as well as his, and asked me to bring the food into his bedroom. When I brought it close to him, he grabbed my arm and said I should lie with him. I tried to talk him out of it, suggesting instead that if he wanted me he should talk to our father to arrange a marriage. But he would not listen. I tried desperately to get away, but he was much stronger than me and forced me into his bed and raped me.

Having gotten what he wanted, his attitude changed. Now he hated me and he told me to leave. I begged him not to turn me out; I felt he was obligated to marry me since no one else would have me now that I was no longer a virgin. He called his servant and told him to get me out of there and bolt the door after me.

I tore my robe in despair and found ashes to put on my head. I could not help but cry as I headed back to the women's quarters. Absalom's house was nearby and I passed it on my way. He heard my crying and suspected what had happened. He asked and, sobbing, I confirmed his suspicions. He told me not to let it bother me, that I should think kindly and forgive Amnon because he was my brother. But my life was ruined. Absalom took me into his house and provided for me. I didn't return to the women's quarters that day.

I know he went to Father and told him what had happened to me. But nothing was done! Father loved his boys and would not, could not, rein them in. He would not punish them, no matter what they did. There was no justice.

I stayed in Absalom's house for two years. When the time for shearing the sheep had come that year, Absalom held a feast and invited all of our brothers. Feasts during shearing are a common practice in our land and I didn't think anything of it until Absalom sent for his wife and children to join him in Geshur.

I was to stay behind with some of the servants. I learned from the servants that Absalom had ordered his men to kill Amnon while at the feast.

The servants were kind to me but without Absalom and his family I was very lonely. I asked permission to return to my mother's apartments and was given it. My mother has since passed away but I am still here. I fill my days helping with the young children of the city. Being a princess, I learned to read and write and do some mathematics. Most of the girls don't normally get that opportunity, so I am sharing with them what I can.

After three years, Absalom was pardoned and brought back to Jerusalem. Still, he was not allowed to see Father for another two years. Four years after that, Absalom rebelled. He had gotten many followers with his charming ways. Being the oldest son of a royal mother, he should have been made king when Father died, or was too old to govern, but Absalom would not wait.

Father still had many loyal men and, apparently, God was on his side. Things went bad for Absalom. Even though Father had told his men not to harm Absalom, he was killed. Joab, Father's military commander, disobeyed those orders.

Even after all the grief Absalom's rebellion had caused him, Father grieved deeply. Was this my father's punishment for not defending my honor? I don't know. But Mother had not done anything to deserve this loss. On top of what had happened to me, her only daughter, now she had lost her son. It took a year, but she finally died of a broken heart.

I rarely see my brother, Hanan. He moved out of the women's quarters years ago and is busy being a prince. He knows he will never be king. He is glad of that; he has seen Father's miseries. He has a couple of wives and some children. I am happy for him.

Ah, time for the children's lessons. Miriam is calling for me.

Abigail bath Jesse

I grew up the oldest of nine children. My father, Jesse, was a self-sufficient man. He worked long hours raising sheep and growing the rest of the food we ate. I particularly liked the almonds we grew. Not only were they delicious roasted, but ground up and mixed with honey and flour, they made wonderful cakes.

Father was not the most important man in the area, or the richest, but he was well respected and we had everything we needed. He was able to provide my sister, Zeruiah, and me with decent dowries. I married Jether the Ishmaelite. We were blessed with five children.

I suppose we would have lived our lives unknown to the world outside our family if not for my youngest brother, David. He got involved with King Saul at a relatively early age. David was an excellent lyre player and had a beautiful voice. Saul sent for him to play and sing when he was in bad spirits. David also distinguished himself on the battlefield, starting with killing the Philistine, Goliath, with his sling and a stone.

After many years, which included running away from Saul, David became king. At first he was king only over our own tribe of Judah. Later he became king over all Israel. With royalty comes strife. Saul had been killed by the Philistines on the battlefield. David was not killed, at least not yet, but only by the grace of God.

He may have wished he was dead. He had a large family which seemed at times to give him nothing but grief. His daughter, Tamar, was raped by his son, Amnon, who was killed by his other son, Absalom, who led a rebellion and was killed by his army commander and my nephew, Joab. David lost a young son shortly after birth. David's family woes were not restricted to his immediate household. They affected mine as well.

My son, Amasa, had joined with his cousin, Absalom, in the rebellion. In an attempt to reconcile the two sides after the rebellion was put down, and because David was angry with Joab for disobeying orders not to harm Absalom and being responsible for his death, David made Amasa the new commander of his army. I loved my nephew too, but Joab later showed he was not willing to stand by idly after being deposed.

After Absalom's rebellion had been quelled, trouble came from another source. Sheba was a Benjaminite, of the same tribe as King Saul had been. While the rest of Israel was rallying to David, Sheba led another rebellion. David told Amasa to summon the men of Judah in defense. Amasa set out to do so but was unable to gather them in the given time period. Since Amasa wasn't back yet and David wanted Sheba taken care of promptly, David told our brother, Abishai, to take his troops and pursue Sheba before he could escape. Joab joined them with his troups.

Amasa met up with them in Gibeon. When he greeted Joab, Joab struck him with the sword. One blow killed my son. As Amasa lay dying, Joab resumed his spot as commander and called all the troops to him. They put down the rebellion and Joab continued to serve as commander for many more battles.

Joab may be a brilliant commander, but he is a murderer at heart. He killed Abner and Absalom, and now Amasa. How many more before he is stopped? I pray he gets his punishment someday.

Needless to say, we do not gather for happy family reunions. There may be peace for Israel at some point, but there will never be peace in the house of David.

Tamar bath Absalom

How dare he? After all I did for Asa, he sends me to the women's quarters? He may think he removed me from the position of Queen Mother, but I was the queen; he cannot take that away. I was mother of King Abijam, not just the grandmother of King Asa. I will be the Queen Mother until I die. He destroyed my image of Ashera, burned it up. He can't remove her from my heart; she is a great goddess still.

If only my father, Absalom, had lived to become king. He would not have given me to Rehoboam. I would have been married to a prince of some other land where my reverence for Ashera would be respected, and I would have been queen there. I would never have been dismissed like this.

I suppose I shouldn't really complain about who my husband was. Rehoboam was a decent husband to me, at least as good as one can be when he has a kingdom to run, seventeen other wives, and 60 concubines. He has 28 sons and 60 daughters and I was fortunate that it was my son, Abijam, who became king after him. But that only lasted for three years. When Abijam died, his son, Asa, became king.

Let me back up. My life was plagued with adversity from the first. My father should have been king, not Solomon. My mother told me how Father had to flee to Geshur for defending the honor of his sister, Tamar, when their father, King David, would do nothing. My father's half-brother, Amnon, had raped Tamar. I can't say for certain, but I think King David may have chosen not to respond because of his own history of adultery with Bathsheba.

It took a few years for the time to be right, but Father eventually had killed Amnon for what he had done. After Father fled, he sent for us to join him in his mother's homeland of Geshur. We stayed there for years.

After we got back, Father attempted to take the kingdom as was due him. My grandfather was old and it was about time for his son to take over. But they acted like Absalom was stealing the crown and he ended up being killed by that coward, Joab. Uncle Solomon became king.

I was given the name Tamar, like my father's sister, when I was born, but adopted the name Maacah when I was married to Rehoboam. I wanted to honor the name of my grandmother who was a princess in Geshur. My brothers had all died when they were very young and I was my mother's only daughter. Like me, she was married for political reasons, just one of many wives.

These Israelite kings like to collect wives, just like all the neighboring kings, even though their God had warned them not to. Solomon was the worst. I doubt he even knew who all his wives were. At least Rehoboam didn't take that many. And, since I was his favorite, I was the recognized queen. Rehoboam was king for 17 years.

At first, Rehoboam ruled over a united kingdom, just like his father and grandfather before him. But then most of the tribes decided he wasn't good enough for them and we were left with just the tribes of Judah and Benjamin. Jeroboam, of the tribe of Ephraim, stole the remaining ten tribes from us. It was that same group of ten who had not joined the kingdom under David for his first seven years. With the rise of Jeroboam, the kingdom based in Jerusalem was known as Judah while the northern kingdom retained the name of Israel. The two kingdoms were in a state of war for all of Rehoboam's reign.

We had more to worry about than Jeroboam. Rehoboam had been king for five years when Shishak, king of Egypt, attacked with his huge army. It didn't matter that one of Solomon's wives was the daughter of an earlier Pharaoh. Maybe they were angry that Solomon had taken so many other wives and they felt their princess was being slighted.

At any rate, they laid siege to Jerusalem. Rehoboam had no choice but to give them all the treasures in Solomon's temple. Judah became a vassal state. The Egyptians had cut off our trade with southern Arabia.

I took refuge in Ashera. Her temple in Jerusalem had been built for one of Solomon's wives. He'd had numerous temples built for his many wives. While queen, I was able to lead the worship of Ashera. When Abijam became king, I kept my position and my quarters in the palace. I thought I could continue with both until I died. But no, Asa had to get picky.

He got rid of all the male prostitutes, those who worked in the temples. He removed all the statues of our gods. That was when he destroyed my Ashera and sent me out of the palace.

But I still have my retinue, and Ashera still has her followers. Asa has no idea of what goes on in the women's quarters. Those of us who worshiped Ashera in the past worship her still. I preside over this worship by my own people and by many of the others here who have their roots in foreign lands. He can take away the images and destroy the high places, but Asa cannot destroy the honor we give her.

Makeda

It has been a long journey, but I have finally returned to my home here in Azeba, the capital I established in Sheba. The journey was long, not just in miles, but in the changes in my life. I am the queen of Sheba, named to the throne by my father, Agabo, on his death bed. My mother is Ismeni. The child I carry is the fruit of my journey.

I had heard stories of the great king of Israel, Solomon. He was reported to be the wisest and richest man in the entire world. As a princess, I had benefited from a good education and thought myself wise. However, I did not have the audacity to declare that there was no one wiser than me, though I must admit I considered it, especially in my younger days. I had to go and see this sage for myself.

After loading up the camels with gifts of gold, spices, precious stones and beautiful wood, we set off on our journey. When we arrived in Jerusalem, we were shown quarters and settled in. The next day I was invited to the palace to meet the king.

Protocol demanded that we exchange gifts before we could get to the questions I had. This done, I proceeded to ask those questions that had been burning in my mind. Solomon did not disappoint. He had a way of simplifying the mysteries of the universe, from the vast orbits of the heavenly bodies to the nature of the smallest chemical reactions. Every answer brought more questions and I could tell this would be a long visit.

One of the treasures of Jerusalem was the temple which Solomon had built early in his reign. I had never seen anything so beautiful; the whole thing was covered with gold. Solomon told me that his father had wanted to build it but their God had designated Solomon to do so. He had received a lot of help with it, especially from Hiram, king of Tyre, who supplied all the lumber. The building of the temple took seven years. Solomon had it built even before he built his own palace.

While showing me this beautiful temple, Solomon also told me about the God he had built it for. Their people had once been enslaved by the people of Egypt, a land much closer to my own than to the land they now lived in. Their God had raised up a prophet named Moses who led them out of Egypt and into what they called the Promised Land. He told me of all the miracles their God had done for them and of the Messiah he had promised them. I could see their God was more powerful than any other god in the world.

I became a proselyte of the Jewish God before I left Jerusalem and gave up worshipping the sun. I brought home with me some of their priests. After I returned, they went out to spread the word among my countrymen, many of whom also became proselytes. All the men in my palace were circumcised and I made Judaism the official religion of the realm.

Solomon and I developed a connection that went deeper than monarch to monarch. He asked me to become one of his wives. I had my own kingdom to rule and could not do that. But we became intimate and I became pregnant. I stayed on in Jerusalem for another two months, but had to return home before my pregnancy became obvious to all.

This child I am about to have will be the next regent of Sheba. He, or she, will be of the most royal blood, a child of the wisest man in the world. Long may he reign.

Sere

I have been a widow for five years, struggling to raise my son, Jonah, who was only three when his father died. Although I missed my husband very much, my son and I were able to manage for the first couple years. Jonath had left us a small barley field and some olive trees. It wasn't much but it fed us and gave us a little money for the other necessities. We were even able to put away some of the grain and oil. Then the drought hit.

By being very frugal, what we had stored lasted us a couple years, but we had reached the end. There was no family to help us; Jonath and I had each been an only child. Our parents were dead. Though I was young enough to remarry, there was no one in or around Zarapeth for me to marry. Having barely anything left, I went to gather sticks for a fire to cook our last meal.

As I was collecting the sticks outside the city gate, I noticed a stranger watching me. When he spoke to me, I could tell that the man was from Israel. He asked a great deal, a drink of water in a land where there had been no rain for years. He had to have known that. But the village still had a small amount of water in the well and I started off to get some for him. Then he added that I should bring him some bread as well.

I told him that I had nothing baked and very little of anything else, that I was preparing to make a last bit of bread for my son and me to eat before we died. He calmly assured me, "Do not fear; go and do as you have said. But first make me a little cake of it and bring it to me, and afterward make something for yourself and your son. For thus says the LORD, the God of Israel, 'The jar of flour shall not be spent, and the jug of oil shall not be empty, until the day that the LORD sends rain upon the earth.'"

I wasn't sure I believed him. Yet, what difference did it make? If I did not do as he asked, would we live any longer? I may have been destitute, but I still believed in hospitality so I went to do as he had asked. Miraculously, each time I went back to the jar of flour and the jug of oil, there was just enough remaining for another loaf of bread. Things went on this way for many, many days. I knew that this man, Elijah, had been sent by his God.

After we had eaten each day, Elijah told me more about that God and all the wondrous things he had done for the people of Israel. He said the reason there had been no rain was because of the wickedness of their king, Ahab, and his wife, Jezebel. Ahab had turned his back on their God and established the worship of Baal. I knew how Jezebel was. She was the daughter of the king of my own country of Sidon and had a reputation for evil long before she married the Israelite king and moved to Samaria.

Despite the steady supply of food, my son took to his bed, sick with a fever. A few days later, he died. I became angry with this stranger I had taken into my home. "What have you against me, O man of God? You have come to me to bring my sin to remembrance and to cause the death of my son!" He said to me, "Give me your son." and he picked him up and carried him to the upper chamber where he had been staying. I heard him cry out to God, though I could not make out the words he was saying.

After what seemed to be hours, Elijah brought Jonah back to me, alive and well. I told Elijah, "Now I know that you are a man of God, and that the word of the LORD in your mouth is truth."

We settled back into our routine. I would make dinner and Elijah would tell us about the God of Israel. Jonah had listened some before, but now it seemed he couldn't hear enough. He had so many questions, questions I had been hesitant to ask. Now Elijah's God was our God too.

A few months later, Elijah said it was time to go. God had told him to return to Ahab. Even in Sidon, we would hear of how Elijah challenged the priests of Baal and won. He destroyed hundreds of Jezebel's priests. After that, the rains returned. Then we heard that Jezebel had become so angry that she threatened Elijah's life. I haven't heard anything about that man of God since.

This morning when I went for the flour and oil, their containers were empty. But it is all right. When God opened the heavens and sent the rain, the crops grew quickly. Today we will go to the field and harvest the barley and pick some olives for fresh oil. It seems we have a bumper crop this year.

This evening, I will again pray for Elijah. I will thank God that he sent him to us. And I will ask God to protect Elijah. I may even ask that Elijah return to visit us. I miss him.

Susannah

Little did we know how much our lives would be impacted when we first met Elisha. We had heard of him long before we laid eyes on him. He was an itinerant preacher, the successor of the prophet Elijah. When I heard Elisha had come to Shunem, I immediately asked him to our house for a meal. He was good company and a man of God so whenever he passed our way we invited him to break bread with us.

After a few visits, I suggested, strongly, to my husband that we furnish the room on the roof for this holy man of God. That would make it easier for Elisha to stay with us whenever he came to Shunem. Jael agreed that it was a good idea and the room was ready well before Elisha next came to town.

On his next visit, Elisha sent his servant, Gehazi, to ask what could be done to repay us for the hospitality. Of course, we were not looking for any kind of payback. God had blessed us with plenty of earthly goods and we were happy to share and provide hospitality. I had no need of anyone to speak to the king or the commander of the army. We were living peacefully among our own people.

Before I go further, let me explain about my circumstances. I had been married to Jael for many years and yet we had no children. I had given up hope of ever having a son. It was a good life however; we had everything else we needed: wealth, respect, good health. But Jael was much older than I and it was likely I would be a widow for a long time. Though I was considered wealthy now, without an heir all our property would go to my husband's nephew and I would be at the mercy of Jael's next of kin.

So I was stunned when Elisha requested my presence and told me that I would have a son in about a year. How, after all this time? I begged him not to deceive me. There was no deception; a year later I gave birth to a son. Like Hannah, whom Elisha had told us about, who had prayed for and received a child after years of being barren, I named my son Samuel.

The years passed and Samuel grew like a weed. Before I knew it, he was almost too big to sit on my lap. He had taken to spending more and more time in the fields helping Jael with the crops. One day at mid-morning, a servant brought Samuel to me. He had complained to his father that his head was hurting. I held Samuel on my lap until noon when he took his last breath. I took him upstairs to Elisha's bed and gently laid him on it. Then I went to find Jael in the field.

When I saw Jael, I did not tell him what had happened. Somehow, I did not cry. I asked for a servant and one of the donkeys, telling Jael that I needed to go see the man of God and that I would return shortly. Jael wanted to know why since it was not the time of the new moon or a Sabbath. I said he should not worry, all was well. I told the servant to urge the animal on and not to slow down the pace unless I specifically asked him to. I had business to tend to.

As I neared the man of God at Mount Carmel, Gehazi came out to greet me. He asked if everything was ok with me, with my husband, with my son. I just said, "All is well". When I came to Elisha, I threw myself at his feet. Gehazi tried to push me away, but Elisha stopped him. He said to Gehazi, "Leave her alone, for she is in bitter distress, and the LORD has hidden it from me and has not told me."

I told him. I was angry. I hadn't asked for a son. I had told him not to deceive me. It would have been better to remain childless than to lose the son I had grown to love. Elisha told Gehazi to go to my house and lay his staff on the child. I would not return home without Elisha. Gehazi quickly went on ahead and we followed. Gehazi met us before we got there. Samuel had not awakened for him; Elisha's staff had had no effect.

When we reached the house Elisha went in and saw the child on his bed. He sent the two of us out of the room and closed the door. Gehazi stayed outside the door while I went down to start supper. After what seemed a long, long time, Gehazi called me back up to the room. There was my son, alive and well. I picked him up as Elisha told me to do and I took him down to the kitchen to finish supper.

Jael returned to the house to find us all laughing and talking. He never knew what had happened and did not have to grieve as I had.

The years continued to pass and my husband did leave me a widow as I knew would one day happen.

But I had my son and my future was secure. At least as much as anyone can say they are secure.

There was another famine in the land. Elisha had come again to Shunem. Before he left he told me, "Arise, and depart with your household, and sojourn wherever you can, for the LORD has called for a famine, and it will come upon the land for seven years." So we packed up and went to the land of the Philistines as David had years ago. The entire household journeyed there for seven years.

When we returned after the famine was over, others had taken over our house and our lands. My now grown son and I went to King Joram to appeal for the return of our property. We arrived to find that the king was talking with Gehazi who was telling him all about the things Elisha had done. We were admitted to the king's presence just as Gehazi was telling him about how Elisha had restored Samuel to life. Gehazi recognized us and introduced us to the king as the very ones he had been talking about.

We repeated to the king what had happened, just as Gehazi had told him. The king must have been impressed. He assigned one of his officials to make sure everything was restored to us. Not only did we receive the house and land, but the king ordered that the limited crops the land had produced in our absence also be returned to us.

With our property restored, we could focus on the next task of life, finding a wife for Samuel. I, who thought I would never have a child, am looking forward to grandchildren.

Jezebel

What is that racket outside? I have heard that Jehu has assassinated my son, Joram, the king of Israel. Is he now after me, the queen mother? I will not cower; I will die with dignity. After all, I am a Phoenician princess, the daughter of Ethbaal, king of Tyre. I will paint my eyes and adorn my head. If I must die, I will die beautiful.

I was married to Ahab while his father, Omri, was still king. It was a political marriage; I had never seen Ahab before the wedding. What a letdown! I came from a land where the king made the rules. I had lived a life of luxury. Now I was married to a man who was afraid to wield his power as king. I had to step in more than once.

There was that episode with Naboth and his stupid vineyard. It was a nice piece of land, right next to our villa in Jezreel. (Not the palace in Samaria.) Ahab wanted it for a vegetable garden and offered Naboth a good price for it. Naboth refused to sell it to his king, claimed that God would not let him sell his inheritance. What did Ahab do? He moped. He went to bed and refused to eat. I told him to act like the king he was, to get up and eat. I would take care of getting the vineyard.

I wrote letters in Ahab's name and sealed them with his seal. I sent them to all the elders and leaders in Jezreel. I said to proclaim a fast and bring Naboth up in front of the people. I had them arrange for witnesses against him, to accuse him of cursing God and the king. Then they were to take Naboth out and stone him to death. The recipients of the letters relied on the good will of the king to retain their positions and I knew they would obey.

When the deed was done and Naboth was dead, I told Ahab to go and claim his garden. Then that meddling prophet, Elijah, came to Ahab and threatened that his whole family would be wiped out. When Ahab heard those words, he tore his clothes and put on sackcloth and fasted. He laid around in that and went about dejectedly. For what? When Ahab died, not one family member had been killed.

That was not the first time Elijah stirred things up. He expected everyone to honor his God but he had no respect for mine. Back in Tyre, my parents were both high priests of Baal and I was a priestess myself. Naturally I brought that with me when I came to Israel. Ahab understood that and had a house built for Baal in Samaria, with a beautiful altar for him. Apparently Elijah took offense at that and at the Asherah which Ahab had made. I fixed him. I outlawed all his precious prophets of Yahweh.

Elijah came and said there would be no rain, or even dew, until his God said it would be different. And there was no rain for three years. Samaria was subjected to a famine. I made sure there was food enough in the palace, but it was hard on the common people. Elijah caused a lot of trouble.

He had hidden out for three years, but finally came to see Ahab. He told Ahab that the famine was the king's fault, brought on because he followed the other gods. It was time for a show down. He challenged Ahab to gather all of Israel at Mount Carmel, along with the 450 prophets of Baal and the 400 prophets of Asherah. My prophets! That one lone prophet of the God of the Israelites was going to go up against all my prophets. Ahab later told me everything that happened.

Elijah told Baal's prophets to choose one of the bulls that had been brought at his request. They were to cut it up and lay it on wood on their altar. He would prepare the other bull. No fire was to be put to either bull. The gods were to start the fires. My people called out from morning until noon. At that point, Elijah mocked them, telling them to cry louder as Baal must be asleep or busy. They cried louder, cutting themselves to get Baal's attention. When the time for the offering arrived, Baal had chosen to not yet answer their plea.

Then Elijah called the people to come to him. He repaired the altar to his God which had been knocked down years earlier. He dug a trench around it, large enough that it could have held about three and a half gallons of water. He put the wood on his altar and laid the pieces of the bull on it. Then he had four jars of water poured over it all. Then he had it repeated a second and a third time. The water ran around the altar and filled the trench.

He prayed to his God loud enough that everyone around heard what he said. "O LORD, God of Abraham, Isaac, and Israel, let it be known this day that you are God in Israel, and that I am your servant, and that I have done all these things at your word. Answer me, O LORD, answer me, that this people may know that you, O LORD, are God, and that you have turned their hearts back." I don't know what trick he was using, or what magic, but suddenly there was fire. It burned up the offering, the wood, the stone altar, and all the water around it.

The common people were fooled by his trickery. They fell on their faces and said, "The LORD, he is God; the LORD, he is God". Elijah said to them, "Seize the prophets of Baal; let not one of them escape." And they seized them. Elijah brought them down to the brook Kishon and slaughtered them there.

Elijah told Ahab to depart and go to eat and drink, that there would soon be rain. A little later, Elijah sent word to Ahab that he should prepare his chariot and get back to Jezreel before the downpour came and made travel impossible. Soon after Ahab departed, it started to rain.

I was furious with Elijah when Ahab told me all that happened at Mount Carmel. Elijah had destroyed my priests and made a mockery of Baal. I sent a message to Elijah. "So may the gods do to me and more also, if I do not make your life as the life of one of them by this time tomorrow." He knew I was serious and disappeared. We never saw him again.

We were having problems enough without having to worry about Elijah. The king of Syria, Ben-hadad, came after us in Samaria and demanded tribute. Ahab mustered his people and set upon Ben-hadad and the 32 kings and their troops allied with him. Ben-hadad was defeated.

The next spring, Ben-hadad came against the Israelites again, this time in the plains of Aphek. Their army was defeated and Ben-hadad was holed up in the city. His servants told him to beg for mercy. Ahab showed his weakness again when he had Ben-hadad brought to him. Ben-hadad promised to restore the cities to Israel that his father had taken in the past and to also set up bazaars in their capital of Damascus. My "genius" husband agreed to those terms and signed a treaty with him.

One of those blasted prophets of Yahweh came to Ahab and said that because he had released Ben-hadad, his life and those of the Israelites would be forfeited. True to form, Ahab returned to the palace in Samaria, vexed and sullen. It was soon after that when Ahab made a fool of himself again with Naboth and his vineyard.

Three years after Ahab had released Ben-hadad, Jehoshaphat, the king of Judah came to visit. Ahab asked Jehoshaphat to have his army join the Israelites and go to war against Syria to regain Ramoth-gilead. Jehoshaphat wanted to get his God's permission first, so Ahab gathered together the 400 prophets who had escaped my wrath years earlier. They told the kings that God would grant them victory. But Jehoshaphat was not content with this and wanted to inquire of still another prophet. Ahab told him about Micaiah, the son of Imlah, but did not want to call him because Micaiah never prophesied anything good regarding Ahab. Jehoshaphat said to summon him anyway.

When Micaiah arrived, Ahab told him to prophesy something good, to agree with all the other prophets. Micaiah said he would only speak what the LORD told him to, but then when he spoke he agreed with the prophecy that Ahab and Jeshoshephat would be victorious. As much as he wanted Micaiah to say exactly that, Ahab did not believe him. I heard Ahab say to him, "How many times shall I make you swear that you speak to me nothing but the truth in the name of the LORD?" Micaiah responded, "I saw all Israel scattered on the mountains, as sheep that have no shepherd. And the LORD said, 'These have no master; let each return to his home in peace.'"

Ahab said to Jehoshaphat, "Did I not tell you that he would not prophesy good concerning me, but evil?" Micaiah had more to say to him, but all I heard was, "The LORD has declared disaster for you."

So they went to war. The next day word came that Ahab had been wounded and had died in his chariot. They brought him home and buried him in Samaria. And our son, Ahaziah, became king in his place.

Ahaziah ruled for two years. One day he fell through the lattice in his upper chamber and was gravely wounded. He sent messengers to ask Baal-zebub, the god of Ekron, if he would recover. The men returned quickly. They had come across a man who told them Ahaziah would surely die. When his servants described the man, Ahaziah knew it had been that meddlesome Elijah.

Twice Ahaziah sent groups of his men to bring Elijah to him. Both times they were destroyed by fire. Elijah came when the third group went to get him. I did not see Elijah, but the servants reported to me that he had said to Ahaziah, "Thus says the LORD, 'Because you have sent messengers to inquire of Baal-zebub, the god of Ekron—is it because there is no God in Israel to inquire of his word?—therefore you shall not come down from the bed to which you have gone up, but you shall surely die.'" And Ahaziah did die. Since he had no son, his brother, Jehoram became king. Jehoram was also known as Joram.

Moab had been paying tribute to Israel for years. After Ahaziah died, Moab rebelled. Since the relationship between Israel and Judah was still friendly when Joram mustered troops against Moab, Joram asked Jehoshaphat to have the army of Judah join them. He also got the king of Edom to join them. When the army had no water, Jehoshaphat wanted to inquire of the LORD as he had years before. One of Joram's servants said Elisha was there. Elisha was Elijah's successor.

So the three kings went to see Elisha. It was only because of Jehoshaphat that Elisha would even speak to them. He said that just as the streambed would fill with water without rain, God would give the Moabites into their hands.

Apparently, when the Moabites saw the sun reflecting on the water they thought it was blood and assumed the three kings and their armies had turned on each other. They rushed into the encampment for the spoil. But when they got there the Israelite army, all alive and well, attacked them. They chased the Moabites away, overthrew their cities, ruined their land, and stopped up all their wells. When the king of Moab took his oldest son and made him a burnt offering, their army was sickened and they returned to their homes.

When Jehoshaphat of Judah died, his son Jehoram became king. Jehoram was succeeded by Ahaziah of Judah. He was actually my grandson. His mother, Athaliah, is my daughter. So when Joram went up against Hazael, king of Syria, Ahaziah went with him.

When Joram was wounded at Ramoth-gilead and returned to Jezreel, Ahaziah came to see him. Which brings us up to now. Jehu showed up here in Jezreel and Ahaziah and Joram went out to meet him. I have heard the cries of the people that Jehu has slain both the king of Judah and the king of Israel. And now I fear he is coming for me….

Athaliah

If not for me, there would not have been peace between Judah and Israel. My father, Ahab was king of Israel. Jehoshaphat was king of Judah. They arranged for the marriage of their children and so I was given in a political marriage to Jehoram, the future king of Judah. Jehoram was co-regent with Jehoshaphat for five years, before reigning alone for seven.

While Jehoram promoted the worship of Judah's God, Yahweh, he supported my worship of Baal. My mother, Jezebel, had been the priestess of Baal in Israel and I became the high priestess of Baal in Judah. Jehoram even had part of the temple of Yahweh taken apart and used to build a temple for Baal. I urged him to kill all his brothers so they could not claim his throne, but it was also because most of them supported the worship of Yahweh without acknowledging the eminence of Baal.

When Jehoram died, our son Ahaziah became king and I was relegated to the role of Queen Mother. Ahaziah was the youngest, and last remaining, son. All his older brothers had been killed by the raiders who had come with the Arabians. Ahaziah was easily influenced and I continued as high priestess.

But his reign did not last long. He had gone to war with Joram, who was my brother, his uncle, and king of Israel. While Ahaziah was with him, that traitor, Jehu, attacked them both and they were killed. Then they had killed all the young men who had traveled to Israel with Ahaziah. Jehu also had my mother killed, thrown from her window. The horses trampled her and Jehu and his men just left her there while they went to eat and drink. He finally sent someone to bury her, but when they went to get her body, there was nothing left but head and feet. Her body had already been eaten by the wild dogs.

When I heard the news, I set out to revenge my mother and protect my position. Jehu had murdered in the name of Yahweh. My husband and son were descendants of David, and supported the worship of Yahweh, at least in part. Their descendants, even if some of them were my grandchildren, could not be allowed to live. I had people who were loyal to me; I ordered them to destroy every man and boy in the family of Ahaziah, including my own grandchildren. It may have been a steep price to pay, but with no apparent heirs, I was able to declare myself sole regent. I have been ruling in Judah for six years now. I may not be popular, but I am queen.

I hear uncommon noise coming from the temple. Is that the voice of their high priest, Jehoiada, saying "Behold, the king's son! Let him reign"? The people are crying, "Long live the king." I must go to the temple to see what this nonsense is about. They can't be presenting the king's son; I had all of Ahaziah's sons destroyed years ago.

I can see him now. It is a youth of about seven years old. He is standing on a raised platform before the temple with some sort of book in his hand. There is a crown on his head. “Treason, treason,” I cry. I’ve got to get away. A few more feet and I will be out the door. Where are my guards?

Jehosheba

The kingdom is at peace and the line of David has been restored to the throne. We had been ruled for the last six years by a daughter of Ahab, of the house of Omni in Israel. That daughter was also my mother, the wicked Athaliah. She had killed all the rightful heirs of my brother, Ahaziah, and set herself up as queen. All except one. I had snatched Joash from his quarters, along with his nurse, and hid them in my own quarters in the temple. My only regret is that I could not have saved any of the other children.

Why the temple? My husband, Jehoiada, is the high priest of the LORD God in Jerusalem and we live within the confines of the temple. Even before Ahaziah had taken the throne, my father, Joram, had agreed to have me marry a priest rather than marry me off to a prince of some other land. I'm glad I was married before my brother ruled. He was as evil and godless as our mother and would never have consented to this marriage. Even though many in Judah had turned away and the temple is in ill repair, there are still many of us that remained faithful. God himself had promised that a descendant of David would continue to rule here. I had but a small part of this.

We kept Joash hidden from the queen and raised him as our own. It wasn't hard to keep him hidden:

Athaliah wouldn't be found in the temple area for any reason. Jehoiada taught him about our God, Yahweh, and I taught him what I knew of palace life. For six years we trained him to take his rightful place on the throne. When he was seven, it was time to place him there.

I knew my mother, and I was afraid for Joash. But Jehoiada had a plan to keep him safe. Jehoiada gathered together some of the faithful who were commanders of hundreds. They went throughout Judah and gathered all the Levites and heads of households. When all were in Jerusalem, the entire assembly made a covenant to put Joash on the throne.

Every Sabbath there was a change of who was on duty at the temple. Jehoiada first gave instructions to those coming off duty and those coming on duty, giving a force double what was normally at the temple. A third of those coming off duty were to guard the king's house, a third to be at the gate Sur and a third behind the gate. Those coming on duty were to guard the temple on behalf of the king. They were to surround and protect the king. No one but the priests and Levites were to be allowed in the temple. Those protecting the king were to stand with weapons in hand and put to death anyone who tried to get at him.

When all was ready, they brought Joash out and put the crown on him. Jehoiada and our sons anointed the new king. "Long live the king" could be heard throughout Jerusalem. Athaliah heard the noise and forced her way into the temple. Seeing the king, she tore her clothes and cried out, "Treason! Treason!" Some wanted to slay her on the spot, but Jehoiada made them bring her out of the temple. Athaliah tried to run but was overtaken by the men. They took hold of her and led her through the horses' entrance to the king's house and put her to death.

Because Joash is too young to rule unassisted, Jehoiada is serving as his counselor. Under the new government, the people renewed their covenant to be the LORD's people. Many went to the house of Baal that my father had built for my mother and tore it down, along with his altars and images. They killed Mattan, the priest of Baal.

I pray that Joash continues in the ways of the LORD all his days. Jehoiada is getting old and may not be around too much longer. I pray for the kingdom of Judah, that we may remain in the LORD God. And I pray for the people of Israel, that they may turn from their worship of false gods and once again come to the house of the LORD.

Gomer

I guess you really do have to lose everything to find out what you had. My story is a lesson, both to individuals and to the people of Israel.

I grew up in the nation of Israel during a period of general prosperity. After a period of frequently changing kings, Israel had been under Jeroboam II for many years. His army had extended the borders further than they had been at any time since King Solomon. While poverty still existed for some, great wealth existed for others. Many people had two homes, one for the hot months of summer and one for the cooler months of winter. Most of these people credited the Baals for their prosperity and presented them with offerings on the high places.

We were not the rich. I learned early on that if I wanted something, it was up to me to find a way to get it. My mother had died when I was young; my father, Diblaim, was a drunkard. I found that if I was nice to the men, they were nice to me. I learned to paint my face in a way that made me even more attractive to them. I gave them what they wanted and in return I received many gifts, including beautiful clothing, jewelry, and even better food than was ever served at my father's table.

In another era, I would have been stoned for my activity. But most of the people around here were followers of the local deities and not only condoned, but encouraged this lifestyle. We had no use for the outdated Torah that Yahweh had given our ancestors.

But we still followed some of the customs. One day a young man came to our door. He did not come alone. Hosea brought his father, Beeri, with him and they negotiated my marriage. They were not of the very rich, but they were well enough off that my father received a decent dowry for me.

At first I was relieved to know where my next meal was coming from. Hosea treated me kindly and seemed to love me. With a young girl's fantasy, I thought I loved him too. Before too long we had a son. Hosea named him Jezreel. He said Yahweh had told him to name him that because God would soon punish the house of Jehu, Jeroboam II's ancestor, for the blood that was spilled on Jehu's behest at the city of Jezreel. He also said that the nation of Israel would be destroyed. I wasn't thrilled with the implications of such a name, but it is the father's right to name a child, not the mother's.

I was happy for a year or so, but began to long for a little more: more excitement, better clothes. So I started seeing other men and receiving gifts from them. I didn't think Hosea knew about it; he was always so busy with his preaching. When I got pregnant, he never expressed any doubts about the child being his. I wasn't sure myself.

When he named my daughter No Mercy, I felt he was using her name to shame me, but did not say anything about it. He said God had told him that was to be her name because God would show no mercy to the house of Israel to forgive them, but would show mercy to the house of Judah.

Two children were a handful. I felt tied down and again started to go out. When I got pregnant the third time, I was sure Hosea knew the child was not his. Hosea's choice of a name, or Yahweh's choice, was worse than the last time. He called him Not My People to signify that the people of Israel were not his people and Yahweh was not their God.

When I took the children out to play or to the market, I could hear the townspeople whispering. I know they were talking about me and calling Hosea a fool for keeping me around. So I left. I figured I did all right before Hosea came along and I could do just fine without him. The children were causing me so much stress anyway. And I really did miss having the finer things in life.

It wasn't long before I found a rich man to take me in. Simeon associated with far more interesting people and, unlike Hosea, Simeon was welcomed by them. I had fine jewelry, lovely clothes to wear. The wine flowed freely and the food was better than I had eaten in years. But I was still restless. Simeon was seeing me less and less, so when Jacob was so sweet to me, I gladly went with him.

This pattern continued for a couple years, but it was getting harder and harder to find new lovers when the current one lost interest in me. I was getting older after all and the men wanted younger women. Finally, there was no one who wanted me.

At first I managed well enough by selling the jewelry I had been given. When I no longer had any jewels to sell, I offered myself as a servant. I figured I would at least have a roof over my head and food to eat. I had never before done the kind of work that was expected of me and apparently I did it poorly. So I was treated poorly, sold by one master to another. I finally ended up on a makeshift stage, offered for sale in the public eye.

I must have been quite a site. I had lost so much weight. My clothes were in tatters. I had no means of even combing my hair. I was dirty. Who in their right mind would even purchase someone like me? But there was someone. I heard a familiar voice from the back of the crowd. It was Hosea! He had come looking for me. I didn't speak as he paid the fifteen shekels of silver and a basket of barley. Neither of us spoke as he took me home.

When we got to the house, the children were kept away from me until I was cleaned up. I hadn't realized how much I'd missed them. Hosea hadn't told them what I had been up to. He simply said to them that I had to be away for a while. They ran to me with open arms and I cried as I hugged them.

After the children were asleep, Hosea told me that God had sent him to find me. He said that I must stay with him this time and not take up with any other men. I must be faithful to him and he would be faithful to me. Hosea had saved me from myself. I now saw how much he loved me and I loved him all the more for it.

Our story was like that of the children of Israel. As I had been unfaithful to Hosea, they had been unfaithful to the LORD God; as I had turned to other men, they had turned to other gods. And as I had returned to Hosea because of his love for me, so Israel would one day return to the LORD because of the LORD's love for her.

Hosea explained all this to me. He told me that the nation of Syria would soon come and destroy the nation of Israel. People here are still in denial. Hosea continues to preach, but will anyone listen?

We have changed the names of my children slightly. No Mercy is now called Mercy. She reflects the mercy God will show to Israel. Not My People has become My People, for God will claim Israel again as his own. The children are grown up now. Thanks to Hosea and the grace of the LORD, they are faithful to Yahweh. Instead of having no use for the Torah, they have no use for the Baals. Unlike me in my younger days, they are content with what they have.

Hadassah

I don't really remember my parents. They died when I was very young and my older cousin, Mordecai, raised me. (My father, Abihail, and Mordecai's father, Jair, were brothers.) It was quite a task for a single man to raise a young girl. I often wondered what my parents were like, but I was still happy. I knew I was well loved.

Mordecai told me stories of our people. We Jews are descended from the great prophet, Abraham. His grandson, Jacob, had twelve sons and the twelve tribes of Israel are from those twelve sons. We are called the sons of Israel because that is the name God himself gave to Jacob all those generations ago.

There was a famine in Canaan when Jacob lived there. His entire family moved to Egypt where there was food. They stayed there for hundreds of years, in an area of their own where they did not intermix much with the Egyptians. The Egyptians forgot about our origins and grew to hate us, enslaving my people. Another great prophet, Moses, with God's help, was able to lead the people out of Egypt and into the Promised Land which became known as Israel.

Israel had no government but God for many years. When there was trouble, God sent judges to lead them. Eventually, the people asked for a king. Saul was the first. David was the second and the greatest.

When David's son, Solomon, died the nation was split in two. The northern kingdom was still known as Israel and the southern kingdom became known as Judah because that was the predominant tribe.

The line of David continued to rule in Judah, but the north was ruled by a series of mostly evil men. The Assyrians came and took over their land and the northern tribes were never heard from again. Oh, there were a few people who remained, but they intermarried with the people Assyria sent to repopulate the land.

The people of Judah didn't learn from the people of the northern kingdom. Eventually, so many people lost sight of the true God that he sent judgment on us too. The Babylonians conquered Jerusalem and transported most of the people to their country. Nebuchadnezzar became our king.

The Babylonians were in turn conquered by the Medes and Persians. When Cyrus took over, he granted the Jews permission to return to Jerusalem. Only about 50,000 took him up on that offer. While some went, my family and many others remained. They had made their lives in this new country. Mordecai worked in the palace in Susa, a large city in Persia.

Within our house, we practiced the traditions of our fathers. But because of Mordecai's placement, very few people on the outside were really aware that we were Jews. Eventually, it became common knowledge.

I lived a normal life until I was fifteen and was taken to the palace grounds. But to explain that, I have to go back five years earlier. The king, Xerxes, had given a great feast. As it was drawing to an end, he sent for Vashti, the queen, to come to the dining hall. I don't know what all the details are, but apparently she refused and as a result was banished from the king's presence. Soon after that, Xerxes went away to war. When he returned, he decided he wanted a new queen. Many of the girls my age were rounded up and brought to the palace. I was one of them.

We were placed under the care of Hegai where we were groomed for the possibility of becoming queen. As time went by, some of the girls were assigned as assistants to the others. I must have pleased Hegai because he made seven of them my attendants and moved us up to the best place in the harem, along with several other similar groups.

Our training and beauty treatments went on for a year. During all that time, no one knew I was a Jew because Mordecai had commanded me not to make it known. Apparently, he walked by the harem every day to check on me, though I saw him only occasionally. I missed him terribly.

Not all of us had arrived at the same time. When the twelve months were up for each of us, it was then our turn to be presented to the king. The girl, now a young woman, was allowed to take with her anything she wanted from the harem, knowing she would be able to keep it whether or not she was chosen to be the next queen. They also knew that with the number of candidates, the chances of becoming queen were slim, so most took everything they possibly could.

She would go to the king in the evening and the next morning she would likely go to the second harem where the rest of the concubines lived. Shaashgaz, the king's eunuch, was likely the only man she would see in the future. Unless the king was taken with her and requested her by name, she would not be called to him again.

I was very nervous when my turn came. I knew what spending the night with the king meant. Hegai was very kind in letting us know what was expected of us. I was uninterested in taking a lot of things with me. What use did I have for jewels or other baubles? So I took only what Hegai advised me, some perfumes which would please the king. If it was my calling to go in to the king, I was going to do the best I could to please him.

Apparently that was the right move. I was called back to the king the next night, and the one after that. I didn't know why at the time, or what plans God had for me, but the king was pleased. He even told me he loved me. I had become very fond of him too. None of the other young women were called to him to audition for the spot and I became his queen.

What a festival that was! I had never imagined that I would have such a wedding. Xerxes gave a feast for all his officials and all the servants too. He granted a remission of taxes and gave gifts to every citizen. I became known by my Persian name, Queen Esther.

Even though I was queen, I did not see Xerxes on a daily basis. I had my own quarters and did not live with the concubines. I pretty much led my own life with my attendants except for those times Xerxes specifically requested my presence. I was again able to see Mordecai openly.

One day Mordecai came to me with disturbing news. He had been sitting at the king's gate when he heard of a plot to take the king's life. Bigthan and Teresh, two of the king's eunuchs, had become angry at Xerxes for some reason and were planning to kill him. Xerxes had requested my presence that evening and I was able to warn him in time. When an investigation showed that the plot which Mordecai had reported was true, the men were hanged on the gallows.

Sometime after this, Xerxes promoted a man named Haman and put him over all the other palace officials. Haman lorded it over everyone he came in contact with. Xerxes had commanded all the king's servants, including his officials, to bow down and pay homage to him. But Mordecai would not. At first, Haman hadn't noticed, but the others who tried in vain to encourage Mordecai to do so went and told Haman.

These others were just trouble makers. They knew Mordecai was a Jew, though they didn't know about our relationship, and they resented the fact that Mordecai held a higher position than they did. They also believed that if they had to bow down, everyone else should. Haman became furious with Mordecai.

When he found out he was a Jew, he started to look for a way to destroy all the Jews in the kingdom. I didn't know any of this at the time.

One day my attendants came to me and said that Mordecai was making a scene in the middle of the city. He had torn his clothes, put on sackcloth and ashes, and was crying out bitterly. He came up to the king's door but could go no further since no one in sackcloth was allowed to enter. I sent him clean clothes, but he would not accept them.

So I sent Hathach, who was now one of my eunuchs, to find out what was going on. Mordecai told him that Haman had promised Xerxes a great sum of money for the privilege of destroying all the Jews in the entire land on a specified date. He even showed him a copy of the written decree issued for their destruction. Mordecai gave the decree to Hathach to show me and told him to tell me to go to the king to beg his favor and plead for the preservation of my people.

Now, you need to remember that up to now, no one in the palace had even known that I was a Jewess myself. I sent Hathach back to Mordecai with a message. Everyone knows that no person, even the queen, can appear before the king unless summoned without endangering her life. Xerxes hadn't called for me in a month. I got back a very direct message. "Do not think to yourself that in the king's palace you will escape any more than all the other Jews. For if you keep silent at this time, relief and deliverance will rise for the Jews from another place, but you and your father's house will perish. And who knows whether you have not come to the kingdom for such a time as this?"

I sent a message back to Mordecai telling him to gather all the Jews in Susa and hold a three day fast on my behalf. I would do the same with my attendants. Then I would go to the king. If I perish, I perish.

Three days later, I made my move. I put on my royal garments and approached the king. I stood in front of his quarters. He was on his throne opposite the entrance to the throne room and could see me waiting. Praise God! When Xerxes saw me, he held out the golden scepter granting me permission to enter. He was happy to see me. Before I could ask anything, he offered me up to half of the kingdom. But would he grant a request to save my people?

I had to wait for the right time. "If it please the king, let the king and Haman come today to a feast that I have prepared for the king." It pleased him. While they were drinking wine, Xerxes asked again, "What is your wish? It shall be granted you. And what is your request? Even to the half of my kingdom, it shall be fulfilled." I still wasn't ready and answered, "My wish and my request is: If I have found favor in the sight of the king, and if it please the king to grant my wish and fulfill my request, let the king and Haman come to the feast that I will prepare for them, and tomorrow I will do as the king has said."

The next day, I saw Mordecai dressed in royal robes and wearing a crown, being led through town by Haman who was calling out, “Thus shall it be done to the man whom the king delights to honor.” I didn’t know what had transpired to cause this turn of events but found out later that Xerxes had been reminded of the time Mordecai had saved his life by bringing to light the plot by Bigthan and Teresh. The treatment Mordecai was receiving was what Haman had suggested when he thought he was “the man whom the king delights to honor.”

That evening, Xerxes again asked what my wish was. The time had come; I asked for my life, and the lives of my people. I told him that there was a plan to destroy us. I said that if it were just a matter of being sold as slaves I would not have said anything. But we were to be killed. Then Xerxes asked who would dare to do this. I said, “A foe and enemy! This wicked Haman!”

Xerxes was furious. I didn’t know if he was angry at me or at Haman. He stormed out of my room and into the palace gardens. Haman stayed and begged me for his life. Haman, who had plotted to destroy me and all my people. Haman was distraught and tripped. When Xerxes returned, Haman was falling on my couch. Xerxes saw that as an attack on me. When he said, “Will he even assault the queen in my presence, in my own house?”, the king’s guard took possession of Haman.

Harbona, one of Xerxes attendants, told him about the gallows Haman had prepared for Mordecai. Haman was going to make a huge public display and had built the gallows 75 feet high so the execution could easily be seen from a great distance. Xerxes said to hang Haman on that and Haman himself became a public example of what happens when you cross the king.

Haman's family did not fare well either. His wife, Zeresh, was left penniless when Xerxes presented all Haman's property to me. I in turn set Mordecai over it. Xerxes also took the signet ring that he had once given to Haman and gave that to Mordecai.

Mordecai and I would be protected but there was still the problem of the edict to destroy the Jews. I fell at the king's feet, pleading with him to avert this evil. Although an edict sealed with the king's ring, as this was, could not be revoked, Xerxes told Mordecai to compose another edict as he thought best could counter the first.

Mordecai dictated the edict and the king's scribes were summoned to write it in all the languages of the kingdom. It was sent to all the satraps, governors, and officials of the 127 provinces from India to Ethiopia. It said that the Jews were to be allowed to gather in every city to defend their lives and to kill any armed force that may attack them, including their women and children. Further, the Jews were allowed to take plunder from their enemies. Instead of wiping out the Jews, the net effect was to make more people claim to be Jews. The fear of the Jews had fallen on the populace. They knew their own lives were in danger if they were to come out as enemies against the Jews.

Almost nine months after the original edict was written to destroy the Jews, on the very day designated for it, the reverse occurred. The leaders in all the provinces actually helped the Jews to lay hands on those who sought them harm. Mordecai was now high in the king's esteem and nobody wanted to cross him. His fame had spread and he had become powerful.

The Jews struck hard. In Susa alone, the Jews killed and destroyed 500 men. It was at this time that the ten sons of Haman were also destroyed, eliminating any danger of their seeking revenge. Although the Jews had been given permission to take plunder from their enemies, they did not do so.

All this was reported to Xerxes. When he told me about it, he asked what else I wanted done. I knew there were still enemies in Susa who continued to pose a risk to my people so I asked for one more day that the Jews would be allowed to continue killing their enemies. I asked also that the sons of Haman be hung on the gallows to serve as an example to others. Another 300 enemies were destroyed in Susa. It was later reported to me that 75,000 of our enemies in the other provinces were also destroyed.

At last the Jews in the empire could relax. The threat of genocide had been removed. We were able to change a time of mourning into a holiday. Mordecai sent another letter to all the Jews. For all time, they were to celebrate this festival each year in the month of Adar. They should feast and give gifts, both to each other and to the poor. The feast became known as Purim, since Haman and his friends had cast Pur (lots) to choose the time of our destruction. It's been a year; a joyful Purim to you.

Vashti

It is good to be back in the palace. My youngest son, Artaxerxes, has taken his rightful place on the throne. Esther is out of the picture and I have resumed my honor.

I was born in the palace, a Babylonian princess. My father was King Belshazzar, his father was King Nabonidus. My grandmother was the daughter of Nebuchadnezzar himself, giving my father royal blood on both sides. When Nabonidus had left Babylon for Tayma where he led the worship of the moon god, Sin, he made my father co-regent. Nabonidus returned when the Persians were advancing on us. He left Father in charge while he went to meet Cyrus in the north. Unfortunately, Nabonidus was defeated and exiled.

Two days later, my father was killed. He had not yet heard the news about his own father and had thrown a great feast. That night, mobs of Medes and Persians attacked and murdered him. When I came to my father's quarters, I was kidnapped by Darius, the man appointed by Cyrus to be king in Babylon. Darius must have had some respect for my grandfather, Nebuchadnezzar. He had mercy on me and married me to his son, Xerxes, whom the Jews call Ahasuerus.

Xerxes had been king for about three years when he gathered the military leaders, the nobles, and the governors of all the provinces. They were planning an invasion to take over the lands controlled by the Greeks. When they weren't arguing about that, they were drinking and feasting. This went on for six months. When they concluded their plans, Xerxes held another feast and invited even the common people. Well, all the male common people anyway.

I had my own feast at that time for the women. We had been partying for a week when the summons came. Xerxes had been showing off all the riches of the kingdom, the cotton curtains, the gold, silver, precious stones. Now he wanted to show off his queen. I would not be displayed like a harlot and refused to go. The very laws of the Persians forbid wives to be seen by strangers. Though he repeatedly sent the eunuchs to get me, I repeatedly refused to come. Xerxes took it personally and became so angry that he broke up the banquet. The next thing I knew I was banished from the king's presence and relegated to the harem.

I still had people in the palace and was kept privy to what was going on. Soon after I was sent away, Xerxes set out from Sardis with his army. A small force of Greek warriors led by the king of Sparta resisted but was defeated at Thermopylae. After that, Xerxes was again triumphant. Athens was defeated and her forces driven back to the Isthmus of Corinth. It was the Persian army that was defeated at Salamis and Xerxes set up camp for the winter in Thessaly.

Instead of engaging the Greeks in spring, Xerxes was forced to send his army home to prevent a revolt. He left part of his army behind with Mardonius in charge. They were defeated at Plataea. The Persian fleet which had remained anchored at Mycale was attacked and burned by the Greeks, cutting off the supplies needed by the army. There was no choice but to retreat and Xerxes lost everything that he had gained. Greece was becoming the new world power.

I think when Xerxes returned home that he may have been sorry he banished me, but his pride would not let him recall me. That and the stupid rule that a king's proclamation could not be undone or reversed. Still, despite all the women in his harem, he wanted a queen. Young women were gathered from throughout every province of the realm. After months of being groomed, Esther was chosen and crowned. Any hope of my restoration was put down.

I could only hope that one day my son would take the throne and I would be welcome in the king's presence once again.

After 20 years in power, including years of leading an army, Xerxes was murdered by a trusted friend, Artabanus, the commander of the royal bodyguard. Artabanus also murdered Xerxes' oldest son, Darius. When Artaxerxes found out, he killed Artabanus and his sons, foiling his plot to take over the kingdom.

With the death of Xerxes and the enthronement of Artaxerxes, Esther was to be moved to the harem as I had been all those years before. But I had pity on her. It wasn't her fault that I had lost my position. Actually, she was the only one besides me who knew what it was like to live as queen to a powerful man whose temper could destroy you in a moment. I had her moved into a small house outside of Susa and sent some from the harem to attend her. I would not say we are friends, but neither are we enemies.

Elizabeth

Look at him, running around and chasing the fireflies. What a joy to watch my son. My son, the child I thought I would never have. I was past the age of childbearing and had finally accepted the fact that I would never be a mother. Then the impossible happened.

Zechariah had been in Jerusalem with his division of priests. He came home at the expected time and I didn't think anything of it…until he tried to tell me what had happened to him. He was mute, couldn't say a word. Now, I know most wives would like their husbands to stop talking sometimes, but this was different. The only way for him to let me know anything was to write it down.

Zechariah had been chosen by lot to go into the temple and burn the incense. All of a sudden, an angel appeared, standing right next to the altar of incense. Now this is certainly not an everyday occurrence and Zechariah was frightened. The angel told him that his prayer was heard and I would bear him a son. The angel even told him what he should name the boy.

The angel, who later said his name was Gabriel, gave him specific instructions. The child was to be a Nazarite. A Nazarite is one dedicated to God. Most often, the vow of a Nazarite is for a limited time during which he is not to drink wine or any other strong drink, nor eat any part of a grape vine, fruit or leaf. He was not to cut his hair or come in contact with a corpse or grave, not even of a close family member. For our son, this was to be a lifelong dedication. Gabriel also said that our son would turn many of our people back to God and make a people prepared for the Lord their God; he would have the spirit and power of Elijah.

This was all too much for Zechariah. Though he had prayed for a son, he didn't think it was really possible. Because of his doubts, Gabriel told him that he would be unable to speak until these words were fulfilled.

Gabriel left and Zechariah stood there in shock. When he finally departed from the temple proper, the people were all wondering what had happened in there. Zechariah was unable to explain, but they must have realized he had seen a vision or something else miraculous. He tried to tell them by making signs, but they couldn't understand. Who would? What had happened was not something one would ever expect. When Zechariah's rotation was completed, he came home.

I was not about to disbelieve or laugh. Sarah had laughed when the angel said she would give birth to a son, but a year later Isaac was born. If God could give Sarah a child, he could do the same for me. And he did.

I knew not to tell everyone that I was pregnant. Who would have believed me? So I pretty much stayed by myself for the first five months. By then, people would be able to tell I was going to have a child and I wasn't just talking crazy. Then, still another miracle happened.

Soon after I started telling my friends about my own miracle, Mary came for a visit. Mary lived quite a ways north of us and I usually only saw her when we went to the feasts in Jerusalem. We are kinswomen. Her parents and mine are of the house of Judah.

When I heard Mary calling my name I felt my child jump for joy. Right away I knew what her news was. She too was going to have a child. Her child would be the Son of God. I could not help but exclaim "Blessed are you among women, and blessed is the fruit of your womb!" I asked why I was privileged to have the mother of my Lord come to me. I knew she was blessed and believed that there would be a fulfillment of what was spoken to her from the Lord.

Mary was filled with a song of praise. She said, "My soul magnifies the Lord, and my spirit rejoices in God my Savior, for he has looked on the humble estate of his servant. For behold, from now on all generations will call me blessed; for he who is mighty has done great things for me, and holy is his name. And his mercy is for those who fear him from generation to generation. He has shown strength with his arm; he has scattered the proud in the thoughts of their hearts; he has brought down the mighty from their thrones and exalted those of humble estate; he has filled the hungry with good things, and the rich he has sent away empty. He has helped his servant Israel, in remembrance of his mercy, as he spoke to our fathers, to Abraham and to his offspring forever."

Mary stayed for several months. We talked about many things, including all the changes that were going on with her body. She asked me how she would tell her parents, afraid they would think poorly of her because she was pregnant and unmarried. I was sure they would understand when she told them exactly what had happened. They were good, faithful people, waiting for the coming of the Messiah as we were. Her betrothed, Joseph, might not be as understanding, but he too was a good man and not apt to make a scene. Not all our talk was serious. We laughed often as we worked on her wedding dress.

Mary stayed about three months. The wedding dress was finished. She had wanted to stay until my baby was born, but also wanted to get home before she started to show. She needed to talk to her parents before her pregnancy became obvious.

Soon after she left, my time had come. Given my age, you can understand that my mother had already passed away. But I had good friends in town and was surrounded by many women when my son was born. Eight days later, the house was full again as friends came to celebrate my son's circumcision and naming.

They all freely suggested names. Some were sure we were going to name him after his father, Zechariah. Some thought Aaron was appropriate. Still others thought Abijah. But I remembered what the angel Gabriel had told Zechariah. When I told them he would be called John, they all objected. We had no one in the family named John. Why would we break tradition and not name him after a relative? Thinking I was wrong, they turned to Zechariah. He motioned for a writing tablet and wrote, "His name is John." At that instant he was able to speak. The people were stunned.

And speak he did. He prophesied saying, "Blessed be the Lord God of Israel, for he has visited and redeemed his people and has raised up a horn of salvation for us in the house of his servant David, as he spoke by the mouth of his holy prophets from of old, that we should be saved from our enemies and from the hand of all who hate us; to show the mercy promised to our fathers and to remember his holy covenant, the oath that he swore to our father Abraham, to grant us that we, being delivered from the hand of our enemies, might serve him without fear, in holiness and righteousness before him all our days. And you, child, will be called the prophet of the Most High; for you will go before the Lord to prepare his ways, to give knowledge of salvation to his people in the forgiveness of their sins, because of the tender mercy of our God, whereby the sunrise shall visit us from on high to give light to those who sit in darkness and in the shadow of death, to guide our feet into the way of peace."

Now, five years later, people are still talking about this throughout the hill country of Judea. We are all wondering exactly what this meant, what would this child be?

Anna

My father Phanuel was a prophet. My husband was a prophet. We are part of the tribe of Asher. Our tribal land was in the north. When Jeroboam became king of the northern tribes, he set up a golden calf to dissuade his people from crossing the border into Judea. Some of my ancestors left and came down here where they could worship in the temple as God had directed. It was a good thing they did. The northern tribe of Israel became more and more godless until the LORD sent the Assyrians to take them away into foreign lands. The southern country of Judea was going down the same path and about 200 years later the LORD sent the Babylonians to take them away and teach them a lesson. The difference in the two countries was that God allowed some of the Judean captives to return to the Promised Land.

I have lived here in the temple in Jerusalem since my husband died seven years after we were married. Now I am an old woman of 84 springs. I have seen countless people come through these gates, most with offerings for one thing or another. Through it all I have been waiting for the coming of the Messiah. My wait is over.

The young couple I saw today looked like any other couple bringing their firstborn to present to the LORD. The mother was carrying the baby. The father had a cage in his hands with two young pigeons for the purification sacrifice. They were of modest means or they would have brought a young lamb instead. Like I said, an average family.

Then I saw Simeon. Simeon was a righteous and devout man whom I saw here daily. He came into the temple with his face aglow like he had seen something wonderful. He reached for the baby. Gazing at the child, he blessed God and said, "Lord, now you are letting your servant depart in peace, according to your word; for my eyes have seen your salvation that you have prepared in the presence of all peoples, a light for revelation to the Gentiles, and for glory to your people Israel." Like me, Simeon had been waiting for the Messiah. He had told me quite some time ago that the Holy Spirit had promised him that he would not die before seeing the Messiah. Today the spirit had told him that this child was the long expected Savior.

The mother was obviously surprised that this man would just walk up to her and take the child from her arms. Simeon blessed the family and said to his parents, "Behold, this child is appointed for the fall and rising of many in Israel, and to be a sign that will be spoken against so that the thoughts of many hearts will be revealed." He looked directly at the mother with sadness and said to her, "And a sword will pierce through your own soul also." Then he returned the child to his mother.

Well, I had to take my turn holding this little one. Having seen the look on the mother's face when Simeon took hold of him, I remembered to ask permission first. I joined in giving thanks to God for allowing me to see this child, the salvation of Israel. Now I, too, could go in peace. Of course, I had to tell everyone who would listen about this wonderful news: the Messiah had come. We may not know exactly how God will work this out, but the time has come at last. This child would grow up to be our salvation.

Mary of Nazareth

I am so excited that Mary Magdalene is coming to visit. I have plenty of friends here in Ephesus, but it is always nice to see the friends from long ago. It's perfect timing too. John has gone to Jerusalem again to see Peter. I used to go along with him on these trips. It was always nice to see James, but it is getting to be too much for me to travel these days.

Actually, I have done a lot of traveling in my time. I was born in Sepphoris in Galilee. We moved to Nazareth when I was young, before Herod died and Judas bar Ezekias attacked Sepphoris, arming his followers in a revolt against Herodian rule. My oldest child was born in Bethlehem and we took him to Egypt and lived there for a while. When my children were older, I traveled extensively around Judea. Now I live here in Ephesus.

I met my husband just after we moved to Nazareth. I had noticed him right away, but it seemed to take him a long time to notice me. Joseph was taller than the other young men he hung around with. Even though his skin was relatively dark, his hair was almost blond. He had a rich, deep voice that I could almost feel.

Our house was in need of some repairs. Joseph was a carpenter like his father, James. One day they came to the house to see what needed to be done. I was in the kitchen with my mother, Anne, when my father, Joakim, brought them in and introduced them. When the repairs were finished, Joseph still found reasons to come around.

After a year and a half, Joseph finally asked my father if he could marry me. We were to be married a year later. Things did not go as planned. One night as I was preparing for bed, an angel appeared to me. I was stunned when he said, "Greetings, O favored one, the Lord is with you!" The angel identified himself as Gabriel and told me not to be afraid because I had found favor with God. Then he told me the most amazing thing! I was to have a son and I was to name him Jesus. He would be called the Son of the Most High and would have the kingdom of his father, David. I may have been young and naïve, but I knew where babies come from. It wasn't that I doubted the words of the messenger, but I knew that I hadn't yet been with Joseph, or any other man for that matter. "How will this be, since I am a virgin?" I asked.

I will never forget how Gabriel said to me, "The Holy Spirit will come upon you, and the power of the Most High will overshadow you; therefore the child to be born of you will be called holy – the Son of God." Who was I to have this honor? I am the Lord's servant. Then he added that Elizabeth, a relative, was also pregnant, even though she was well past child bearing age and had been considered barren. As suddenly as he had appeared, Gabriel was gone.

When I woke up the next morning, I knew that it hadn't been a dream. I really was going to have a child, a son. I needed to speak to someone about this. Mother was wonderful, but would she understand or would she doubt my virginity when she found out I was pregnant? The angel had said Elizabeth was pregnant. Elizabeth would understand this miracle.

As calmly as possible, I suggested to Mother that it was about time I visit Elizabeth. I insisted I could make the trip myself. After all I was not a child anymore; I was about to be married. I really did have another good reason. Elizabeth had a reputation for making beautiful dresses. She could help me pick out the fabric and make my wedding dress, or help me make it. Reluctantly, Mother agreed to let me go.

There were other people going to Jerusalem and I was able to travel with them. From there I found a family returning to Hebron. It was a long trip. I was tired when I arrived, but felt exuberant that I had made the journey without difficulty.

Not only did Elizabeth greet me but she said the baby jumped for joy when he heard my voice. They had been told she was going to have a boy and he was to be named John. I have always loved Elizabeth, but now, with our babies just months apart, we had much more in common. We stayed up so late that first night.

I stayed several months. We found the perfect material and completed my dress in a relatively short time. I did wonder if I was going to get to wear it. Would Joseph understand that this child is from God or would he accuse me of unfaithfulness and divorce me?

It would have been nice to have stayed with Elizabeth until after her baby was born but I had to get back. Joseph had to be told, and so did my parents. That needed to be done before I started to show that I was pregnant. Also, if I waited too long, I would have difficulty traveling. The nausea had ended and it was time to return home.

I saw Joseph the day after I got back to Nazareth. I told him about the angel and everything Gabriel had told me that night. Joseph was a good man, but this was a little hard to believe. He could have taken me to the city elders and accused me in public. Stoning was no longer common but I would have been ostracized at the least. Gentle Joseph, he would just divorce me quietly. He even said he would go with me to tell my parents the next day.

The next day, Joseph came running to my house. He said an angel had appeared to him in a dream, telling him not to be afraid to take me as his wife, convincing him that I was pregnant by the Holy Spirit and not because of any infidelity. Joseph said he was told to name the child Jesus because he would save his people from their sins.

Mother and Father believed us. We had a quick, quiet wedding and I moved in with Joseph. We did not have marital relations until after Jesus was born. Before my child was born, we were on the road.

What a journey that turned out to be. A decree had come from the Roman governor. Quirinius was going to tax all the people under the rule of Rome. Herod may have been king, but the governor was even more powerful in this area. In order to be taxed, everyone was to register in the location from which their family had come. And it didn't matter if the women were pregnant or the elderly found it hard to travel.

So a small group from Nazareth headed south to Bethlehem. Both my father and Joseph's could trace their heritage back to Kind David. Both our families, and a few of our neighbors, made the trip together. Many walked. Most of the elderly had donkeys to ride on. Because I was nine months pregnant, Joseph had also procured a donkey for me to ride.

Half way between Jerusalem and Bethlehem, I went into labor. By the time we arrived at Bethlehem, the child would wait no longer. There were so many people on the road that rooms were all but impossible to find; Joseph had knocked on many doors. Finally he found someone who could provide a covered, relatively warm area, a cave where the farm animals were kept.

Mother and I, with some of the other women of our party, went into the cave while the men and children set up the tents around it. Our forefathers had once lived in tents. They were sturdier than the ones we have now which are used mostly for the Festival of Tents and only secondarily for travel. No way was Mother going to let her grandchild be born in a flimsy tent.

When Jesus was born, Mother made him a bed in the feeding trough. When Joseph came in to see his son, the baby and I were both sleeping. Mother and the other women quietly left the cave to join the men and children. Joseph and I were left alone with the baby.

We had visitors that night. Upon entering the cave, the shepherds fell on their knees and worshiped Jesus. They told us how the angle had appeared in the sky and told them about his birth, that their Savior had been born and could be found lying in a feeding trough. Overjoyed with the news, they had rushed to Bethlehem to see for themselves. After they departed, I was left thinking about everything they had said. I still remember every detail.

The next day, most of the group went into town to register and pay the tax. Joseph and I waited three days and then we did the same. The landowner graciously allowed the entire family to extend their stay in their tents on the grounds. On the eighth day we had Jesus circumcised according to the Law of Moses. It was only then that Jesus formally received the name Gabriel had told us. After the celebratory meal, the rest of the family returned to Nazareth.

Rather than make the arduous trip back to Nazareth with the others so soon after I had given birth, Joseph found us a small house to rent in Bethlehem. Business wasn't very good back home anyway. We were hoping he could find more work in Judea than was available in Galilee.

He did do well; there was plenty of work to be done in Bethlehem and the surrounding area. And since we were not that far from Jerusalem, it was a simple matter to take Jesus to the temple when the time of my purification had arrived a month later. This was the first time I went out in public, except for that time I had no choice and went to register. The Romans didn't care if I was impure.

I was taken back when a man walked up to us and took the baby into his arms. His name was Simeon. After he gave us a blessing, he praised God for letting him see Jesus. He also warned me that I would face sorrow because of my son. Without really understanding, I felt something pierce my heart already.

Next, an old woman approached us. I thought at first the women had just come to admire the baby, as older women are prone to do. But she too, took the child in her arms. Unlike Simeon, she was aware of a mother's feelings of possessiveness and asked permission first. She introduced herself as Anna, and then she began to praise God as well. After she had returned the baby, I noticed that she was talking to many others in the courtyard and pointing out Jesus. I remarked to Joseph how curious the morning had been as we walked over to find a priest for the sacrifice.

Life settled into a routine in Bethlehem. Joseph kept busy with his carpentry, I with homemaking and taking care of Jesus. I made friends in Bethlehem. Because we were so close to Jerusalem, Jesus and I accompanied Joseph to each of the feasts while we lived in Bethlehem. I even made another trip to see Elizabeth, since she was no longer quite so far away. It was good to see her and John.

We had been living in Bethlehem for about a year and a half when we received visitors that changed our world again. I was cleaning up in the kitchen after supper, with Jesus playing at my feet, when the knock came at the door. After a few minutes Joseph came in to the kitchen. We had guests; they had come to see Jesus.

I brought the baby into the living area. The five men all stood when I entered the room. They greeted me, but their eyes were on Jesus. The oldest appearing man said, "We have come to worship him, the one born King of the Jews." They approached Jesus and, like the shepherds in the cave, they fell on their knees to worship him. They brought out gifts: gold, frankincense, and myrrh. Neither Joseph nor I had seen such wealth before.

I brought out the dishes and food I had just put away and while the visitors were eating, they told of their journey. They were part of a group of people in their country to the east who had been waiting for the promised birth of a king. Their lore told of a special star that would appear when that child was born. They had been following the star since its appearance and it led them here. At first it had been a little difficult to determine exactly where that star was pointing to. Thinking that a king must certainly be born in the capital city of Jerusalem, they first went there and started asking around. Herod heard of this and invited them to the palace.

"Herod was very interested," said Jaspar. "He even called some of his advisors together to ask where we should be looking. They said Bethlehem, so we came here. The star seemed to hold its course right over this house."

"Yes, Herod was very interested," added Melchior. "He wants us to return and let him know where exactly we found the child so he can also come and worship him."

The next morning, the men were talking to each other excitedly. They had each dreamed a dream telling them to return to their own country without returning first to Jerusalem. After they ate breakfast, I loaded them up with bread and fruit for their long journey home. Joseph walked with them to the edge of town and then returned home. We spent the rest of the day preparing to host the king, certain Herod would find us without the aid of our recently departed visitors.

But we did not greet the king at our door. That very night, Joseph had a dream of his own. An angel of the Lord appeared to him and warned him that Herod would be searching for Jesus to kill him. Joseph rose and woke me before sunrise. He loaded up the donkey with as much as he could, including the gifts we had just received. We took Jesus and left for Egypt without telling anyone.

There was a large Jewish community in Egypt and we settled in, not knowing how long we would have to stay there. Eventually Joseph had another dream. An angel of the Lord told him that Herod had died and we should return home. This time we did say goodbye to our friends before setting out to return to Bethlehem.

Shortly after crossing the Jordan, we heard from other travelers that Archelaus had succeeded his father as ruler over Judea. Adding that to another dream warning, we turned north to return to Nazareth in Galilee.

We also heard what had happened in and around Bethlehem after we'd left. Herod was so angry when the men from the east didn't return to tell him where we were. He was so afraid of the one they'd called the King of the Jews that he ordered the murder of all the boys in the area who were two years old and younger. I was happy we had escaped, but felt so sorry for the families of the other little boys.

It was good to be back among old friends and family. My sister, Salome, had married while we were away and had given birth to a son. We were back in Nazareth just in time to witness his circumcision. They named the baby James.

Soon after, I found I was pregnant again. We named him James also. It was customary to name children after relatives, and Joseph's father's name was James. As time went by, we had more children: Joseph, Judah, Mary, Simeon, Martha, Ruth. Because some names were so common, we called Joseph Joses, Judah was Jude, and Mary was Miri. Salome was my only sibling and I loved all those children running around the house.

Salome and her husband, Zebedee, had another son during that time and named him John. We didn't see them much except for during the festivals and special family gatherings because Zebedee had a fishing business to run and you can't fish if you aren't by the water. The Sea of Galilee was a full day's journey from Nazareth.

We would go to see them sometimes, but most often our trips were to Jerusalem. The men were obligated to go to the festivals there three times a year. If I wasn't pregnant or nursing I would go too. One of those trips still stands out in my mind more than the others.

Jesus was 12 years old and had gone with Joseph and me for the Feast of the Passover. There was nothing remarkable about the trip until we were on the way home. At the end of the first day traveling back, we couldn't find Jesus. I thought he was traveling with the men; Joseph thought he was with me. The two of us hurried back to Jerusalem to find him.

We finally found him in the temple after three days. There he was, sitting among the teachers. He was listening intently. We had taught Jesus about the Law of Moses, the prophets and the writings, but he was asking questions you would only expect from someone far older.

I felt a mixture of relief that he was ok and anger that he had put us through this. I asked him what in the world he was thinking and told him how worried we were about him. He answered me with a question, "Why were you looking for me? Did you not know that I must be in my Father's house?" We didn't understand at the time that he was talking about his heavenly father. We all went back down to Nazareth and for almost twenty years he didn't worry us like that again.

Joseph taught his carpentry trade to all the boys. James wasn't especially good at it, Joses and Jude were so-so, but Jesus and Simeon were naturals. Since Jesus was the oldest, everyone assumed he would take over the family business. But Jesus had other plans.

Jesus was not only good at carpentry; he had an uncanny understanding of the scriptures and a talent for explaining them to others. It was common for different people to do the readings in the synagogue and he was often called upon to do so. He started traveling to different parts of the country and speaking both in the synagogues and out in the open.

But I'm getting ahead of myself. I need to tell you a little about John, Elizabeth's son. We heard he was preaching in the wilderness of Judea, calling people to repentance and baptizing them in the Jordon River. Because of this, he became known as John the Baptist. He was living out there, eating wild honey and pods from the locust tree. Some said he looked like a madman, dressed in a garment of camel's hair with a leather belt around his waist. Many people came to him and he had some dedicated disciples. It was his preaching that was later to get him killed by Herod Antipas.

I knew Jesus had gone to Judea but didn't find out until much later that he had been to see John and be baptized. I didn't hear about it until later because Jesus had just disappeared after that. No one had seen him for well over a month. When he showed up again, he never told anyone where he had been or what he had been doing.

I didn't get the details, scant as they were, until five years later when I was living with Salome's John. Right after he was baptized, Jesus had gone out into the wilderness. He didn't eat; he didn't even have water. He had been tempted by Satan over and over again.

Shortly after Jesus returned to Nazareth, we heard that John the Baptist had been arrested and put into jail. It was after that when Jesus started to be gone for longer periods of time. As he traveled, Jesus collected his own band of disciples. There were a lot of people who followed after him, but twelve men in particular who spent the most time with him.

Naturally, his cousins James and John were part of that group. They actually left their father's fishing business to follow Jesus, but Zebedee didn't seem to mind too much. First though, Jesus recruited Simeon and his brother Andrew who were also fisherman. (Jesus later called Simeon "Peter" and that name stuck.) Then there were Philip and Nathaniel, Thomas, another Simeon and another James, Matthew Levi, and a couple of men named Judas.

Jesus came home from time to time, usually with at least some of these men, but those visits became further and further apart. One of those visits was to attend a family wedding in Cana.

It was a lovely wedding. Rebecca was a beautiful bride and Benjamin was grinning ear to ear the whole time. There was a problem though. I heard the steward talking about the wine running out. I knew Jesus could somehow take care of the problem and save Benjamin and his father from embarrassment. When I told Jesus about it, he just said that his hour hadn't yet come. I was sure he would still do something, so I told the servants to do whatever he might tell them to do. The next thing I knew, there was more wine. I heard the taster say it was better than what had first been put out. Jesus had told the servants to put water in the stone water jars and then told them to take it to the master of the feast. It was no longer water, but wine. This was the first of the wonders that Jesus was to do.

After the wedding, we all went to Capernaum for a few days. Jesus came home to Nazareth less and less often. Finally he stopped coming all together. The way the local people treated him that one Sabbath, I couldn't blame him.

Jesus had gone to the synagogue as he had done many times before and stood up to read. The reading for the day was from Isaiah. "The Spirit of the Lord is upon me, because he has anointed me to proclaim good news to the poor. He has sent me to proclaim liberty to the captives and recovering of sight to the blind, to set at liberty those who are oppressed, to proclaim the year of the Lord's favor." Then he told them that that Scripture had been fulfilled.

At first they listened intently. But they were expecting him to do in Nazareth the kind of wonders he had done in Capernaum. Jesus was not going to do that. He told them the no prophet is acceptable in his home town. Then he talked about how during the famine in the days of Elijah, God sent him to stay with a gentile widow even though there were plenty of widows in Israel. He reminded them that Elisha healed Naaman, the Syrian, of leprosy when there were plenty of lepers in Israel.

When they heard this, the congregation became furious. The chased him out to the edge of town. James heard them say they were going to throw him off the cliff. James and Joses tried to get to Jesus first, but it seemed like Jesus just walked away without being seen.

Jesus only returned to Nazareth once after that. James and Joseph had been to Bethany and Jerusalem on business. A short time after they returned, Joseph had taken to his bed with some sort of illness. We sent word to Jesus in Capernaum and he came home. Two days later, Joseph died. Jesus was a big help in making arrangements for the funeral. Some of his disciples came with him and stayed a couple days after the funeral. Jesus stayed for the rest of the month-long mourning period and then he was gone again.

After Joseph had died, I would go up to Jerusalem with my other sons. On one trip we all went to see Jesus when we heard that he was preaching in a nearby town. We knew he had been making enemies and wanted to try to talk him into coming home. We got the attention of one of his followers who told Jesus we were outside and wanted to talk to him. The door was open and we could hear as Jesus said, "Who is my mother, and who are my brothers?" Then we saw him stretch out his hand toward his disciples and say "Here are my mother and my brothers! For whoever does the will of my Father in heaven is my brother and sister and mother." We returned to Nazareth without getting a chance to talk to him.

We heard of more and more almost unbelievable things. Jesus healed people of all sorts of diseases: blindness, leprosy, palsies, hemorrhages, you name it. All these were meant to show them who he is and to reinforce his preaching. I finally understood what he meant when he stood in the temple when he was 12 and said he had to be in his Father's house. I should have understood then; God is his Father. Now he was telling everyone what his Father wanted. I started traveling with Jesus whenever I could. His words were the words of life.

Jesus went through the country, preaching and teaching and doing miracles, for about three years. Then the real trouble started.

The family had gone up to Jerusalem for the Passover. Jesus had been traveling with his disciples and I hoped to see him in Jerusalem. We were staying with Elizabeth who had moved to Jerusalem after Herod had John beheaded early in Jesus' ministry. Zechariah had died some years before that and Elizabeth was alone.

Friday morning came and I still hadn't seen Jesus. I was going to send James and his brothers to see what they could find out, but they were already gone by the time I got up. After several hours, a young man came to tell us that Jesus had been arrested and was being taken to Golgotha, a place where the Romans crucified criminals. I rushed to the hill. Salome was already there with John. I didn't see any of the other disciples. My sister-in-law, Mary, was there with Salome and so was Mary Magdalene. Seeing my son on that cross reminded me of what Simeon had said to me so long ago, that a sword would pierce my soul. I don't think anything could have hurt more.

While we stood there at his feet, Jesus looked down at us. He said to me, "Behold, your son." He turned to John and said, "Behold, your mother!" From that day on I lived with John. You might ask why Jesus would have done that when I had four other sons who should have been looking after their mother. At that time, none of them believed that Jesus was the Son of God. I had to continue his work. James and the others already objected to my traveling with Jesus. They would not have been happy with me if I continued to travel on my own.

It got very dark that afternoon while Jesus was hanging on the cross. And there was that earthquake. Because it was so dark that nobody could see a thing, the earthquake was even more terrifying. Even when the darkness passed I could hardly see anything through my tears. John had to guide me home like he would a blind person.

The disciples were all pretty worried that they would be targeted next. When they wanted to get together, they would do so in the upper room where they had last met for supper. The house was owned by one of the women who traveled with them. Jesus had many followers besides the 12 disciples, including Mary Magdalene, Salome, my sister-in-law, Mary, Joanna, and other women and men. The upper room was large enough for many more than the thirteen who had been there that Thursday night. More importantly, it also had good locks on the doors.

I wasn't there with them on Sunday, I had gone back to Elizabeth's home to gather my things and tell here where I would be staying. We decided I would spend the night with her before going back to Galilee the next day with John. When I saw John on Monday, he had wonderful news.

Some of the women had gone to the grave to finish preparing the body. When they got there, the grave was empty. Some men were there, probably angels. They told the women that Jesus was living. The women told the others and then John and Peter had gone to see for themselves. They too were told by angels that Jesus had risen. Mary Magdalene had gone back a second time and reported actually seeing Jesus, but no one could quite believe her.

That evening when they were all gathered together in that upper room, Jesus had appeared to them. Yes, the doors were locked. Nobody let him in, he just appeared. My heart sang with joy when John told me all this. I would see my son again in Galilee.

Within a week, Jesus also appeared to James. Now at last James was also a believer. Joses, Jude, and Simeon also came to believe. A lot of people saw Jesus and believed in him in the weeks after his resurrection. But some still refused. The Pharisees had paid off the guards and spread the story that Jesus' body had been stolen in the night.

Jesus was not to stay with us forever. Forty days later, John was with the other disciples on a hillside near Jerusalem. John said Jesus told them to preach the good news to all the people in the world. Then Jesus rose up from the earth and was hidden by a cloud. No one ever saw him again. But he is with us still. He promised to be and he is. I can't explain it fully, but he lives in us, his followers.

John frequently traveled back and forth between Galilee and Jerusalem. Many times I went with him. We had important work to do, spreading the news of what Jesus' death and resurrection meant to us and to everyone in the world. John made longer trips as well, and finally we settled here in Ephesus.

John still travels. He is much younger than I and still full of energy. I don't often go along, just a trip to Jerusalem now and then to visit friends and relatives. James took over leadership in Jerusalem when Peter left for other mission fields. He married Mary of Bethany and they live in Jerusalem with their children.

Fortunately, many of my friends are younger than me and they come to Ephesus to visit me. Like I said, Mary Magdalene is coming today. She should be here any time now. I had better go check on the cakes in the oven.

Riva

I've had bouts of fever before, but this time was different. While it's true I was pretty sick when I first got malaria and thought I was going to die, I didn't. It started like a common cold. Then the cough was followed by nausea and vomiting, back pain, headache, chills and fever. Somehow, I recovered.

I'd had a few relapses which were anything but fun. I usually took to my bed for a couple weeks and then gradually returned to normal. This last time I had been sick for a month and there was no sign of improvement. The pain in my head was agony. I could keep nothing down, not even water. It was hard to breathe. My fever got higher and higher, despite all the cool cloths that were placed on me. They tell me I became unconscious. Then suddenly I woke up and I was well.

How could this happen? It is because of my son-in-law's friend. My son-in-law, Simeon, and his brother, Andrew, were fisherman. They often fished with Zebedee's sons, James and John. All four of them were following a man named Jesus. I had met Jesus before. He had been to our house (I live with Simeon) several times.

I was already out of it when they arrived this time. They tell me that when Jesus heard I was sick with a fever, he came in and just touched my hand. When he did I woke up. I can tell you that I felt wonderful. In fact, I felt so well that I was able to get up and cook a meal for them right then. I had no residual weakness or anything. In fact, I had never felt better.

The word of my miraculous recovery spread fast. It seemed like the whole town came to our house that evening. Those who were sick came for healing. If they couldn't come on their own power, their friends or relatives brought them. And Jesus healed them all. Some were even possessed by demons and he cast them out with a single word.

Jesus must have been drained after that. But he was up early the next morning. I'm an early riser, but by the time I got to the kitchen to fix breakfast, Jesus was gone. Simeon went looking for him. They returned to the house long enough to get their few possessions and then they left again.

I was used to Simeon and Andrew leaving. They would be gone for weeks at a time. At first their absences were related to their fishing and to taking the fish to market. After they met Jesus, they fished far less often and spent their time with him. I asked Simeon once why they did this. He told me that Jesus was the Christ, the Son of the Living God. I wasn't sure about that at the time, but let me tell you…I am convinced now without a doubt.

Levona

I had heard so much about this man named Jesus. He seemed to have his base in Capernaum, but he had been going throughout Galilee, preaching and healing people. Recently he had been in the city of Nain where, according to the story going around, he had even brought back a young man from the dead.

I was fortunate enough to not have any life threatening diseases. I didn't need to be cured of blindness, or leprosy, or any of the other diseases Jesus was said to have cured. I didn't need to have demons cast out.

The troubles I had were of a different sort. I had done so much in my past which the Torah had forbidden. I excused myself for a long time, saying I had no choice. My husband died not very long after we were married and left me with a three month old child. My parents had died years earlier and I had no brother to take me in. What was I to do?

At first I tried begging, but the people walked right past me. Desperate to feed my daughter, I started to steal food to supplement what I could glean from the edges of the fields. It was so easy; I soon progressed to stealing money. I was quite good at it actually. I could take money from strangers as they passed by and they wouldn't even know it until I was long gone.

When the weather turned foul, the people passing by were in more of a hurry and bundled up more. That made it more difficult to get anything from them. The fields had been picked clean long ago. We were going to starve if I didn't think of something else.

And so I sold myself. Because I was still young, I had no shortage of customers. Even some of the Pharisees were my lovers; they paid well for secrecy.

Then I heard this Jesus preaching. I felt like he was speaking directly to me when he called us to repent. He told of God's love and how God would forgive me. I started to follow him from place to place just to hear his words. Somehow, I was able to subsist on intermittent odd jobs. I guess that's what happens when you trust Jesus; things just work out. Sometimes I even followed him to Judea.

I remember the time he told the parable about a Pharisee and a tax collector. The Pharisee stood in the temple bragging about how good and holy he was and thanking God for it. What a pompous and arrogant individual. But all the tax collector could say was "God, be merciful to me, a sinner." That was exactly how I felt. Jesus said that tax collector was the one who was justified. If the tax collector could be forgiven, maybe I could too.

Then some of us with little children came to have them blessed by the holy man, Jesus. His close followers didn't seem to like that and told us to leave. They even asked Jesus to send the children away. But Jesus said, "Let the little children come to me and do not hinder them, for to such belongs the kingdom of heaven." Then he put his hands upon them and blessed them.

Back in Galilee, Jesus and his disciples went to the house of a Pharisee for supper. Now, there are several kinds of Pharisees. Some are actually very good people. But most are either self-righteous, like the one Jesus had talked about in the temple, or secret sinners, like the ones who were my customers, or both.

The host of this particular dinner, Simeon, was both. He was self-righteous and he had, at one time, been one of my customers. Anyway, I heard he had invited Jesus to his house and, since I now lived nearby, I thought it would be a good time to honor Jesus.

I was nervous, but I went into the house. Being that close to Jesus, I could only stand there and cry. As I stood near Jesus, I wet his feet with my tears. I loosened my hair to wipe his feet dry. Then I poured out ointment from an alabaster jar I had with me and anointed his feet, kissing them as I did.

Simeon was mumbling to himself loudly enough that some of us could hear him. He said "If this man were a prophet, he would have known who and what sort of woman this is who is touching him, for she is a sinner." Of course Simeon knew of my sins; he had participated in them. But men like him held a double standard, believing they could do what they wanted with impunity; that it was always the sin of the woman.

Jesus said to him, "Simeon, I have something to say to you." And he answered, "Say it, Teacher." Jesus said, "A certain moneylender had two debtors. One owed five hundred denarii, and the other fifty. When they could not pay, he cancelled the debt of both. Now which of them will love him more?" Simeon answered, "The one, I suppose, for whom he cancelled the larger debt." And he said to him, "You have judged rightly."

Then turning toward me he said to Simeon, "Do you see this woman? I entered your house; you gave me no water for my feet, but she has wet my feet with her tears and wiped them with her hair. You gave me no kiss, but from the time I came in she has not ceased to kiss my feet. You did not anoint my head with oil, but she has anointed my feet with ointment. Therefore I tell you, her sins, which are many, are forgiven—for she loved much. But he who is forgiven little, loves little."

Then he said to me, "Your sins are forgiven. Your faith has saved you; go in peace." And so I left, more peaceful than I had ever been in my life. He was right, of course. I had many, many sins to be forgiven. I couldn't have been more grateful.

I can't say I have not done anything wrong since that day. But I have not stolen and I have not sold my body since I heard Jesus preach about God's love. What I have done is follow Jesus.

Photina

I found it odd that the man was sitting there, even odder that he spoke to me. I could tell he was a Jew by the fringes on his clothing. When he asked for a drink, I knew by his accent that he was from Galilee. In those days it was very rare for a Jew to pass through Samaria, but there he was, sitting at Jacob's well near Sychar. It was around noon and the sun was hot. Anyone who had been out walking about would be thirsty. What he asked wasn't unusual. That he asked me, a woman and a Samaritan, was.

I had gone to the well to draw water for my own household. When he spoke to me I had to ask, why me? His answer baffled me, "If you knew the gift of God, and who it is that is saying to you, 'Give me a drink,' you would have asked him, and he would have given you living water." I could see he had nothing to draw water with; that's why asked me in the first place. The well was too deep to get anything out of it without some kind of utensil.

I asked, "Where do you get that living water? Are you greater than our father Jacob? He gave us the well and drank from it himself, as did his sons and his livestock." He said to me, "Everyone who drinks of this water will be thirsty again, but whoever drinks of the water that I will give him will never be thirsty again. The water that I will give him will become in him a spring of water welling up to eternal life." That made about as much sense as a Jew talking to a Samaritan, but I said, "Sir, give me this water, so that I will not be thirsty or have to come here to draw water."

Jesus, that was his name, said to get my husband and bring him to the well. But I had no husband and I told him that. I was amazed at what he said next. How could he know? "You are right in saying, 'I have no husband'; for you have had five husbands, and the one you now have is not your husband. What you have said is true."

Of course it was true. I tried to be a good wife, but I was barren, could not have children. None of the men I had been married to could tolerate that. None except for Asher, but I lost him in a farming accident. The others divorced me when I could not produce an heir. It is very hard on a woman alone but no one else would marry me. So I lived with the one man who would have me, who'd already had children by the wife of his youth.

We Samaritans believe that Moses was a great prophet and there could be no other until the Messiah comes, but this man appeared to be a prophet. My ancestors worshipped here on Mount Gerizim, but the Jews say that Jerusalem is the only proper place to worship. What would this prophet say? "The hour is coming when neither on this mountain nor in Jerusalem will you worship the Father. You worship what you do not know; we worship what we know, for salvation is from the Jews. But the hour is coming, and is now here, when the true worshipers will worship the Father in spirit and truth, for the Father is seeking such people to worship him. God is spirit, and those who worship him must worship in spirit and truth."

I said to him, "I know that the Messiah is coming. When he comes, he will tell us all things." He said, "I who speak to you am he."

Just then the men who were traveling with Jesus came up to us. They were polite enough not to question me. I left my water jar there and went back to town. I said to everyone I saw, "Come, see a man who told me all that I ever did. Can this be the Christ?" They were as curious as I and headed to the well to hear more. Many asked Jesus to stay and tell us more. He and his friends stayed for two days. Almost everyone in the city believed what he said. When he left, the people of Sychar told me that it was no longer because of what I had told them that they believed, but because they had heard for themselves. We all knew that this was indeed the Messiah, the Savior of the World.

I am one of six sisters. Anatole, Photo, Photis, Paraskeve, and Kyriake all had children and had been shunning me, saying I was under a curse for having none. After Jesus spoke to us, they also believed and welcomed me back into the family. Asher also believed and married me. The curse was lifted from me and we had two sons, Victor and Joses. It took my father longer to come around, until Victor was born. I thank God I was able to reconnect with him before he died.

Over the next couple years, Jesus gained a reputation for healing. He hadn't healed physical ailments in Sychar, but he had healed a lot of hearts. It seemed Jesus was there for anyone who needed him, even if they didn't know they did. Many people loved him. Many hated him.

The time came when Jesus was taken captive by the authorities in Jerusalem and was crucified. We thought it was the end of us. But less than a week later, word came that Jesus had risen from the dead. Wonder of wonders, he gave his life and rose again so that we could be with him in heaven. About a month later, Jesus disappeared from the earth with a promise to someday return.

Not long after that, his disciples, the men I had seen with him at Jacob's well, started to spread out across the land sharing the good news. Many of their converts also went out. Then they went beyond the boundaries of Judea and Galilee. At first they didn't go really far, some went to Antioch and established a church there. That's where the believers, the followers of The Way, came to be known as Christians. A man named Philip came back to Samaria. That's when we were baptized. Later, some of the believers went to Greece, Asia, and Mesopotamia.

Asher died when Joses was four years old. Being a single woman was not a problem like it had been before. The Christians made sure everyone was taken care of. Everyone pitches in.

The boys are young men now and we are going to do our part. We have said goodbye to most of the people here in Sychar and are headed to Carthage in Africa. It's a little scary but we go with our Lord and Savior.

Martha

I guess what I remember most about when Jesus was going about preaching was the time he brought my brother back to life. But that wasn't our first encounter.

We had known Jesus back when we still lived in Nazareth. Our families were close. In fact, when our parents died, it was Jesus' mother and sisters who had come to try to nurse them back to health. But it didn't help and Jesus wasn't yet performing miracles. We buried our parents and then, after the period of mourning, my brother, Lazarus, moved us to Bethany.

We maintained contact with the family. When they came to Jerusalem for the festivals they sometimes stayed with us. Jesus' father, Joseph, would often come to Jerusalem with one or more of his sons to deliver furniture that had been commissioned. He was a really good carpenter so, even though there were plenty of men in Jerusalem who could do the job, some people still wanted Joseph to do the work

It was only natural that when Jesus started his ministry that he would stay with us in Bethany when he was in the area. He even stayed with us the week before that horrible Passover when he was crucified.

I had to learn an important lesson about hospitality early on. It wasn't that I was not a good hostess. I just didn't have my priorities straight. Lazarus had invited Jesus and his disciples to our house for dinner. When you have that many people, there is a lot of preparation and I was very busy. While I was bustling about, my sister, Mary, was just sitting there, listening to Jesus talk. To be honest, I was more than a little miffed that she was letting me do all the work.

So I wiped my hands on a towel and went to Jesus. What was I thinking? I said to him,

"Lord, do you not care that my sister has left me to serve alone? Tell her then to help me." Jesus had a great deal of sadness in his eyes when he said, "Martha, Martha, you are anxious and troubled about many things, but one thing is necessary. Mary has chosen the good portion, which will not be taken away from her." Let me tell you, I quickly learned to take more time to listen and not to worry so much about the other things.

I had learned my lesson. What Jesus had to say was important. It was more important than all the miracles he had been performing. But that didn't stop us from asking for a miracle when Lazarus got sick. Remembering the illness that had taken our parents from us, Mary and I sent messengers to Jesus to let him know what was happening, hoping for a miracle to cure Lazarus.

When the messengers returned without him, they said Jesus had told them that the illness would not lead to death, but was for the glory of God. By the time they got back here though, Lazarus had already died. Jesus and his disciples arrived days after he'd been buried.

A lot of our friends and neighbors were still at the house, trying their best to console us. When I heard Jesus was near, I went out to meet him while Mary remained seated in the house. I said to Jesus, "Lord, if you had been here, my brother would not have died. But even now I know that whatever you ask from God, God will give you." When he said, "Your brother will rise again" I replied, "I know that he will rise again in the resurrection on the last day." Then Jesus said, "I am the resurrection and the life. Whoever believes in me, though he die, yet shall he live, and everyone who lives and believes in me shall never die. Do you believe this?" I did, but apparently misunderstood. I said, "Yes, Lord; I believe that you are the Christ, the Son of God, who is coming into the world." Then I left him outside the village and went to tell Mary that Jesus was there and wanted to see her.

I think our guests thought she was going to the tomb to cry and they followed her. I knew where she was headed and I followed too. When Mary got to Jesus, she fell at his feet, voicing my very thoughts, "Lord, if you had been here, my brother would not have died." Everybody was crying, including Jesus.

Then Jesus asked where Lazarus was buried. He followed the crowd to the tomb. Most of the people understood how much Jesus loved Lazarus, but some of them were critical, asking things like "Could not he who opened the eyes of the blind man also have kept this man from dying?"

You need to understand that our tombs were not holes in the ground, but caves with large boulders as doors. When Jesus said, "Take away the stone," I reminded him that Lazarus had been dead for four days and there would be a foul odor. Jesus said, "Did I not tell you that if you believed you would see the glory of God?" So they took away the stone. Jesus lifted up his eyes and said, "Father, I thank you that you have heard me. I knew that you always hear me, but I said this on account of the people standing around, that they may believe that you sent me." Then he cried out with a loud voice, "Lazarus, come out." I learned another lesson; never doubt the Lord. Lazarus came out, his hands and feet still bound with the strips of linen, his face wrapped with a cloth. Jesus said to them, "Unbind him, and let him go."

I knew that some of the Jews, mainly the Temple scribes, Pharisees, and Sadducees, had been upset with Jesus and wanted to kill him. After raising Lazarus from the dead, they plotted to kill my brother also. It was because many people were coming to see Lazarus and believing in Jesus because of it. The temple authorities were losing their followers.

Lazarus was spared, but we all know what happened to Jesus shortly after that. He was arrested, tried in an illegal court, turned over to the Romans, and crucified. Jesus had raised Lazarus, but who could raise Jesus?

It turned out he raised himself. None of us really expected it, but on the third day, a Sunday, Jesus raised himself. When some of the women went to finish the burial process, the stone had been rolled away and the tomb was empty. That night, Jesus showed himself to his followers who were gathered in a locked room. He kept showing up for 40 days before he returned to heaven.

Jesus promised to come back to us some day. While we wait we try our best to spread the word, what we call the Good News. There were a lot of people in Jerusalem for Pentecost when Peter and the others preached openly and 3000 people came to believe. Many of those people lived in faraway places and took the word with them when they returned home. When the persecutions started, many of the disciples left Jerusalem and established churches wherever they went.

Meanwhile, life does go on. I married and had my children. Jesus' brother, James, finally got around to asking Mary to marry him and they also had children. James became the leader of the church in Jerusalem after Peter left. Simeon took over after James was killed. We all do what we can to bring as many people as possible to know and love the Lord, spreading the word and leaving the conversion up to the Holy Spirit.

Mary of Bethany

I had known Jesus and his family when I was a child living in Nazareth. After my parents died, my brother, Lazarus, moved my sister, Martha, and me to the town of Bethany in Judea. On the one hand, I didn't want to leave the only home I'd known. On the other hand, we would be close to Jerusalem. I didn't know then how much Joseph's family would affect my life.

One would have thought that Jesus would take over his father's carpentry business since he was the oldest. But he was gone so much that his brother, James, was the one to inherit it. I'm sure his mother, Mary, missed Jesus when he was gone, especially after Joseph died. But after a while, Mary started to travel with Jesus.

Jesus was a preacher. He preached some in Galilee, mostly in or around Capernaum. The people in our hometown of Nazareth didn't seem to appreciate him much. They just didn't understand. His mother didn't even seem to fully understand at first. When he died, his brothers still didn't believe in him.

I did. Every time Jesus came to Judea I tried to find a way to see him. It was usually pretty easy because he often stayed at our place. I remember the time I was so wrapped up in listening to him that I got Martha really upset with me. Maybe I should have been helping her fix the meal, but I just couldn't tear myself away from him. His words held the promise of peace.

Did you know Jesus could raise the dead? It wasn't too long before Passover one year when Lazarus got deathly ill. It seemed to be the same illness that had taken my parents' lives some ten years earlier. We sent for Jesus because we knew he could heal him. But Jesus didn't come until Lazarus had been dead for four days. When Jesus arrived, he called Lazarus out of the grave and Lazarus came walking out, death linens and all. What a joyful reunion that was.

Jesus had been staying with us one year before Passover, going back and forth between our house and the temple in Jerusalem. He was invited to the home of Simeon, still called the Leper, even though he had been healed by Jesus a year before. Something drove me to take an alabaster flask of expensive ointment I had been saving and go to anoint Jesus' feet.

I came into the house and went straight to Jesus and poured the jar of nard on his head as he reclined at the table. I could hear some of his disciples mumbling indignantly. Apparently they thought I had wasted the ointment when it could have been sold for a large sum of money for the poor and they scolded me about it. Jesus said to them "Why do you trouble the woman? For she has done a beautiful thing to me. For you always have the poor with you, but you will not always have me. In pouring this ointment on my body, she has done it to prepare me for burial. Truly, I say to you, wherever this gospel is proclaimed in the whole world, what she has done will also be told in memory of her." He said they could always help the poor but he would not always be around.

I didn't know what he meant about preparing him for burial. I didn't think he was going to die. I just wanted to show him my love. And his not being around? I was sure he would be there for a long time yet. I didn't understand until much later.

Of course, "a long time" ended far sooner than I expected. Jesus was killed in just a matter of days after that. Because it was only a couple hours before the start of the Sabbath, there was little time to do all the ointments and such that are normally done before a proper burial. But the ointment I had poured was still on him when they laid him in the cave.

Such grief! Jesus had raised Lazarus from the dead, but who would raise Jesus? I didn't realize at the time that he would raise himself. When I'd heard that he had shown himself to some of the women and then to the disciples who were cowered in the locked room I could hardly believe it! But later on, I saw him for myself. He walked among us for almost six weeks before he went up into heaven. And he left us with a promise that he would come again to take us with him to heaven. Not only that, but he would be with us here in our hearts, even though we would be unable to see him. I talk to him daily.

Life here goes on. Many of us are busy with spreading the Good News of salvation. Lazarus travels frequently to do just that. Martha married and started a family. Her son, Ben, often travels with Lazarus.

I ended up marrying Jesus' brother, James. James was one of the first people, other than the closest disciples, to whom Jesus appeared after his resurrection. James may not have believed in Jesus before that, but how could he deny what he had seen with his own eyes? He turned over the family business to their brother Simeon and moved to Jerusalem even before Jesus departed this world the last time. We have seen some wonderful things. But we have also seen some sad ones.

Herod had the other James, Jesus' cousin, killed to please the temple authorities who had conspired to have Jesus killed. It was not in the master plan to resurrect James before the end days. Then Herod had Peter jailed with the intent of killing him too. Peter was a leader of the church in Jerusalem. Thankfully, his death was not to be at that time; an angel led Peter out of jail.

Then there was Saul, or Paul, as he later came to be known. Saul was there when Stephen was stoned and the persecutions started. Saul was one of those Pharisees who hated everything Jesus stood for. After the incident with Stephen, Saul became one of the worst enemies of The Way, bringing soldiers, arresting the followers of The Way and having many of them killed.

Then came the day Jesus appeared to Saul on the road to Damascus. Saul became an ardent supporter of The Way, traveling to far lands to spread the Good

News. He always started in the Jewish Synagogues, but ended up preaching to the Gentiles when most of the Jews rejected the Word. Saul's former colleagues orchestrated his arrest and Saul ended up in prison in Rome.

When Peter left Jerusalem, James took over the leadership of the church here in Jerusalem. Our home near the temple served as a gathering spot for those of The Way. One of our visitors was Simeon, James' cousin on his father's side. He came to us with the good news that Saul had been released from prison.

That was the last bit of good news that James was to hear. The very next day I received the worst news of my life. James and our houseguest, Joram, had gone to the temple early. Simeon had business across town and was to join them later. Something didn't seem right when Simeon returned alone.

James and Joram had been taken while they were preaching in the temple. The followers of The Way who had been there were unable to stop the high priest's henchmen from condemning James and Jorem and taking them out to be stoned.

I started to cry, but remembered Jesus' promise of resurrection. I would miss James, but I would surely see him again someday. Meanwhile, there was work to be done here in Jerusalem. We would have the funeral, but that would not stop the efforts to spread the Good News which outweighed this bad news.

There were many of the brethren at the funeral. They came from Antioch, Galilee, and Samaria. Our children all returned and Martha came to sit with me.

After the funeral, they prayed to determine the new leadership in Jerusalem and chose Simeon. He was a close relative of Jesus, had been among the followers before the crucifixion, and had been one of the first to see him after his resurrection. More importantly, he was filled with the Holy Spirit.

And I will stay here in Jerusalem too. Simeon isn't married and needs a home base. I will stay here and serve my Lord until I am born to new life and rejoin my husband, my friends, and my Savior.

Joanna

He has left us again, only this time we know he will return. He is gone, but not completely gone, for he is in our hearts and souls. I was privileged to be with him as he told us, “All authority in heaven and on earth has been given to me. Go therefore and make disciples of all nations, baptizing them in the name of the Father and of the Son and of the Holy Spirit, teaching them to observe all that I have commanded you. And behold, I am with you always, to the end of the age.” When the clouds had taken him, the angels were there, telling us that Jesus would come again. Until then, we had work to do.

I had met this Jesus of Nazareth some years earlier. Though my family originally came from a small city in Judah, I was living in Galilee at the time. My husband, Chuza, was employed as a steward in the palace of Herod, the tetrarch of Galilee. Chuza was kept busy at the palace and I had the opportunity to go out and about freely. But I was sick and wasn’t free to mingle with the people. I was on the fringes of the crowds when Jesus was speaking. Moved by his words, I was soon following him around the country as he preached. I eventually joined with some of the other women, including Susanna and Mary Magdalene.

I didn't just hear Jesus, I benefitted from his miraculous healing. That was another thing I had in common with some of these women; we had all been healed by Jesus. Mary had been plagued with seven demons. Jesus threw them out. Susanna had been deaf and her speech was barely distinguishable. When Jesus healed her, we found she had a beautiful, clear voice. I had a horrible lung disease. Had I not been healed, I'm sure it would have killed me. It had already taken the lives of my parents and some other people who were close to me.

I coughed all the time. I spit up blood. That is why I was always on the fringes of the crowds. Coughing up blood, I was considered unclean. I was short of breath, feverish, and plagued with chest pain. I had lost so much weight and strength that sometimes I could hardly stand. A good wind off the Sea of Galilee could have blown me over.

The words of Jesus drew me to him, as it drew many. I thought he might be the promised Messiah, which of course it turned out he is. I won't ever forget the day he came over to me and touched me. No normal person would touch a person like me. I felt his power course through my body. The pain was gone; the fever was gone; the cough was gone.

Soon after that, I met the other women and we became good friends. Jesus had a dozen men who followed him almost everywhere. They were called his disciples. We called them the Twelve. But there were many more of us who followed whenever we could. Some, like Mary, Susanna, and me, had money we could contribute to their upkeep. We did whatever we could to take care of the others.

When I wasn't following Jesus, I was at Herod's palace with Chuza. After I was healed, I was able to share the teachings of Jesus with many of the servants in the palace. I tried to talk to Herod and his pseudo wife, Herodias, but they wouldn't listen. Herodias even banned me from coming into contact with her.

Because Chuza took care of Herod's finances, we often traveled with them, especially when they went to Jerusalem for the feasts. I was there after Jesus was arrested and brought to trial. He had been dragged before Pilate, the Roman prefect, for judgment. Pilate knew Jesus was innocent and when he found out that Jesus was from Galilee he saw an opportunity to hand off his problem to Herod.

At first, Herod was happy to have this chance to meet with Jesus. He had heard about the miracles Jesus had done, including my own healing. Herod wanted to see more, a magic show of sorts. But Jesus did not entertain him. As Herod questioned him, Jesus stood there without saying a word. Before sending Jesus back to Pilate, he let his soldiers abuse the innocent man.

When Jesus was returned to him, Pilate gave in and gave the order for Jesus' crucifixion. Our Lord was crucified as a common criminal, hung between two other men who really were criminals. What a terrible, terrible day that was.

My heart broke for Mary, the mother of Jesus. I had gotten to know her well in recent years. She had lost her husband two years earlier and now it was her firstborn son. Seeing her son hang there, on that cross, with nails in his hands and feet, bloodied up from the abuse of the soldiers…that alone was almost too much for the rest of us to bear.

Jesus had always looked out for her, even when he wasn't around. Now that he was facing death, he still showed his concern. None of his siblings supported Jesus' mission and it may have been doubtful that they could have provided the support she would need in the near future. With a great effort, Jesus called down to her from the cross, "Woman, behold your son." Then he spoke to his beloved disciple, John, saying "Behold, your mother." John took her home with him.

A man named Joseph took Jesus' body from the cross. We women followed as he and Nicodemus carried the lifeless form to the tomb. Then we went to Mary's house to prepare spices and perfumes for the body. We would need more, but that would have to wait until Sunday morning. For the time being we would rest on the Sabbath in obedience to the commandment.

Early Sunday morning we took the spices and headed for the tomb. As we walked, we considered the difficulty we would have when we got there. A large stone would be sealing the entrance to the tomb. It was bound to be very heavy. Who would roll it away for us?

That did not prove to be a problem. When we got there, the stone had already been moved. But when we went into the tomb, we were even more surprised to find no body. All that lay there were the cloths he had been wrapped in. As we stood there, looking at each other, two men appeared. Their clothes gleamed like lightning. Stunned, we bowed to the ground. The men said to us, "Why do you look for the living among the dead? He is not here; he has risen! Remember how he told you, while he was still with you in Galilee: 'The Son of Man must be delivered over to the hands of sinners, be crucified and on the third day be raised again.'" We did remember, but we hadn't understood what he meant.

We hurried back to Jerusalem to tell the disciples. Mary Magdalene had started back with us, but stopped and returned to the tomb where she later saw Jesus with her own eyes. The disciples were skeptical. They didn't believe us and, for the most part, they didn't believe Mary either. Peter and John must have considered that maybe we women weren't all crazy. They took off to the tomb to see for themselves.

That night, while we were all gathered in the upper room which Mary of Jerusalem had provided for a meeting place, Jesus appeared. The doors were locked, but all of a sudden he was just standing there. Then they believed.

Jesus showed himself to different groups of people many times in the next forty days, once to 500 of us at one time! He showed up in his brothers' carpentry shop in Nazareth and talked to James. James gave up his carpentry and moved to Jerusalem to be with the disciples the very next day.

Not all the disciples stayed in Jerusalem at first. Peter, James, Andrew, and John went back to Galilee to fish now and then. Sometimes a few of the other disciples went with them. Mostly they, and the rest of us, were just trying to keep out of the way of the temple authorities.

We were all together forty days after the resurrection. Jesus led us out to Bethany. He told us that repentance and forgiveness of sins should be proclaimed in his name to all nations, beginning in Jerusalem, throughout Judea, to Samaria, and throughout the world. But we were to stay in Jerusalem until the Comforter came to us.

So that is what we are doing. We stay at Mary's house in Jerusalem, praising God, serving each other, and waiting for the Comforter. When he comes, we will know what we are to do next.

Mary of Emmaus

Some people still call me Mary of Galilee. That is where I lived for many years. But I was born and raised in Emmaus. I moved to Galilee when I married my husband, Cleopas. His family is from Galilee. Two years ago, when my mother became ill, we moved south to Emmaus so I could care for her. I am known most often through my sons, Joses and James, both of whom were married and stayed behind in Galilee. But Cleopas also has a son, Simeon, from a previous marriage. Simeon's mother died in childbirth. Simeon lived with us. I will tell you later how Simeon fits into my account.

Cleopas is a brother of Joseph who is married to Mary, Jesus' mother. So it was only natural that we knew who Jesus was and paid attention to what he was saying and doing. I often joined Mary and the other women in traveling with Jesus and his disciples. We knew that Jesus was a great prophet. We witnessed the miracles he performed which could only be done by the will of God. I was there when Jesus preached and I was there when Jesus was crucified.

The crucifixion was a terrible thing to witness. Mary's sister, Salome, and I tried to comfort her, but what could we say? No parent should have to bury their child; it's not natural. But this, this was even more terrible. Jesus was unrecognizable, a bloody mess from the beatings he had endured and the crown of thorns pounded into his head.

When Joseph of Arimathea took the body of Jesus to his own newly cut tomb, we women went along to see where he was laid. It was almost the Sabbath and there was no time for a proper anointing and wrapping of the body. We planned to purchase additional spices when the Sabbath ended and wrap the body properly on Sunday morning,

When we got to the tomb on Sunday, the stone which had sealed the doorway had already been rolled away, but Jesus' body was missing. We suddenly noticed the two men in white. The one asked us, "Why do you seek the living among the dead? He is not here, but has risen. Remember how he told you, while he was still in Galilee, that the Son of Man must be delivered into the hands of sinful men and be crucified and on the third day rise." Then we remembered, and finally understood, what Jesus had said would happen to him.

We hurried back to where the disciples and some of the other followers, including Cleopas and Simeon, were staying in Jerusalem. We had all been so frightened that the authorities would come after us next that we stayed off the streets and in the house of John Mark and his mother, Mary. Anyway, we told them what we had found at the grave site but they didn't believe us. Peter and John went to see for themselves. I could not wait for them to return as I needed to get back to my mother. I didn't find out until the next day what transpired with Cleopas and Simeon.

Early that afternoon, Cleopas and Simeon were headed home. It is only about seven miles from Jerusalem to Emmaus and they planned to get home by supper time. As they were talking about the events of the past week, Jesus joined them. For some reason, they did not recognize that it was him. When he asked them what they were talking about, they were amazed that this stranger hadn't heard about what had happened. Not knowing it was Jesus they were speaking to, they said that Jesus was a prophet whom they had hoped would redeem Israel. Instead, the chief priests and rulers took him to be condemned to death. Jesus was crucified.

When Cleopas told him about when we women had gone to the tomb and what we found there, he said to them, "O foolish ones, and slow of heart to believe all that the prophets have spoken! Was it not necessary that the Christ should suffer these things and enter into his glory?" And beginning with Moses and all the Prophets, he interpreted to them in all the Scriptures the things concerning himself.

When they got to Emmaus, Cleopas urged him to come in for supper and spend the night. They didn't want the conversation to end and, besides, it was just common hospitality to provide a meal and lodging for this stranger since dusk had arrived and it would soon be dark.

Cleopas set the table with some of the bread I had made that morning before going to the tomb, along with some fig cakes and wine, and they sat down to eat. It was when Jesus took the bread, blessed and broke it and gave it to them that they finally recognized him. Then Jesus suddenly vanished from their sight. They said to each other that they should have known. "Did not our hearts burn within us while he talked to us on the road, while he opened to us the Scriptures?"

So they immediately hurried back to Jerusalem to tell the disciples and the others what had happened. Before they could say anything, the disciples told them, "The Lord has risen indeed, and has appeared to Simeon!" Then Cleopas and Simeon told what they had experienced with Jesus. Now they all believed what we women had told them earlier that day.

While they were gathered in that room discussing all the marvelous things that had happened that day, Jesus appeared to them. Because the door was locked and nobody had gone to open it, they thought they were seeing a ghost. But Jesus greeted them and told them to be at peace. He showed them the wounds in his hands and his side. If anyone had remaining doubts, that removed them.

Jesus showed himself to us numerous times in the next 40 days. Then he went up into heaven. He will return someday; he promised. Until then we will tell others of his life, his sacrifice, and God's great plan of salvation.

All that was years ago. So much has happened since. Cleopas has died and was buried. The disciples and many others of the original followers have left

Jerusalem, taking the good news with them to other parts of the world. Peter headed up the church in Jerusalem for a time, with our nephew, John, assisting him. When Peter went to Antioch and John went to Ephesus, the leadership fell to Jesus' brother, James.

James was recently stoned to death by the unbelieving Jews. Annas, the high priest, was taking advantage of the lack of a Roman leader in Jerusalem at the time. The previous Roman procurator had been dismissed and the new one had been delayed in coming. Annas demanded the presence of James in the temple for an inquisition. When James would not condemn the followers of Jesus, Annas urged the unbelieving Jews to take James out of the city and stone him.

We are saddened by our loss, yet we do not mourn as the unbelievers do. We know that we will be reunited with James, with Cleopas, and with all those who have died in the faith. We will see them again when we have also died, or on that day when Jesus will return in all his glory.

Meanwhile, a new leader had to be found for the church in Jerusalem. Jesus' brother Simeon was still living in Nazareth doing carpentry. His other brothers, Judas and Joseph, were out somewhere in the world spreading the message. As I said earlier, the other disciples were also scattered around the world. My Simeon, Cleopas' son, was the nearest relative of Jesus who was living in or near Jerusalem. The task fell to him.

Soon I will be joining my husband in the afterlife. I have been privileged to witness the fulfillment of the promises made to our fathers, the establishment of the new covenant, and the spread of the Good News of salvation. I have had the honor of knowing first hand my Lord and Savior. I am content.

Mary Magdalene

I remember my life before Jesus. I was very young when I became possessed by demons. They would often throw me to the ground and put me in convulsions. Other times they would speak terrible things through me, often lies about my parents and other people I knew. My parents loved me but were embarrassed by me. As a result, I was kept in the house as much as possible. But the demons would take hold of my body and I would escape. Later, I would be found wandering the streets of Magdala. You can see why I had no friends and, when I grew older, no suitors.

There would be stretches of time when the demons would leave me alone. I knew in my heart that they hadn't left, but I took advantage of the lull. During those periods, Solomon, a kind fishmonger, would let me work in his market. There was a young man who came to the market whom I really liked. He seemed to like me too. But I never knew when the demons would awaken and become active. One day they returned just as he stepped up to my booth. Because I didn't really know what was happening when the demons took over, I can only imagine the look on that poor man's face when he saw me writhing on the ground. I never saw him again.

While I was at the fish market, I would try to listen to people as they walked past. One day I heard people talking about this man called Jesus. He would walk through our country talking about the kingdom of God. What really caught my attention was their talk about him healing people and casting out demons. Casting out demons? Maybe there was hope for me after all.

These people had just come from the other side of the sea, in the country of the Gerasenes. They said Jesus had arrived in a boat and as soon as he stepped out of it, a madman came to him. This man had been possessed by demons. No one could control him. They tried shackles and chains, but he always broke away. It had gotten to the point that they couldn't even lay hold of him to try the shackles again. The man had run over to Jesus and fallen at his feet, crying out "What have you to do with me, Jesus, Son of the Most High God? I adjure you by God, do not torment me." Jesus asked him, "What is your name?" He replied, "My name is Legion, for we are many." And he begged him earnestly not to send them out of the country. The voice of the man, for I know from experience it wasn't the man himself, begged Jesus to send them into the herd of nearby pigs. Jesus agreed and the demons entered into the pigs. There must have been thousands of them because every one of the 2000 or so pigs rushed down the bank into the sea and drowned.

The people telling about this were upset because they had owned some of those pigs. But I was hopeful. If Jesus could do something like this for that man, he was someone I had to go see. I wiped my hands on my apron and said goodbye to Solomon. The people had said Jesus was going to Capernaum and I had to get there before he left.

It was not difficult to find Jesus; a huge crowd had gathered. A man had come up to Jesus, begging him to heal his daughter. The crowd followed them to the man's house. Suddenly Jesus stopped. Looking around he asked, "Who touched my garment?" At first, no one responded. In that crowd it could have been anyone. Then a woman came and fell at his feet. Jesus said, "Daughter, your faith has made you well; go in peace, and be healed of your disease." I found out later that the woman had been bleeding for twelve years. The bleeding had stopped immediately when she touched his robe.

As Jesus spoke to her, someone else came up to him and the man he had been speaking to. This newcomer said, "Your daughter is dead. Why trouble the Teacher any further?" Jesus said to the man who had asked for his help, "Do not fear, only believe." A few moments later, they disappeared into the house. I don't know exactly what went on in there but later on I had a chance to talk with that twelve year old girl. If she'd been dead, she was no longer.

Gradually, the crowd dispersed. But I waited, and waited. The next morning, Jesus came out of the house with some of his followers. Trembling, I approached him to ask release from my own demons. He touched my shoulders and I felt the demons leave.

I knew that this time it wasn't temporary. Then Jesus said, "Follow me." And I did.

I found that in addition to the twelve men who followed Jesus, there was a band of women who went along to minister to them. They weren't all with him all the time, only as their responsibilities allowed. Some of them, like Joanna, were wealthy and provided for the necessities of the traveling band. All of them, including sometimes Jesus' own mother, were kind and welcomed me into their mist. I loved traveling with these people. I had the opportunity to hear Jesus preach about his father's kingdom. Even then, I knew Jesus was a great prophet and taught the way to heaven.

Over the course of the next two years I learned so much about God's plan of salvation. But I didn't understand the whole thing; I didn't even understand as much as I thought I did. Then came that final week.

We had gone up to Jerusalem for the Passover. Sunday was great! The crowds welcomed Jesus and cheered him on as he entered the city. That was followed up by his rampage in the temple courtyard. For the second time, he upended the tables of the money changers, declaring, "'My house shall be called a house of prayer,' but you make it a den of robbers." Like the day he cast the demons from me, and many since, a crowd gathered. Though Jesus had healed many in his three years of ministry, there were always more who wanted healing.

As if the chief priests and scribes weren't upset enough about the upheaval in the courtyard, even the sound of the children in the temple was disturbing them. The children were crying out, "Hosanna to the Son of David" and the priests and scribes were indignant. They thought Jesus should be indignant as well and asked him, "Do you hear what these are saying?" Then Jesus asked them a question, "Have you never read, "Out of the mouth of infants and nursing babies you have prepared praise'?" With that, we left. Jesus and some of the men went to Bethany to stay at the house of Lazarus, whom Jesus had recently raised from the dead. Some of us women went with Mary, Jesus' mother, to stay with her relative, Elizabeth. The rest dispersed to the homes of various friends and relatives or to their own homes in the area.

Early Friday word came that Jesus had been arrested. They said that Judas, one of Jesus' close disciples, had betrayed him, bringing the temple authorities to the Garden of Gethsemane where Jesus had been praying. After being found guilty of blaspheme by the illegally convened Sanhedrin, Jesus had been dragged to Pilate at the governor's headquarters where he was sentenced to die by crucifixion.

We three Mary's, Jesus' mother, her sister-in-law, and myself, along with her sister Salome, went as quickly as we could to the crucifixion site, which was known as Golgotha. We found Jesus' close friend and disciple, John, but the rest of the disciples were gone.

When Jesus died, John took Jesus' mother to the house he had in Jerusalem. When Joseph and

Nicodemas removed Jesus' body from the cross for burial, we women followed them to see where the grave would be. Because there was little time for proper preparation due to the Sabbath approaching, we intended to return Sunday morning to finish the job. It was with sad hearts that we all went back to our various lodgings.

Very early Sunday morning we headed to the grave. We wondered how we would get past the large stone which had been rolled in front of the door to the tomb. But when we got closer, we saw that it had been rolled away. Closer still and we saw some men sitting there. One asked us why we were looking for the living among the dead. He said Jesus had risen and we were to tell the disciples.

We quickly started back to the city. The disciples didn't believe us but Peter and John did run off to the grave to see for themselves. I headed back with them, but running faster, they got there before I did. By the time I arrived, they were inside the tomb. When they came out they acknowledged my presence and simply said, "No, he's not in there" and headed back to Jerusalem.

I couldn't bring myself to leave; I was so confused. Jesus had been my life for the last two years. What was I to do now? I stooped to look inside the tomb once more. There were the two angels again, sitting on the ledge where his body had been laid. They asked me, "Woman, why are you weeping?"

I said to them, "They have taken away my Lord, and I do not know where they have laid him." Then

I stood up and turned around. I saw a man standing there whom I thought had to be the gardener. He too asked, "Woman, why are you weeping? Whom are you seeking?" Through my grief and tears, all I could say was, "Sir, if you have carried him away, tell me where you have laid him, and I will take him away."

Then he spoke my name. I knew instantly that he was Jesus himself. "Teacher!" I exclaimed as I reached for him. He said to me, "Do not cling to me, for I have not yet ascended to the Father; but go to my brothers and say to them, 'I am ascending to my Father and your Father, to my God and your God.'" I hurried back and told the disciples that I had seen the Lord and gave them the message as he had asked. I didn't know if they believed me or not. I knew it was a difficult concept to grasp. But I was elated.

When Jesus appeared to some of them that night they had to believe Jesus was alive. Still, things weren't back the way they had been. We no longer could follow Jesus as he went preaching and teaching. He appeared to us many times over the next 40 days, but not teaching the crowds as he used to. When he appeared to 500 of us, every one of us was already a follower. The time for reaching the masses was over. Jesus had some final instructions for us before he ascended into the heavens.

Ten days after he went up to heaven, we were gathered at the home of John Mark and his mother, Mary. We were still leery of the temple officials and stayed off the streets as much as possible. All of a sudden we heard what sounded like a strong wind, but we were in the building. Then we saw what looked like flames of fire hovering over each of our heads. We were speaking in languages we had never learned. We were all filled with the Holy Spirit, the Comforter that Jesus had promised us had come.

Leaving the confines of the house, we started sharing God's plan of salvation with the people who had crowded into Jerusalem for Pentecost. Every visitor could hear one of us speaking in his own language. Then Peter got up to preach. Three thousand people joined with us that day. We had the makings of a church. Jesus had said to start in Jerusalem and that is exactly what happened.

Peter, who had once denied even knowing Jesus, emerged as the leader of the church in Jerusalem. John also became a pillar of the church which grew daily. People were sharing the love of Jesus and taking care of each other. No one lacked for anything. Men were appointed to take care of the distribution of food, especially to the widows. But not everything was good.

Stephen was one of the men appointed for the distribution of food. He and the others like him were called deacons. Loved by members of the church, they were not thought so well of by the temple authorities. Stephen was stoned to death. That set off a general persecution of the church, members who called ourselves followers of "The Way".

A young Pharisee named Saul was sitting on the side lines, holding cloaks while Stephen was being stoned. He turned out to be one of the worst of those who were against us. He would lurk about Jerusalem, trying to find out who were followers of The Way. Then he would have them arrested and often put to death. The persecutions motivated people to move away from Jerusalem and that just gave Saul the challenge of finding them in the distant cities.

But God had other plans for Saul and his church. Saul had gotten a letter from the temple authorities granting him the right to arrest the followers of The Way who were in Damascus. That wasn't even a Jewish city! So Saul gathered his henchmen and went down from Jerusalem, heading north to Damascus.

Peter and John had been arrested by the temple authorities more than once in the past and warned to stop preaching of Jesus. Of course they went right on doing so, putting God's authority and commands above those of the priests and scribes of the temple. Then the enemy got an additional ally. Herod had arrested and killed James, John's brother. When he saw how much that pleased the temple authorities, he arrested Peter, intending to do the same to him. God had other plans. Peter was led out of jail by an angel and resumed his preaching.

We got word that Saul was preaching in the synagogue in Damascus. Was this a ruse? Saul had been chief among the persecutors. Could he really have switched sides? We heard that he had been met by Jesus while on the road to Damascus, repented of his sins and the persecution he had led, and became a follower of The Way himself.

The Jews felt betrayed and plotted to kill him. Saul escaped and made his way back to Jerusalem where he tried to join the disciples. But at that time nobody here trusted him. No one except for Joseph Barnabas. He brought Saul to the disciples and told how Saul had seen Jesus on the road and how he had been preaching boldly in the name of Jesus.

So Saul was allowed to go about in Jerusalem, preaching the good news. He spoke and disputed against the Hellenists and they plotted to kill him. When the disciples heard of it, they took Saul to Caesarea and sent him off to Tarsus where he had been born. With the immediate threat of persecution removed, the church had a period of peace.

As I said, because of the persecution, believers spread out all over the county and even beyond. There was a large group who went to Antioch. It was there that the followers of The Way first were called Christians. Peter spent as much time there as he did in Jerusalem and Jesus' brother, James, became recognized as the leader of the church in Jerusalem.

After a period of time, Barnabas went to Tarsus to get Saul. They spent a year in Antioch and then the Holy Spirit indicated that they should be sent off. That was the start of Saul's journeys among the gentiles. Dealing with mostly gentiles, he began to go by the Greek form of his name, Paul. Where he went and the people he helped bring to the faith would be a story far too long for me to relay to you now.

As for me, I did what I could. I became very close to Jesus' mother, Mary, and with John who was caring for her. John had been making trips to Ephesus and eventually moved there. Mary was quite advanced in age by then so I often visited her to help. And that is where we are now. You know, after that fateful day when I first spoke to Jesus, I never did go back to Magdala.

Salome of Capernaum

I knew in the very beginning that Jesus was the Son of God. Mary told me so. I just didn't understand what that meant. As we all grew older, I even put it in the back of my mind.

I remember a bright spring morning. The weather was glorious and I wanted to do something fun. But Mary was pensive; her mind seemed far away. She wouldn't tell me then what was going on. She left the next day and didn't return for three months. It wasn't until she came back from her trip to Elizabeth's that she finally confided in me.

Mary and I were always close. She told me what was happening even before she told Mother. An angel had appeared to her and told her she was going to have a baby. Mary was promised to Joseph but they had not yet had the marriage feast and she had not been living with him. I may have been younger than she was but even I knew you had to have sex in order to have a baby. Mary swore she hadn't done that and I had to believe her. So how could this have happened?

Mary said the angel told her that "The Holy Spirit will come upon you, and the power of the Most High will overshadow you; therefore the child to be born of you will be called holy – the Son of God." I was excited for her, but what would Joseph say? And our father? I was surprised at Father's reaction. He took it very calmly. I guess both he and Mother believed everything Mary said about it.

Joseph was another story. I heard he was going to divorce Mary quietly. At least he wasn't calling her a whore and publicly ridiculing her. But the very next day after she told him he showed up at the house to work out a quiet marriage ceremony with Father's blessing. Mary moved in with Joseph.

Everybody's lives were turned upside down after that. The Roman governor put out a decree that everyone had to go to the land of their heritage and register. The registration would be used to set taxes. As if that weren't disruptive enough, Mary was far along in her pregnancy and just about to give birth at the time the trip was to be made.

I don't think Mary, or even Joseph, was as excited about the trip as I was. Joseph was worried about her. So was Mother. I only thought about how much fun we could have traveling with the whole family to Bethlehem. What do children know of reality? All I saw was picnicking, playing with cousins, and spending time with grandparents and extended family. We'd always enjoyed our trips to Jerusalem for the feasts and Bethlehem wasn't that far from Jerusalem.

We had stayed in our tents on the trip and planned to spend our time in Bethlehem in those tents as well. But Mary went into labor and Mother and Joseph sought out a more private place for her. The guest rooms in town were all filled with other travelers and the only place available was a stable in a cave. Mother and some of the other adult women went in there with Mary but I had to stay outside and wait with the others. Mother said there just wasn't room in the small stable for me.

After the baby was born, I was allowed in just for a few moments. With that many relatives around and wanting to visit, there was a constant flow of in and out until Mother put her foot down and said, "Enough".

Most in our group were sleeping when the shepherds appeared. They had arrived moving awfully quickly and when they left half an hour later they were going just as speedily. Mary later told me that angels had come to the shepherds telling them that the Messiah had been born so they had rushed to see for themselves.

After everyone had registered and Jesus had been circumcised, most of us returned to Nazareth. Joseph chose to stay in Bethlehem with Mary and Jesus at least until Mary had recovered. I didn't know then that it would be years before we saw them again.

Sometime later we heard that King Herod had ordered the death of all the baby boys in Bethlehem under the age of two. We were so worried because Mary and her small family were still there. A few months later we got word that they had escaped to Egypt and were living in the Jewish settlement there. But we were still worried about them.

Some years had passed when they showed up in Nazareth again. I had become a woman, married and moved to Capernaum by then. Zebedee and I had a son whom we named James. Mary and Joseph returned just in time for his circumcision.

As time went by, Joseph built up his carpentry business and Zebedee built his fishing enterprise. Mary and I each had more children and got together whenever we could. Those gatherings sometimes proved very interesting. Zebedee was a good, but shall we say, loud man. He was eager for the Messiah to show up and deliver our nation from the Roman rule and made his opinion well known. He was thunderous when he got on that subject.

We heard that a relative of ours, Elizabeth's son, was preaching in the desert. His name was John, the same as my second son. My John and his brother, James, were excited about him; they thought that maybe he was the promised Messiah and frequently left their fishing to go listen to him near the Jordan River. John the Baptist, as he became known, called for repentance of sins and dunked his followers in the river as a sign of repentance.

John the Baptist wasn't the Messiah. In fact, he said there was someone greater than him who was to come later. One day when James and John were in the crowd listening to John the Baptist, Jesus arrived. The Baptist said "Behold, the Lamb of God, who takes away the sin of the world! This is he of whom I said, 'After me comes a man who ranks before me, because he was before me.'" Then, over the Baptist's initial objections, he baptized Jesus. Those closest to them, my sons included, saw what looked like a dove coming down over Jesus and they heard, "This is my beloved Son, with whom I am well pleased."

Jesus disappeared for weeks after that. When he returned, he started gathering followers of his own. He called James and John to leave their fishing boats and follow him. He gathered a dozen men in all who spent most of their time with him and were his students, or disciples. A lot of other people took the time to go and hear Jesus preach. Knowing Jesus to be a great prophet, I was one of them.

My understanding of Jesus' purpose wasn't always on target. I thought he was the Messiah that Zebedee was waiting for. I was so wrong that one day I even caused dissention among the disciples.

We were all traveling up to Jerusalem. I caught up to Jesus and knelt to ask him a favor.

"Say that these two sons of mine are to sit, one at your right hand and one at your left, in your kingdom." Jesus knew I was asking on their behalf. It wasn't that I thought they were better than the others. Well, maybe I did a little. I was asking because they were his cousins. Jesus looked at me sadly and said to them, "You do not know what you are asking. Are you able to drink the cup that I am to drink?" They answered, "We are able." He told them, "You will drink my cup, but to sit at my right hand and at my left is not mine to grant, but it is for those for whom it has been prepared by my Father."

When the other disciples heard the request, they became angry with James and John; they were indignant at the request of the two brothers. Jesus used the occasion to make a point. "You know that the rulers of the Gentiles lord it over them, and their great ones exercise authority over them. It shall not be so among you. But whoever would be great among you must be your servant, and whoever would be first among you must be your slave, even as the Son of Man came not to be served but to serve, and to give his life as a ransom for many." But none of us really understood at the time what he meant.

We were to find out. On another trip to Jerusalem, Jesus was captured by the temple authorities. The Pharisees, scribes, and Sadducees had hated what Jesus was preaching and were jealous of his following. They may have even believed he was the Messiah and would lead an uprising. While most of us Jews wanted relief from the Romans, the temple authorities were worried that if there was an uprising the Romans would take away the powers that the Jewish leaders clung to.

Because they could not sentence anyone to death, the temple authorities brought Jesus to Pilate, the Roman prefect, who sentenced him to be crucified. I was there with his mother and some of the other women when he was put up on that cross. We heard the people in the crowd loudly mocking him.

Jesus seemed to be speaking several times, but because we were standing at a distance from the cross we could not hear everything. I did hear him when he told John to take care of his mother. Mary was my sister; of course we would take care of her.

Suddenly, everything became dark. I can't explain it; it wasn't an eclipse of the sun and there were few clouds in the sky. But it got so dark, one could hardly see his hand in front of his face. The darkness lasted for three hours. Out of the darkness I could hear Jesus speak. "My God, my God, why have you forsaken me?" Shortly after, he cried out, "Into your hands I commit my spirit." I think that is when he died.

Normally, bodies are left on the crosses as a warning to others. Then they are often just thrown into a pit somewhere. Partly because that day was the day of preparation for Sabbath, the Romans allowed Jesus' body to be removed. A man named Joseph, who came from Arimathea, got permission to take the body. There was no time for full preparation of the body, so it was wrapped in linen with minimal spices and put in Joseph's own grave.

On Sunday morning, when the Sabbath was over, some of us women brought additional spices with which to anoint the body. As we were walking, we remembered the large stone that had been placed in front of the entrance to the tomb. It had taken two strong men to put it there. Who would roll it away for us?

When we got closer, we saw that the stone had already been rolled away. There were two young men sitting there, dressed in bright white robes. We were startled and scared. Then one of them spoke to us. "Do not be alarmed. You seek Jesus of Nazareth, who was crucified. He has risen; he is not here. See the place where they laid him. But go, tell his disciples and Peter that he is going before you to Galilee. There you will see him, just as he told you."

We hurried from the tomb back to Jerusalem where the disciples and some others had gathered. When we told the disciples, they didn't believe us. Who could blame them? We could hardly believe it ourselves.

John and his friend, Peter, went to see it themselves. John later told me he had gotten there first but stood at the entrance waiting for Peter. When he looked in he could see the linen cloths lying there, but no body. The face cloth was neatly folded and sat separately from the other cloths. When Peter got there, he went right into the tomb and John followed. Then they believed us. But they still did not understand.

Jesus had risen from the dead. He no longer went about preaching but he showed himself to us many times over the next forty days. He came to some of us individually and sometimes to groups of us.

The time came, however, when he would say goodbye. He left and nobody saw him again. But he promised he would return and take us with him to heaven. What a glorious reunion that will be.

Meanwhile, he left us work to do here. We were to spread his message of God's love and everything else Jesus had been speaking about during his time here on earth. How were we to be able to do all this?

Ten days after we'd seen him for the last time, a large group of us were waiting in Jerusalem as Jesus had told us to do. Suddenly, there was a great gust of wind and it seemed like flames danced above our heads. We all began speaking in languages we had never known before. All the people who had gathered in Jerusalem for the feast of Pentecost could understand what we were saying in their own languages. Peter said it was the fulfillment of what the prophet Joel had said hundreds of years earlier. "And in the last days it shall be, God declares, that I will pour out my Spirit on all flesh, and your sons and your daughters shall prophesy, and your young men shall see visions, and your old men shall dream dreams; even on my male servants and female servants in those days I will pour out my Spirit, and they shall prophesy". That day, 3000 people heard and believed in Jesus.

Not everyone was happy about that. The temple authorities who went after Jesus were now focused on his followers. Peter and John were arrested. Fortunately that time they were let go. Then a follower named Stephen, who had been named a deacon to manage the distribution of food, was attacked. Some liars had claimed "This man never ceases to speak words against this holy place and the law, for we have heard him say that this Jesus of Nazareth will destroy this place and will change the customs that Moses delivered to us." They brought him before the high priest. Stephen tried to explain God's plan of mercy, going back to the days of Abraham. But the crowd was stirred up and merciless. They dragged him outside the city and stoned him.

Even Herod got involved in the persecution. Not because of strongly held beliefs or even fear of Jesus' followers, but because he saw that it pleased the Jews who were against us. Herod had my son, James, killed with a sword. I felt some of the pain my sister Mary felt when Jesus was killed. But my son would not be rising from the dead. He is, however, at home in heaven with Jesus as the rest of us will one day be.

The priests were so happy with the death of James that Herod arrested Peter also. But God was not yet ready for Peter to die. Peter was to remain the leader of the followers in Jerusalem, at least until God's plans changed.

John comes and goes. He assists Peter when in Jerusalem. Sometimes he travels, mainly to Ephesus, to tend to other groups of believers. Our numbers grow each day as we wait for Jesus' return.

Veronica

I was desperate. I was married once; I guessed I still was, but I hadn't seen my husband or my daughter for years. I had spent the last twelve years trying to deal with constant bleeding. I was drained, literally and figuratively. I was weak from the loss of blood. I had inherited a fair amount of money, but had spent it all on doctors who only made things worse. Nothing helped.

Because I was always bleeding, I was always unclean. And being unclean meant that no one would have anything to do with me. At first my husband tried to find a cure for me but finally had sent me away; he couldn't deal with a perpetually unclean wife. I was always alone. I wanted to die.

But I had heard about Jesus and how he healed people from all kinds of diseases. I had listened to him from the edges of the crowd. His words alone had a way of comforting me. He spoke of the love of God, his father, and the forgiveness of sins. Once, in Nazareth, I heard him say he was the fulfillment of the promises of scripture. The people from his village turned on him, but I believed.

He had been away for a while. As usual, when he returned there was a large crowd gathering around him. I heard a man come to him and beg him to go with him and heal his twelve year old daughter who was close to death.

The crowd grew larger and pressed in around him. I thought it might be my only chance to get close to him. If only I could touch the fringe of his garment, I was sure even that minimal contact could cure me. As soon as I touched his robe, I could tell that the bleeding had stopped. I felt renewed.

When Jesus asked who touched him, I was too frightened to speak up. Everybody else around him denied it. His disciples were amazed that he would ask because with so many people around someone was bound to bump into him. But Jesus said to them that he had felt the power go out from him. I knew that he knew and that I could not remain hidden. Trembling, I fell at his feet and told him why I had done it and how I had been healed immediately. He spoke directly to me saying, "Daughter, your faith has made you well; go in peace."

I set out to show myself to the priest and to offer a sacrifice to God. (By the way, the young girl was healed. I heard she had died and Jesus raised her from the dead.) Then I went back to my home town of Caesarea Philippi to see if I could find my husband. I did not find him for he had died some years earlier, but I did find my daughter. What a wonderful reunion that was.

Because I wanted her to come to know Jesus, we eventually returned to Judea. It was at the time of the feast of Passover. We arrived at Jerusalem on a Sunday and happened upon a large crowd of cheering people. There was Jesus, riding into town on a donkey. People were putting their coats and palm branches on the road ahead of him, shouting "Hosanna! Blessed is he who comes in the name of the Lord! Blessed is the coming kingdom of our father David! Hosanna in the highest!"

Later in the week we were able to hear his preaching. Some was in parables, the little stories he was prone to tell. At other times he spoke directly to the scribes and Pharisees. There was that one incident I particularly remembered.

The Pharisees were always trying to trap Jesus in his words, and Jesus was always outsmarting them. This time they asked him if it was lawful to pay taxes to the Roman government. They prefaced the question with the comment that they knew he didn't care about anyone's opinion but taught the way of God. Big words, considering they didn't believe it; what hypocrites. Jesus knew they had asked him just to try to trick him into saying something they could hold against him.

Jesus asked them, "Why put me to the test? Bring me a denarius and let me look at it." They brought it to him and he asked, "Whose likeness and inscription is this?" They said to him, "Caesar's." Jesus said to them, "Render to Caesar the things that are Caesar's, and to God the things that are God's." They were stunned. They couldn't get him on treason because he supported taxes. But he did it in such a way that they couldn't use it to turn the people against him either.

Another time, it was the Sadducees who tried to trap him. These Sadducees don't believe in the resurrection, something Jesus often preached about. They presented him with this scenario. "Teacher, Moses wrote for us that if a man's brother dies and leaves a wife, but leaves no child, the man must take the widow and raise up offspring for his brother. There were seven brothers; the first took a wife, and when he died left no offspring. And the second took her, and died, leaving no offspring. And the third likewise. And the seven left no offspring. Last of all the woman also died. In the resurrection, when they rise again, whose wife will she be? For the seven had her as wife."

Jesus said to them, "Is this not the reason you are wrong, because you know neither the Scriptures nor the power of God? For when they rise from the dead, they neither marry nor are given in marriage, but are like angels in heaven. And as for the dead being raised, have you not read in the book of Moses, in the passage about the bush, how God spoke to him, saying, 'I am the God of Abraham, and the God of Isaac, and the God of Jacob'? He is not God of the dead, but of the living. You are quite wrong." What he was saying was that if God was the God of the patriarchs, then they must be living.

It was only a few days later when things took a turn for the worse. The temple authorities had found an excuse to arrest and try Jesus. The next time I saw him, he was carrying part of a cross to his crucifixion. I had seen and heard the crowd gathering.

I could hardly believe my eyes when I saw him there. The same crowd that was cheering for and praising him earlier in the week had called for his death.

Jesus hardly resembled a man; he was a bloody mess. His back was torn up from where he had been whipped. Blood was running from his head where a crown of thorns had been beaten into his brow. I watched as he stumbled along toward his demise. When I saw him fall, I pushed my way through the crowd to wipe the mud, sweat, and blood from his face. I had just wiped it the one time when the Roman soldiers pulled me away.

It was then that they took a man from the crowd and forced him to carry the heavy beam. I learned later that the man's name was Simeon and he came from Cyrene. I got to know him later when we both joined with the followers of Jesus.

Like so many others, I followed the parade to the crucifixion site. I was there when they nailed him to the cross and when they took him down. I saw them put his lifeless body in the grave and roll the large stone in front of it. And I was there when he appeared to the disciples that Sunday night.

He is gone now, gone for who knows how long. But he said he will come again. And he gave us a job to do, to tell others about him, about the forgiveness of sins he has given us by that death and resurrection. And so I'm telling you. Repent and take the forgiveness he offers. You too can have life everlasting.

Herodias

Lugdunum is a large city and a favorite of emperors. It is the most important city in the western part of the Roman Empire, but it isn't Rome and I am not the queen. I deserve more than this. After all, my grandfather, Herod the Great, was the greatest king Judea ever had and my grandmother, Mariamne, was a Hasmonean princess.

When I was young, I was married to an uncle, the son of Herod the Great. My husband, Herod Philip, was to be the next king. Another uncle, Antipater, objected and Herod demoted my husband. Philip ended up ruling over Gaulanitis, Batanaea, Trachonitis, and Auranitis, just a small portion of my grandfather's kingdom.

When my daughter, Salome, was just a baby, Philip and I were living in Rome. Another uncle of mine, Herod Antipas, stayed with us when he came to Rome. Antipas was the tetrarch of Galilee and Perea, another portion of Grandfather's kingdom. Antipas was younger than Philip and much more interesting; I was drawn to him. There was a problem though. I was married to Philip and Antipas was married to Phasaelis, the daughter of King Aretas of Nabatea. I told Antipas that if he would divorce Phasaelis, I would divorce Philip.

A divorce in Rome was not that big of a deal. Neither was marrying one's ex-husband's brother. But it was a problem in Galilee and Judea. There was a man called the Baptizer, who was preaching in the wilderness of the Jordan. His name was John. He had the nerve to condemn us for following our hearts. He wouldn't shut up about it and I finally convinced Antipas to put John in jail. He sent him to the fortress of Machaerus. What I really wanted was for John to be silenced permanently, but Antipas was afraid of the people's reaction because the preacher had such a large following.

I finally had a chance to get rid of the pest. We were at Machaerus and we were going to have a birthday feast for Antipas. I arranged for Salome to do a little dance as part of the entertainment. Antipas had always enjoyed watching her dance and play. I knew that after a few drinks, Antipas would want to show his appreciation for her antics and I knew just how to take advantage of it.

Sure enough, Antipas was so pleased, he offered Salome whatever she wanted, up to half the kingdom. While I knew he was exaggerating, I also knew he could not renege on his offer, not in front of his friends and all those important people. Salome wouldn't know what to ask for and she would come to me. I told her to ask for the head of John the Baptist on a platter. She did and that was the end of the Baptizer.

Then there was this new fellow, Jesus of Nazareth, who was causing trouble. Like John, he had people following him around everywhere. Antipas was almost in a panic; for a long time he thought that Jesus was John raised from the dead.

In the end, Jesus was disposed of also. It was while we were in Jerusalem for the Passover. Jesus had been arrested by the temple police and brought before Pilate, the Roman prefect of Judea. Pilate couldn't find a reason to condemn him so he sent him to Antipas. Antipas had realized by this point that Jesus was not John. He had heard about some wonders that Jesus was said to have performed and was happy to have the man in front of him, expecting to see some of those miracles for himself. Antipas was not so happy when he came into my quarters that evening.

Antipas had questioned Jesus at length, but got nothing from him. All the while, the chief priests and scribes stood by, vehemently accusing Jesus. Finally, Antipas joined his soldiers in ridiculing the pathetic man. Then he sent him back to Pilate. The whole episode had a strange result. Pilate and Antipas had never gotten along before, but because of the shared experience of Jesus, they became friends.

Sepphoris had been the capital of Galilee and we lived there for a while. The city needed to be rebuilt after it was ruined by Judas after the death of Herod the Great. Antipas restored the city and renamed it Autocratoris in honor of Caesar Augustus.

When we weren't in Jerusalem, Machaerus, or Sepphoris, we lived in Tiberius. Some years after Tiberius became emperor, Antipas built a new city on the Western shore of the Sea of Galilee and named it Tiberias. As soon as the city was ready, we moved the capital there. The city was populated with non-Jews because it was supposedly built over an old cemetery. That was fine with me. Tiberias was a beautiful Greek-Roman city in the midst of a country of barbarians. It was good to have it populated with Romans.

A few years after the Jesus incident, King Aretas attempted to get his revenge on Antipas for divorcing Phasaelis. It was really as much because of earlier disputes over the border area of Perea with Nabatea. That war was a disgrace; Antipas' troops were totally defeated. Emperor Tiberius ordered the two legions under Vitellius to make a counter offensive, but that didn't happen. When Tiberius died soon after the order, Vitellius claimed that he didn't have the authority to continue. Vitellius had been delaying the onset because he held a grudge against Antipas from an earlier incident. For some unknown but fortunate reason, Aretas withdrew to Nabatea.

While Tiberius was still emperor, my brother Agrippa fell into debt, despite the ties he had with the imperial family. I was able to persuade Antipas to help him out but they had an argument. Later, Agrippa was heard telling his friend Caligula that he was anxious for Tiberius to die so Caligula could succeed him. Agrippa was imprisoned.

Caligula did, in fact, succeed Tiberius. He not only released Agrippa from prison, but gave him the territory of Philip, who had died a few years earlier.

In fact, he gave him even more territory and gave him the title of king, while Philip had been only a tetrarch.

Antipas was the one who should have been named a king and I persuaded him to request that title from Caligula. It might have been granted, except that Agrippa presented Caligula with a list of charges against Antipas, including that Antipas had conspired against Tiberius and was now plotting against Caligula. When Antipas admitted to having a stockpile of weapons, Caligula believed the other charges of conspiracy.

That summer, Antipas was stripped of his holdings and his territory and money was turned over to Agrippa. Antipas was disgraced and exiled to Lugdunum in Gaul. Caligula offered to let me stay in Rome, but I had been through too much with Antipas. And I didn't trust my brother to not come after me in Rome. So I came to Lugdunum with Antipas.

And now Antipas is dead and I am alone and without honor. Even my daughter has no time for me. I have not seen her for several years and have never met my grandchildren. I don't even know how many children Salome has.

Now what do I do?

Salome Herodias

My husband, Aristobulus, has finally been given his father's territory to rule. When Herod of Chalcis died, Claudius gave it to Agrippa. Nero later gave Armenia to Aristobulus. Now Vespasian has taken away Armenia and given Aristobulus his heritage. In addition to Chalcis, some of the other non-Jewish provinces in the area were put under his jurisdiction.

We have been in Chalcis for just a short while. The news came today that my mother died in Lugdunum. No surprise, she was at that age. I had wanted to see her again years ago when Herod Antipas died, but I was going through a rough pregnancy. After Herod was born, I was still too ill to travel. Then there was always some other reason. My next two pregnancies were little better. Then I had three boys to care for. Herod was followed by Agrippa and Arisobulus. I suppose I could have left them in the care of their nurses, but the time never seemed right. I did try to go a couple years ago, but by then Mother had gone into seclusion and would not receive visitors, not even her only daughter. Now it's too late.

My mother and I have had a strained relationship anyhow. She divorced my father, Herod Philip, when I was a baby and married his brother, also her uncle, Antipas. When I was still a child, Antipas offered me half his kingdom for entertaining him and his friends at a birthday banquet. Because I was so young and inexperienced, I followed Mother's recommendation and asked for the head of a man he had jailed, John the Baptizer. When they brought me the head on a platter, I took it to my mother. She was delighted, but the bloody head turned my stomach. I had nightmares for years.

Early on, I married Philip the Tetrarch of Ituraea and Trachonitis. We had no children. Philip and my father died around the same time, while Tiberius was still emperor. I soon fell in love with Aristobulus, even though he was ten years my junior. It was years before we had any children. I got pregnant easily, but had trouble bringing a child to term.

It has been a long time getting to this point. My youngest will soon be joining his brothers in Rome where all the sons of aristocracy go for their education at some point. Aristobulus will be busy with his government and I will need to find myself a purpose. Maybe I will travel to Corinth. I have been hearing about a group there established by a man named Paul. They seem to have a special purpose in life. I should find out more about it.

Claudia

I was raised in Rome under the protection of my grandfather, Augustus. When Tiberius, his step-son, became Emperor, he married me off to Pontius Pilate. Pilate was 30 years old. I was 16. It may have been an arranged marriage, but it was a good one. Pilate was assigned to the post of Judea to be its prelate. Unlike many Roman wives, I went with him instead of staying in Rome. I loved him.

Parts of Judea were really beautiful. Caesarea was once an insignificant Phoenician town called Strato's Tower. It was captured by the Hasmonean, Alexander Jannaeus, over a hundred years ago. 30 years later, it was captured by General Pompeii and became Roman territory. About 40 years after that, Herod, known as "The Great", turned it into a beautiful, large harbor and built a beautiful palace there. An aqueduct was built to bring in fresh water from Mount Carmel. There was a hippodrome and an amphitheater. The Herodian temple he built contained large statues of Augustus and Roma. The city became a huge trading center, drawing people from all over the world. Caesarea was to be our home for ten years. It was populated to a great extent by Syrian Greeks, but many wealthy Jews lived there also. And, of course there was the Roman contingent, of which we were a part.

Jerusalem was the next greatest city in Judea. Herod had built a theater and amphitheater here also. His most magnificent building project was the reconstruction of the Jewish temple. It stood on a giant white platform and was gilded with gold. The gleaming temple was easily seen when approaching the city. Part of the building was the Tower of Antonia where soldiers were stationed and where we stayed when in Jerusalem.

While life in Caesarea was generally calm, the same could not be said of Jerusalem. Although it was part of the Roman Empire and came under Roman jurisdiction, the city was in reality mostly ruled by the Sanhedrin, or Jewish council. And that was made up of the temple authorities. Things went smoothly only as long as the Roman prefect and the Jewish High Priest could get along.

When we first got to Judea, Pilate sent his troops into Jerusalem with their standards. They had arrived at night and in the morning the Jews saw them and took offense. The Jews appealed to Pilate to have the standards removed but Pilate felt his authority was being challenged. After all, he had told the soldiers to remove all the images and effigies, thinking that would meet the Jews' requirements. How could he now back down and yet save face?

Five days later, after much deliberation, Pilate sent the soldiers to surround the protesting Jews. The demonstrators fell on the ground, baring their necks and saying they would rather die than suffer this desecration of their Mosaic law. Pilate was impressed with their dedication and ordered the standards removed.

Sometime later, Pilate wished to honor Tiberius by setting up golden shields in the Herod's palace in Jerusalem. The Jews didn't like that either. They were simple, gold plated shields without any images on them at all. How picky were these people? They appealed to Pilate to remove them. When he saw no reason to do so, they sent letters to Tiberius. Tiberius wrote to Pilate, rebuking him for violation of precedent (previous prefects were apparently more considerate of Jewish customs) and ordering the removal of the shields and their transfer to Caesarea.

Pilate tried to do good for these ungrateful people. The city of Jerusalem had a need for a reliable water supply. Pilate wanted to put in an aqueduct like the one in Caesarea. Rather than put an additional tax on the people, Pilate worked out a deal with the high priest to use some of the temple funds to pay for it. The people were incensed that the temple money was used for a secular purpose, never mind that it was for their benefit. The high priest acted like he knew nothing about any agreement and that Pilate had stolen the money.

Pilate had had it with these Jews. He sent mercenary soldiers into the crowd, disguised as locals, while he spoke to the people about the good reasons for the aqueduct. When the Jews again protested, he signaled the soldiers to randomly attack, beat, and kill. It silenced the protestors, but for how long? And Pilate was again rebuked by Tiberius. Is it any wonder that Pilate was cautious after that when dealing with the Jews and their complaints?

We were again in Jerusalem for the Jewish Passover. It wasn't that we wanted to participate. It's just that the population in Jerusalem grew so much during this feast that Pilate had to be there in person to keep a lid on things. The trouble started early on Friday morning. The temple authorities brought a man named Jesus of Nazareth to be judged by Pilate. Apparently they had found him guilty of some Jewish law and wanted Pilate to pronounce a death sentence. Whatever their original complaint had been, when they brought him to Pilate they accused Jesus of claiming to be a king.

When Jesus was standing before him, Pilate asked, "Are you the King of the Jews?" Jesus answered him, "You have said so". But while the Jews were accusing him, he had nothing to say. Pilate asked Jesus if he could hear the things he was being accused of. Jesus still didn't answer. Pilate was amazed and said to the chief priests and the crowds, "I find no guilt in this man." But they were urgent, saying, "He stirs up the people, teaching throughout all Judea, from Galilee even to this place."

When Pilate heard that Jesus was a Galilean, he thought he could pass him on to Herod, who was also in the city for Passover. But Herod sent him back with no judgment having been made. Despite being still stuck with the Jesus problem, Pilate became friends with Herod from that day on.

Pilate brought Jesus before the crowd again. He told them that he could not find Jesus guilty of any of the charges, nor could Herod. Then he said he would punish Jesus and release him. But they continued their cry, "Crucify him, crucify him."

Of course, I didn't know all this at the time; Pilate related all of it to me later. I had had a dream during the night. The trial of Jesus was well underway when I awoke. When I heard the crowd outside, I asked my servant what the commotion was. When she told me what was going on, I had to send a message to Pilate right away. "Have nothing to do with that righteous man, for I have suffered much because of him today in a dream." I couldn't even explain the dream. There was just this feeling of impending doom. I stayed behind the pillars, watching what next occurred.

Pilate made another attempt. There was a custom among the Jews that the prefect would release one prisoner at the time of their Passover feast. Pilate was certain they would not want someone like Barabbas. Barabbas was truly a criminal. He had been leading a group he said was going to bring back the land to the control of the Jews and throw off the Romans. That alone would have been a crime against the state. In reality he was just a thief and murderer and his followers a malicious band of brigands. Barabbas was the one who deserved to die, so that is whom Pilate offered. But he also offered to release Jesus instead, believing the crowd would take the meeker man.

They surprised him. The temple authorities persuaded the crowd to ask for Barabbas and destroy

Jesus. Pilate again said to them, "Which of the two do you want me to release for you?" And they said, "Barabbas." Pilate said to them, "Then what shall I do with Jesus who is called Christ?" They called out, "Let him be crucified!" Pilate asked, "Why, what evil has he done?" But they shouted all the more, "Let him be crucified!" Then they added, "If you let this man go, you are no friend of Caesar."

Pilate saw that he was gaining nothing and a riot was beginning. He felt he could not risk another letter being sent to Tiberius. Trying to rid himself of the whole thing, he took water and washed his hands before the crowd, saying, "I am innocent of this man's blood; see to it yourselves." The people called down a curse on themselves, yelling, "His blood be on us and on our children!"

Barabbas was released. The innocent man standing before Pilate, already beaten and bloody with a crown of thorns on his head, was ordered scourged again. Then Jesus was delivered to be crucified. It was ironic. The master criminal was released while two of his band were to be executed along with an innocent man.

I retired to my room and stayed there until it was time to go back to Caesarea. But rumors still reached my ears. They said that two days after Jesus was crucified he was seen by some of his followers. Others said his followers had stolen the body on Sunday morning. All I knew was that Jesus had not been an ordinary criminal.

I could tell Pilate was shaken. He spent as little time in Jerusalem after that as he possibly could. He was cautious about doing anything to upset the temple authorities, but he had nothing but disdain for them. He knew his career was going nowhere, no matter what he did.

Part of Pilate's area of responsibility included Samaria, a nation that lay between Judea and their northern province of Galilee. Someone had spread the word that it was in his power to find the sacred vessels that Moses had hidden on Mount Gerizim. Moses was the greatest prophet of both the Samaritans and Jews. Large numbers of armed Samaritans gathered at the mountain. Pilate was certain that the reason given was a smokescreen for some other, more important, plot and quickly sent forces to attack them at a village named Tirathana. The Samaritans were routed and many were captured and killed that day. The Samaritans appealed to Vitellius, who was the legate in Syria and ranked between Pilate and Tiberius. The Samaritans claimed that nothing political had been planned and they complained about Pilate's entire administration.

That was the last straw. Pilate was summoned to Rome to answer the charges. Before we got there, Tiberius died. By itself, his death would not have been damning, but it coincided with the downfall of Pilate's mentor, Sejanus. Without the backing of Sejanus, Pilate could not keep his position in Judea. Judea wasn't the best spot in the world, but it had been profitable. And who knew what he would get instead?

Caligula became emperor. Any friend of the disgraced Sejanus was his enemy. Pilate was exiled to Gaul. I could have stayed in Rome and lived an easier life. But what is life without the man you love?

We had been here for almost three years when I got the worst news of my life. Pilate was late coming home. I was greeted by Pilate's servant. He told me Pilate had committed suicide. I think life defeated him. He did his best for Rome and for me. For Rome, it never was enough.

Strangely, I received word from Caligula that I am welcome back in Rome. Maybe I should go. There is nothing left for me here. I've heard there is a group in Rome made up of followers of this Jesus of Nazareth. Perhaps they will have some answers for me, answers to the questions I have been asking myself since his death. Could he really be a son of a god? I should go. They tell me I should look up a woman named Prisca, the wife of a tentmaker named Aquila. Yes, I will leave tomorrow.

Mary of Jerusalem

Sometimes people ask me if I miss my privacy. Many different people have walked through my door over the years. At times there have been so many people here that one could hardly turn around without bumping into someone else.

Looking back, that first group of people seems small compared to those who meet here now. I had sent my son, John Mark, out to draw water. He met up with two men whom he brought to the house. They were disciples of Jesus, whom I knew to be a great prophet. They asked where the guest room was because their teacher wanted to have the Passover supper here. Naturally, I showed them the large upper room which would be appropriate for a group of thirteen.

That was the night Jesus was captured. He was crucified the next day. The evening of the third day, the disciples and some of Jesus' other followers were gathered here in my house with the doors bolted shut. We were afraid that the authorities would be after the disciples next. They might actually be after all of us. There were stories from some of the women that Jesus had been seen alive that day, but most of us could not believe that. Then, suddenly, he was standing right there in the middle of us.

This convinced all of us that he was truly risen from the dead. Jesus continued to show himself to us for more than a month after that. Sometimes he would come to individuals, like he did to his brother, James. Mostly he came to just the eleven disciples, but he came to many others of us as well. One time he showed up where 500 of us had gathered to pray.

Eventually the day came when he left us again. Thomas, one of his disciples, told me later that they had been on the mountain side near Bethany. Jesus had said to them, "All authority in heaven and on earth has been given to me. Go therefore and make disciples of all nations, baptizing them in the name of the Father and of the Son and of the Holy Spirit, teaching them to observe all that I have commanded you. And behold, I am with you always, to the end of the age." He told them to stay in Jerusalem to wait for the Holy Spirit.

Where would they wait? My house was big enough for far more than 13. There were about 150 of us gathered here when, ten days later, it happened. There was a sound like a rushing wind. When we looked around there seemed to be flames of fire hovering over everyone's head. People were filled with the Spirit and began speaking in languages they had not known before.

We went outside to where there were people gathered from all over the world to celebrate Pentecost in Jerusalem. Everyone there was able to understand one of us as we spoke of the kingdom of God. The priests thought we were babbling drunkenly. It was only nine in the morning! Peter got everyone's attention and preached his first sermon.

He quoted the prophecy of Joel where it was written, "And in the last days it shall be, God declares, that I will pour out my Spirit on all flesh, and your sons and your daughters shall prophesy, and your young men shall see visions, and your old men shall dream dreams; even on my male servants and female servants in those days I will pour out my Spirit, and they shall prophesy. And I will show wonders in the heavens above and signs on the earth below, blood, and fire, and vapor of smoke; the sun shall be turned to darkness and the moon to blood, before the day of the Lord comes, the great and magnificent day. And it shall come to pass that everyone who calls upon the name of the Lord shall be saved."

The first part of the prophesy had come to pass. The second part would occur when Jesus returns. Peter said Jesus was the fulfillment of other prophesies. Jesus, who was crucified and whom God raised up from the dead. Many, cut to the heart, asked what they should do. Peter said to them, "Repent and be baptized every one of you in the name of Jesus Christ for the forgiveness of your sins, and you will receive the gift of the Holy Spirit." He continued to exhort them, saying, "Save yourselves from this crooked generation." So those who received his word were baptized, and there were added that day about three thousand souls. The church was born.

We called ourselves followers of The Way. The disciples preached of Jesus every day and every day more joined our numbers. We worked together, many selling much of their properties and contributing to the common fund so that no one was in need. My nephew, Barnabas, sold everything he had. I sold some of my property, but kept my house. It would remain a meeting place for the church.

Some of us had been given much in terms of worldly goods. Others were not so richly gifted. As I said, no one was in need, but it took a lot of work to see that everyone was given what they needed from the common storehouse. The disciples found that so much of their time was taken with that that they didn't feel they had enough time for teaching. So they appointed some of the others as deacons to handle the food issues.

One of these men was Stephen. Even though the deacons' main job was to take care of the food distribution, Stephen found time to do some preaching himself. But he ran into trouble. There was a synagogue called that of the Freedmen. Some of those men rose up and disputed with Stephen, but they could not withstand his wisdom and the Spirit with which he was speaking. They stirred up some other men to accuse Stephen of blasphemy against Moses and God. Then they grabbed him and brought him before the council.

When the high priest heard the accusations he asked Stephen if they were true. Stephen answered with a retelling of our history, starting with Abraham. This did not satisfy anyone and they became enraged, but Stephen remained calm. He said, "Behold, I see the heavens opened, and the Son of Man standing at the right hand of God." The ones causing the trouble only got angrier. They cried out with a loud voice, stopped their ears, and rushed together at him.

They dragged him out of the city and stoned him. Some of us had followed, but we were unable to help. As they were stoning Stephen, he called out, "Lord Jesus, receive my spirit." Falling to his knees he cried out with a loud voice, "Lord, do not hold this sin against them." When he had said this, he died.

The incident with Stephen seemed to set off a larger persecution against the followers of The Way. Our worst enemy was a man named Saul, who had been at the stoning, holding the cloaks of those who were throwing the stones. He was a Pharisee and a friend of the high priest and so was easily able to get permission to arrest and jail, and sometimes order the killing of, any member of the church.

Then even King Herod got into the picture. He arrested and killed James, one of Jesus' closest disciples. When he saw how it pleased the temple authorities, Herod had Peter arrested as well. The rest of us gathered at my house to pray for his release.

We were sitting around the fire late that night, focused on our prayers. My servant girl, Rhoda, came running to us out of the darkness. She was so excited, she could hardly get her words out. She said Peter was at the gate. We knew she had to have been mistaken; Peter was in jail under lock and key. Some of those gathered said Rhoda was out of her mind. When she insisted, they said it was probably his angel.

We believe that God has given us each a guardian angel who reflects the appearance of the one they are guarding. She kept insisting and everyone became silent. Now we could hear the knocking. I went to open the gate myself. We couldn't have been more astonished; it was Peter!

Everyone was now clamoring, asking how he had escaped. Peter motioned with his hand for all to be quiet and told us what happened. He had been sleeping, chained to two soldiers with additional sentries guarding the door. He was struck on the side and when he woke up and looked, there was a light in the cell and an angel standing there. The angel said, "Get up quickly," and the chains just fell off. They clanked onto the floor, but nobody else noticed anything. The soldiers remained sleeping.

The angel told him to get dressed, put on his sandals, and wrap his cloak around him. Then they just walked out. The angel was real but Peter said he thought at the time that he was seeing a vision. When they had passed the sentries and reached the iron gate, it opened on its own accord. They started down the street and the angel just disappeared. Looking around, Peter realized that it was not a vision. He said to himself, "Now I am sure that the Lord has sent his angel and rescued me from the hand of Herod."

When he realized this, he came straight to my house, knowing there would be a group of us gathered here. He told us to let James, who was Jesus' brother and a leader of our group, know what happened. Then, not being a fool, Peter left the city.

It wasn't long after that when Herod got what was due him. Herod had gone from Judea to Caesarea. While there, some of the people of Tyre and Sidon came to sue for peace. Herod had been upset with them and they wanted to smooth things out because they depended on Herod's domain for their food. Herod put on his royal robes, took his seat on the throne and delivered a speech. The sycophants shouted, "The voice of a god, and not of a man." The egotistical man accepted the praise instead of giving God the glory. An angel of the Lord struck him down. His stomach was eaten by worms and he died five days later.

Things settled down a little in Jerusalem. Barnabas and Saul returned from their mission trip and brought my son with them. I was able to enjoy his company for a while until Barnabas took him on another trip.

Sapphira

Where is that man? Ananias went to the temple two hours ago to deliver the proceeds from selling that extra property. Our neighbors should have heard about it already and be knocking on our door to thank us.

Let me explain. I had heard of Jesus before, even listened to his talks once or twice. I knew he was more than the run of the mill prophet that pops up here in Judea and even Galilee every so often. When he was seen walking around after he had been crucified and buried, a lot of people were convinced that this was the Son of God. Ananias and I joined the followers of The Way. Ever since Peter gave that sermon on Pentecost, more and more people have been joining the followers of Jesus.

Peter and John are the leaders of the group. They had been some of Jesus' closest associates. Jesus had done many miracles and healed many people in his time here on earth. Since he left, his disciples were also able to heal people.

There were so many people among the followers of The Way that a system was set up to handle the money. There is a common treasury through which all the widows and children in need are provided for. That is all well and good as far as it goes. But don't you think people need to hang on to some of their property too so they don't become a burden on the church?

Ever since Barnabas sold his land and turned over the money, people have been saying how kind and wonderful he is. And he acts like it doesn't matter to him and he did it from the goodness of his heart. Well, maybe he did. But there's no reason other people can't get some praise for doing the same, or at least doing something similar.

Ananias had a piece of property that had been sitting idle for the last year. We figured that since we managed without it being productive for that length of time it wouldn't hurt us to sell it and give some of that money to the church. We thought about giving it all to Peter for the church, but then we thought about some of the things we had been wanting to get and decided to keep some of the proceeds.

Surely the church wouldn't miss ten percent or so. That still left a lot of money to give. Peter, nor anyone else, would never even have to know how much we sold it for. If Ananias said what he gave them was the sale price, who could say differently? If we wait a while before spending the money we kept, no one would even make the connection.

It has been a while since Barnabas sold his property and people are still talking about how generous he was. Even after taking our ten percent, the balance was more than what Barnabas had given. Surely the praise heaped on Ananias would be even greater than that given to Barnabas. I could hold my head up high when I go walking in the streets.

It's been three hours now and he is still not home. I want to hear how he was thanked. I want to be able to tell people what we did, but I can't do that until I know it has been taken care of. I guess I'd better go to the temple myself and find out what is going on.

Tabitha

I had never been really sick before. Sure, I got the sniffles once in a while, but I never had to take to my bed. I was the one they called on when someone else was sick or in need.

I guess you could say I made a name for myself with the clothes I made, but that was never my goal. I had a talent for sewing, so that is what I did. Unlike the other widows in Joppa, I was well off. When they needed a garment and could not afford one, I could. I was able to just look at a person and know what size to make it.

I was also able to take food to the widows and the fatherless children. If I was able to help anyone, I did. I wasn't trying to win any popularity contests; I just wanted to help.

As a child of Abraham, I went to the temple in Jerusalem as often as I could. And I always went to the synagogue here in Joppa on Sabbath. I followed all the prescribed rituals and thought I was doing God's will by following all the rules.

Until that Pentecost. When Peter was standing there preaching, I felt something in my heart and soul. Peter said Jesus was the fulfillment of the prophesies. I knew and understood. I was baptized that very day along with a multitude of others.

So I was no longer doing things to fulfill the requirements in the Law of Moses. I was doing things in response to the love of Jesus, who died on that cross for me. If he did that for me, I had to do whatever I could for others.

But then I got sick. At first I just seemed to be incredibly tired. When I got weaker and feverish, I took to my bed. The tables were turned. I could no longer help the other widows. No, they came to comfort me. Then I fell into a deep sleep.

The first thing I saw when I opened my eyes was Peter. What was he doing in my room? He gave me his hand and helped me up. Then he took me to see the others who were waiting downstairs. While I had felt wrung out when I'd gone to sleep, I was now feeling better than ever.

My friends had to explain to me what had happened. My servant girl had found me unresponsive. When she could not wake me, she called some of the other women in town, women I had previously helped. I was dead! They washed my body and brought it to the upper room.

The other believers, the disciples here, heard that Peter was in nearby Lydda and sent for him. When he arrived, these people I had helped were weeping. They hurried to get some of the garments I had made for them so they could show Peter. Peter sent them all out of my room. And I woke up. His friends told me that after sending my friends out, he knelt down and prayed. Turning to me he said, "Tabitha, arise." And that's when I woke up.

I asked Peter and those with him to stay awhile in my house. He thought it would be more appropriate to stay in the house of my neighbor, Simeon, who was a tanner. It took me a bit to see the statement he was making by choosing to stay with Simeon.

Most of the people in Joppa still lived within the Law of Moses. Tanners worked with animal corpses. Touching a dead animal, according to the law, made a person unclean. Peter was showing that this was no longer the case.

Word got around that I was alive again. Peter was busy for days, preaching the good news of what Jesus did for all of us. Many more believed on the Lord. My dying and coming back to life seemed to help people believe in him.

Lydia

My husband and I came down to Philippi from Thyatira about ten years ago. He was a merchant, dealing with the sale of purple cloth. He had heard that there was a large population of murex off the coast of Philippi. It was more profitable to deal in purple if one had direct access to the source of the dye. Murex was a certain type of ocean mollusk, the only type to produce this dye.

Two years after we got here we had established a booming business. Unfortunately, this made our shop a target for thieves. My husband was killed in an attempted robbery. The townspeople took care of the would-be thief and I have not had any trouble since. I do miss Ari though.

I guess what got me through it all was my faith in the God of the Jews. I am not Jewish myself, but I learned of their God from some of the God- fearers in Philippi. I knew that their God had promised to send someone, the Messiah, to rescue them. I wasn't sure what that meant though. Their God, whom they addressed as Adonai, was the God who created the world. I knew him to be the only true God, not like the multitude of pretenders we Greeks had learned about from childhood or the deified Roman emperors.

Somehow, I became a leader of the God-fearers in Philippi. A group of mostly women, we would meet for prayer every Sabbath at the riverside. Normally, this meeting would occur in a synagogue, but there were not ten Jewish men in the entire city so there was no synagogue. Many times some of the others believers would meet at my house to read from their scriptures.

So the riverside is where we were one Sabbath when we were joined by some visitors to the city. Their leader's name was Paul. He was accompanied by his friend and personal physician, Luke, and another friend named Silas. We sat there for hours as Paul told of the man they believed to be the long awaited Messiah. They said his name was Jesus and that he had been punished for our misdeeds. They said that Jesus was God and the Son of God. I found this difficult to believe because the Jews had always said that there is only one God. To complicate matters more, Paul said there was also the Holy Spirit who was God. He explained that this didn't mean there were three Gods, but that there are three persons in one God. I still can't really explain that but I do believe it.

Paul's preaching moved my heart. By the end of the afternoon, I too was a follower of The Way, one of those who believed that Jesus was indeed the Son of God, the promised Messiah, and that he suffered death and rose again. He took our punishment for our sins upon himself and suffered the consequences so we don't have to. Someday he will come again and take all those who believe in him to heaven to be with him. What joy I felt!

Some of the women, myself included, were then baptized by Paul in the name of this Triune God. Even greater joy! When the other women returned to their homes, I invited Paul and his group to mine. I gathered my entire household together to listen to this good news Paul was bringing to us. Then we headed back to the river so they could all be baptized as well.

Paul and Luke indicated that they were going to stay in Philippi for a while and I prevailed upon them to stay at my home. Thanks to the success of my business, I was able to maintain a large home with enough servants to provide for many guests.

One day when we were again headed out to the river we were followed by someone who was possessed by a demon. She was but a young girl and a slave who, by her fortune telling, brought much wealth to her owners. This was not the first time she followed us. She followed Paul anytime he stepped out of the house. She would cry out, "These men are servants of the Most High God, who proclaim to you the way of salvation." Although this was certainly true, it became annoying for Paul and his fellow travelers because she was so loud and disturbing everyone around her, making it difficult for him to preach. After many days of this, Paul turned and said to the spirit, "I command you in the name of Jesus Christ to come out of her." And it came out immediately.

This was a blessing for the girl who was now in her right mind. However, when her owners saw that their hope of gain was gone, they seized Paul and Silas and dragged them into the marketplace before the rulers. They accused them saying, "These men are Jews, and they are disturbing our city. They advocate customs that are not lawful for us as Romans to accept or practice." The crowd which had gathered joined in attacking them, and the magistrates tore the garments off them and gave orders to beat them with rods. After they had inflicted many blows upon them, they threw them into prison, ordering the jailer to keep them safely. Paul, Silas, and Luke were all put into the inner prison and had their feet fastened in the stocks.

After they were released, Paul came and told me the rest of the story before leaving the city. About midnight Paul and Silas were praying and singing hymns to God. The prisoners were listening to them when suddenly there was a great earthquake and the foundations of the prison were shaken. I could feel the quake in my house too. Immediately all the doors were opened and everyone's bonds were unfastened. The jailer woke up and drew his sword to kill himself. He figured the prisoners had all escaped and he would pay for it with his life after being tortured. But Paul cried with a loud voice, "Do not harm yourself, for we are all here." The jailer called to the other guards to light the lanterns and he rushed in. He was trembling with fear when he fell down before Paul and Silas.

The jailer had heard about what Paul and Silas had been preaching and asked "Sirs, what must I do to be saved?" They told him what they had said to us, "Believe in the Lord Jesus, and you will be saved, you and your household." Then they all went to his house where Paul and Silas continued to preach. The jailer tended to their wounds from the beating. He and his family were then baptized. After feeding them, the jailer returned them to the prison.

The leaders of the city must have seen the girl's owners had no real case, for they sent the police to the jail to release Paul and his associates. When the jailer told this to Paul, Paul said "They have beaten us publicly, uncondemned, men who are Roman citizens, and have thrown us into prison; and do they now throw us out secretly? No! Let them come themselves and take us out."

The police reported these words to the city leaders who were afraid when they heard that Paul and his company were Roman citizens. It was against the law to treat citizens in this manner, so the city leaders came and apologized to them. They took them out of jail and asked them to leave the city.

First Paul returned to my house and told us all that had transpired. We gathered everyone who had been meeting in my house. When greetings and encouragements had been exchanged, Paul, Silas, and Luke went on their way, their next destination being Thessalonica.

While they were here in Philippi, they had preached to many people. We had established a good sized group who met regularly in my house. I served them with joy and we studied the scriptures in the light of the good news that had been shared with us. Little by little, our church continued to grow. Praise God the Father for sending his Son!

Prisca

Originally from the area of Pontus, we had been living peacefully in Rome before the expulsion. Aquila and I are tentmakers. We are also Jews, and that was our crime under Claudius.

We are Jews, but we are also Christians. We had been to Jerusalem several times for the various feasts that are held there three times each year. On one of those trips, we stopped to listen to a man named Peter who was preaching in the temple. He told of Jesus, a man who was at the same time God himself. He told how this Jesus had lived a perfect life and died a horrible death, all to save us from being punished for our sins. On the third day he raised himself from death. This was the Messiah, the Anointed One, or Christ, who had been promised to our forefathers. Our hearts stirred within us and we knew the truth of what he was saying. We were baptized that same day.

At first, those who trusted Jesus had been called followers of The Way. In some circles we still are. Some of the people around the believers in Antioch derisively called them Christians. They took pride in being called after the name of Christ and we now wear it as a badge of honor.

We were not a new religion by any means. Those of us who were Jews are still Jews. The life, death, and resurrection of Jesus was the fulfillment of the prophecies. He did not come only to the Jews, but for all mankind. We do not require the believing non-Jews to convert and become God-fearers. The rules of Torah were fulfilled by Jesus and we are no longer commanded to fulfill them ourselves. We were never really good at that anyway. We are joined by the term Christians, people who believe that Jesus lived and died for us.

When we arrived in Rome we found a gathering of like - minded people, fellow Christians, and settled in. We started holding meetings in our own house when the group became too large to meet in one place. We tried to live peacefully, but some people had conflicts.

There were some Jewish Christians who still thought we should be strictly obeying Torah, including having all the males circumcised. There was a large group of Jews who still rejected Jesus. And there were some Christians who tried to convert others by force. These three groups would occasionally have run-ins, drawing the attention of the Roman authorities.

The population of Rome had grown beyond its capacity, as it often does. The emperor Claudius was looking at ways to control the growth. Seeing the friction among the Jews, he ordered all Jews to leave Rome.

Though we were leaving a profitable business behind, Aquila and I moved to Achaia, to the city of Corinth. It was a fairly large metropolis, near the port of Cenchrea where we thought we could reestablish ourselves.

We had been going to the synagogue in Corinth each Sabbath. It was there we first heard Paul speak, not long after we had arrived. He was a fiery preacher, telling about Jesus as we had heard Peter do back in Jerusalem. There was always a crowd gathered and we hadn't had a chance to talk with him yet.

Early one morning, Paul found us. He was also a tentmaker and was looking for work. We offered him work and invited him to stay with us in our home. He stayed with us in Corinth for a year and a half. We became very close in that time and Paul started calling me Priscilla, which only my closest friends and family did. A short while after Paul had joined us, two of Paul's fellow preachers came from Macedonia and we made room for them as well.

At first Paul preached only in the synagogues. Some of the Jews violently opposed him and the day came when Paul had enough of their harassment. He shook out his garments and said to them, "Your blood be on your own heads! I am innocent. From now on I will go to the Gentiles."

With that, he moved his preaching station to the house of a man named Titius Justus, a worshiper of God whose house was next door to the synagogue. Many of the Greeks believed and were baptized. Crispus, the ruler of the synagogue, also believed in the Lord, along with his whole household.

The Jews would not tolerate Paul's presence indefinitely. One day they united to make an attack on him, bringing him before Gallio, the proconsul of Achaia. They complained that Paul was teaching people to worship God contrary to the law. Paul did not get a chance to speak before Gallio said, "If it were a matter of wrongdoing or vicious crime, O Jews, I would have reason to accept your complaint. But since it is a matter of questions about words and names and your own law, see to it yourselves. I refuse to be a judge of these things." With that he abruptly dismissed them.

When Crispus had been baptized, the Jews made Sosthenes the ruler of the synagogue. But he too had come to trust in Jesus. Not being able to do anything to Paul, the Jews abducted Sosthenes and beat him in front of the tribunal. But Gallio paid no attention to any of this.

After this, Paul stayed about a month before he moved on. Aquila and I went with him. Our first stop was in the port of Cenchrea where Paul cut his hair and made a vow. Then we went to Ephesus. Aquila and I established our business there and opened our home to the church as we had done wherever we lived. Paul tried again to reason with the Jews in the synagogue. We settled in Ephesus while Paul moved on to Syria, to the church in Antioch. We had asked him to stay longer, but his plans were set. He promised to come to us again if it was God's will.

While we were in Ephesus, a young Jew came to us from Alexandria. An eloquent man, Apollos was very learned in the Scriptures and a Christian. Excited about the good news of Jesus, he spoke and taught about him constantly. But his knowledge was incomplete; he knew only the baptism of John.

Aquila and I heard him while he was speaking in the synagogue. We took him aside and explained to him the way of God more accurately.

Apollos wanted to go throughout Achaia to spread the word. Having been instructed more fully, the brothers encouraged him and wrote to the disciples to welcome him. We received good reports of his teaching. He greatly helped those who through grace had believed, for he powerfully refuted the Jews in public, showing by the Scriptures that Jesus was the Christ.

Paul was able to return to Ephesus but we missed him; we had gone back to Rome for a time. Paul eventually went back to Corinth. While we were in Rome, the church received a letter from him there, brought by our friend Phoebe who had been living in Cenchrea when we met her. We had again gone to Ephesus by the time Paul ended up in Rome. Our paths were not to cross again.

Paul's first trip to Rome was not at all as he had planned. When he was in Jerusalem, the Jews had attacked him in the temple. The Roman authorities had to step in to rescue him. He was kept as a prisoner, first in Caesarea, then in Rome where he remained under house arrest. He was released after two years in Rome but eventually returned on his own volition. Rome had a new emperor by then. Nero was a madman. He blamed the Christians for everything, including a devastating fire which he is rumored to have started himself. Nero had both Paul and Jesus' disciple, Peter, executed before taking his own life.

Meanwhile, a large church has been established in Ephesus. We have many different house churches, but remain one church in the Lord. We have seen quite a few of the church leaders here. Paul's close friend, Timothy, is here. The Lord's dearest friend, John, has been here with Jesus' mother, Mary. They had a home here until she went to heaven. Now John travels throughout and beyond the empire.

Jesus may have seemed insignificant to some, but he has changed the world. His church exists to spread the Good News of salvation. We are sinful creatures and deserve nothing but eternal damnation. But his love for us caused him to take that sin upon himself and pay for our transgressions. What should we do? As Paul said to the jailer in Philippi, "Believe in the Lord Jesus, and you will be saved, you and your household." And as Peter told those in Jerusalem, many years before that, "Repent and be baptized every one of you in the name of Jesus Christ for the forgiveness of your sins, and you will receive the gift of the Holy Spirit."

Phoebe

It was good to see Priscilla again. We had become good friends when she lived in Corinth and I lived in nearby Cenchrea, the port of Corinth. I had opened my home to the few others in my city who had become Christians before Paul first arrived in Achaia. Priscilla had heard about our church and sought us out when she and her husband, Aquila first arrived from Rome.

When Paul came to Corinth, Priscilla and Aquila invited him to stay with them. We all became good friends, busy with spreading the Good News of Jesus the Christ. Between those efforts, we conducted our businesses. They made tents; I had a weaving business. We dealt with many of the same customers. That was how we supported ourselves, but our real vocation was spreading the Good News.

There was a lot of travel in the early days of the church. Their group left Corinth, stopping in Cenchrea before heading out to Ephesus. Priscilla and her husband eventually went back to Rome. Paul traveled all over the place and ended up back here in Corinth. We visit each other's homes whenever the opportunity presents itself.

Paul has established many churches throughout the world. He travels often, but also writes many letters. He sends those letters out with whoever is headed in the direction of his audience. When I had to go to Rome for business, Paul had a letter for me to take along for the churches there.

Although Paul dearly wanted to get to Rome himself, he had not yet been able to do so. The church there was started by Jews, like Priscilla and Aquila, who had been in Jerusalem when Peter had preached to the crowds there for Pentecost and, in effect, started the church. Until Paul could make the arrangements, the letter would have to do.

Paul had issues to address with the Romans. For one thing, he needed to clarify to some that this life was not about obeying the laws of the Jewish patriarchs. The law shows sin; it does not bring salvation. Breaking one law is the same as breaking all. None of us can keep the law and that is why we need Jesus. It isn't circumcision of the body that is important, but circumcision of the heart. So, Jew or Greek, we are all the same.

The emphasis is really that we are not saved by law but by grace. And that is not something we do for ourselves, it is something Jesus has done for us. I guess that is too "easy" for some to accept. That doesn't mean we are free to do anything we want though. As Christians we are to do good, not to gain forgiveness, but because we have received forgiveness.

I remember reading the letter to those gathered to hear it. Paul said, "Let love be genuine. Abhor what is evil; hold fast to what is good. Love one another with brotherly affection. Outdo one another in showing honor. Do not be slothful in zeal, be fervent in spirit, serve the Lord. Rejoice in hope, be patient in tribulation, be constant in prayer. Contribute to the needs of the saints and seek to show hospitality. Bless those who persecute you; bless and do not curse them. Rejoice with those who rejoice, weep with those who weep. Live in harmony with one another. Do not be haughty, but associate with the lowly. Never be wise in your own sight. Repay no one evil for evil, but give thought to do what is honorable in the sight of all. If possible, so far as it depends on you, live peaceably with all. Beloved, never avenge yourselves, but leave it to the wrath of God, for it is written, 'Vengeance is mine, I will repay, says the Lord.' To the contrary, 'if your enemy is hungry, feed him; if he is thirsty, give him something to drink; for by so doing you will heap burning coals on his head.' Do not be overcome by evil, but overcome evil with good." Wow, a tall order but again, not to earn forgiveness but because we have been given forgiveness.

It is difficult living under Roman rule. But Paul points out that it is our responsibility to support those who rule over us because God put them there. Therefore we are to pay our taxes and obey their laws, as long as those laws aren't contrary to the higher laws of God.

The only debt we should owe anyone is the debt of love. We ought not pass judgment on others; that is not our place. Nor are we to do anything that may cause another to stumble. For example, while we are free to eat whatever we desire, we are not free to cause our brother or sister despair by doing so.

Paul plans to go to Rome so he can encourage the faithful who are in Rome and they, in turn, can encourage him. As many of the churches have contributed to the charity sent to Jerusalem, those in Rome would have the opportunity to support the mission to Spain which Paul hoped to make after seeing the Roman Christians.

I have now taken care of sharing the letter. I have greeted my brothers and sisters in Christ, both old friends and new. I guess it's about time I head to the market place to take care of other business. To God be the glory.

Eunice

I have often wished I could have raised Timothy in the conventional Jewish tradition. I was raised that way. My parents were devoted Jews, and I'm sure they were very disappointed when I went off and married a Greek. My father died not long after that. I was sure it was of a broken heart.

When I was younger, I believed in God. I just didn't think we Jews had a monopoly on him and I didn't think we had to adhere to all that Jewish nonsense about rules and Sabbath and everything else that made us seem strange to the gentiles. I was only partly right. It wasn't nonsense.

My mother, Lois, and I reconciled when I became pregnant with my son, Timothy. She patiently re-introduced me to the faith of our fathers, the way it was meant to be. She said all our ceremonies were important because they pointed to the promised Messiah. The prophecies went all the way back to the beginning of time, when Adam and Eve sinned in the garden and were promised deliverance.

My husband, Alexander, was a good man. But part of what brought us together was that neither of us was really big on religious tradition. I already told you how I scorned my Jewishness. Alexander thought all the Greek and Roman gods were products of someone's imagination, which of course they were. Unlike me, he didn't believe in a god at all.

Getting back with my mother and my faith, I wanted to have Timothy circumcised when he was eight days old, according to tradition. Alexander wouldn't hear of it. Timothy was twelve when his father died and it just didn't seem right to put the boy through that at his age when he had just lost his father. Still, my mother and I had been able to teach the Jewish writings to Timothy from the time he was a baby. He had a good understanding of God's word.

We ran into Paul early in his travels. He had come to Lystra with his partner, Barnabas. The very first time we saw them, they were performing a miracle. There was a man sitting in the crowd who could not walk. I had seen this man many times, begging from all who passed him. I knew he had been crippled since birth. Yet Paul looked at him and said loudly, "Stand upright on your feet." We were all amazed when he sprang up and began walking.

On seeing this, those in the crowd who believed in the Greek gods, raised their voices to praise the strangers. "The gods have come down to us in the likeness of men!" they shouted. They called Barnabas Zeus, and Paul, Hermes, because he was the chief speaker. Even the priest of Zeus, whose temple was at the entrance to the city, brought oxen and garlands to the gates and wanted to offer sacrifices with the crowds.

When Barnabas and Paul heard that, they tore their garments and rushed out into the crowd, crying out, "Men, why are you doing these things? We also are men, of like nature with you, and we bring you good news, that you should turn from these vain things to a living God, who made the heaven and the earth and the sea and all that is in them." Despite what they said, they could hardly restrain the people from offering sacrifice to them.

But Jews had come from Antioch and Iconium. Paul and Barnabas had run into trouble there before coming to us. Now those Jews persuaded the crowds to drag Paul out of the city and stone him. They left him there, thinking he was dead. Those of us who had heard what he had really been saying gathered around him to help him. He was able to get up and reenter the city. The next day he went on with Barnabas to Derbe.

After a while, they returned to Lystra and preached to us some more. That was when we got the details about how Jesus had lived and died in our place. We could not have fulfilled the law, but he did. And then he took our punishment for us. We were forgiven. Even I was forgiven for my apostasy. Timothy, my mother, and I were among those who repented and were baptized before Paul and Barnabas returned to Antioch in Syria.

When Paul next returned to Lystra, he asked Timothy to accompany him. I hated to let him go, but I knew it was something he had to do. Because everyone knew that Timothy's father was a Greek and because they would be associating with traditional Jews, Paul had Timothy circumcised. Timothy has been traveling with Paul for years now. Sometimes

Paul sent him off on his own; sometimes Timothy came home for a visit. I may not have been able to raise Timothy in all the Jewish traditions, but there is no doubting his faith now.

Alexia Maria

It is tough being related to one of the most loved, hated, famous, infamous men in the known world. It isn't much easier being seen by Romans as a Jew and by Jews as a Roman.

I was born and raised in Tarsus. Years ago, in the time of Pompey, it was made the capital of the Roman province of Cilicia. Augustus made Tarsus a free city because that is where his friend, Athenodorus, was from. Most of her citizens at the time were granted Roman citizenship. My grandfather was one of them, thus my father and his children are also Roman citizens.

But we are Jews as well. My name reflects this. Alexia is Roman; Maria is from the Hebrew Miriam. I moved to Jerusalem when I married my brother's friend, Asher. You have probably heard of my brother, Saul. He is now known by the Greek form of his name, Paul.

Saul and Asher studied under the great rabbi, Gamaliel. Their faith was strong and they became good Pharisees. When people started calling Jesus of Nazareth, a crucified criminal, the Son of God, they were incensed. It was blasphemy, was it not?

Saul had always been a zealous person, but I think he went a little too far with his hatred of those who followed The Way. With the full backing of the Jewish council, the Sanhedrin, Saul went after the infidels, capturing many and putting them to death. Asher wasn't as outgoing as Saul, but he quietly backed up his efforts.

Imagine our surprise when we heard that Saul was going around telling everyone that this Jesus really was the Son of God. Asher was so upset that he stopped speaking to him. And he ordered me not to either. Saul, now called Paul, came back to Jerusalem from time to time and I heard more about what he was preaching.

There was real trouble this last time that Paul was here. He had gone to the temple daily as he usually did. After a few days of this, a group of Jews from Asia grabbed him and accused him of perdition. They said, "Men of Israel, help! This is the man who is teaching everyone everywhere against the people and the law and this place. Moreover, he even brought Greeks into the temple and has defiled this holy place." What I heard later was that he had really only brought them as far as the court of the gentiles. But these people were looking for trouble and bending the truth to support their accusations. They seized Paul and dragged him out of the temple in an attempt to kill him.

This was one time I was glad for the Roman troops stationed at the Fortress of Antonia adjacent to the temple. They rushed to the crowd and when the people saw the soldiers, they stopped beating Paul. Then the tribune came up and arrested him and ordered him to be bound with two chains. He inquired who Paul was and what he had done. Some in the crowd were shouting one thing, some another. Unable to get the facts, the tribune ordered Paul to be brought into the barracks. They actually had to carry Paul because of the press and violence of the crowd.

As he was being brought into the barracks, Paul asked the tribune for permission to speak to the crowd. Probably impressed that Paul spoke Greek, he granted permission.

Paul told them, “I am a Jew, born in Tarsus in Cilicia, but brought up in this city, educated at the feet of Gamaliel according to the strict manner of the law of our fathers, being zealous for God as all of you are this day.” He then summarized his persecution of The Way and how he had been converted by Jesus himself on one of his murderous trips. When the Jews heard the words of Paul’s conversion, they cried out for his death.

The tribune ordered Paul to be brought into the barracks to be examined by flogging to find out what was behind the uproar. When they stretched him out for the whips, Paul asked the centurion standing there if it was lawful to flog an uncondemned Roman citizen. Paul knew that it wasn’t. The centurion told the tribune what Paul had said. The tribune had bought his own citizenship, but Paul had gained it by birth. It frightened the tribune that they had even bound a Roman citizen.

The next day, Paul was brought before the council and set before them. The tribune wanted to know what was behind the commotion and hate. Paul set the Jews against each other instead of against him by bringing up the fact that the Sadducees disagreed with the Pharisees about the resurrection. The Pharisees took Paul's side as a dispute arose between the two parties. When the dissension became violent, the tribune, afraid that Paul would be torn to pieces by them, commanded the soldiers to go down and take him away from among them by force and bring him into the barracks.

I know all this because of what happened next. My son, Aaron, was in the crowd listening and overheard a plot against Paul's life. I told him he had to let Paul know. Then Paul called for the centurion to hear it.

More than 40 of the Asian Jews had made a vow to not eat or drink until they had killed Paul. They conspired with the chief priests and elders to have Paul brought to them for more questioning, planning to kill him before he got there. The centurion wanted to avoid a riot, so he got together a large contingent of soldiers, horsemen, and spearmen to escort Paul to Felix, the Roman governor, thereby averting the threat.

Paul's accusers came to Felix and made their case, poorly. Felix would not be fooled by them because he had a rather accurate knowledge of The Way, being married to Drusilla, a Jewess who had sought out the information. Felix put off the accusers and ordered Paul into liberal custody.

I don't know any of the details after that, but Paul was kept in Caesarea for years. Even Felix left before Paul did. When Porcius Festus took over, Paul was still in prison. Apparently, at some point, Paul appealed to Caesar. Since Paul is a Roman citizen, Festus had no choice but to send him to Rome.

That was the last I heard of Paul. As far as I know, he is still in prison in Rome.

Bernice

Word has just reached us of the volcano eruption in Pompeii. It has wiped out the entire city. I think my sister, Drusilla, was living there. Serves her right. We are both of the Herodian line, daughters of Agrippa I; I am no less a royal princess than she. In fact because I am the oldest, I should be held in higher regard.

I live in Rome now, the consort of Titus Flavius Vespasianus. I have a good deal of wealth and am using it to back Titus as the next emperor. I expect to be empress. Even now I am living as his wife.

Being married just didn't work out for me in the past. My first marriage was to Marcus Julius Alexander of Alexandrea. I suppose he was my one true love; but he died far too soon. I was then married to my uncle, Herod of Chalcis. We had two sons, Bernicianus and Hyrcanus. When he died, I went to live with my brother, Agrippa II. After several years there, I married Polemon II, king of Cilicia.

I had asked Agrippa to arrange this marriage to dispel the rumors that Agrippa and I were having an incestuous affair. I will not say if the rumors were true. If they were, it was nobody else's business. Polemon readily agreed to the marriage because of the wealth I brought with me. But Polemon was impossible to live with. Agrippa had made him be circumcised in order to marry me. I think he resented that and took out his resentment on me and my sons. I packed up my things and left, with my sons and my money, and returned to Agrippa. Because he never married, I functioned as his queen.

As royalty, we were obligated to call upon the new procurator in Judea soon after he took office. It was an extended visit and while we were there, Festus presented before us a case of a prisoner that had been left to him by his predecessor, Felix. When Felix had been in Jerusalem, the chief priests and elders presented their complaints to him and asked for a sentence of death. He told them he would honor custom and not make a judgment until the accused met the accusers face to face and had opportunity to make his defense concerning the charge laid against him.

As soon as he returned to Caesarea, Felix had the man, Paul, brought before him. The charges they brought were about their own religion, not Roman law. They had certain points of dispute with him about their religion and about a certain Jesus, who was dead, but whom Paul asserted to be alive. Not knowing just how to investigate those charges, he asked Paul if he wanted to go to Jerusalem to face the charges there. Paul, being a Romans citizen, appealed to the emperor. He was sitting in jail waiting to be sent to Rome. When Agrippa said he wanted to hear from Paul himself, Festus promised it would be done the next day.

The next day came and we entered the audience hall with the military tribunes and the prominent men of the city. Then, at the command of Festus, Paul was brought in. Festus presented Paul and said that he had found nothing in the man deserving of death. His problem with sending him to Caesar as requested was that he had no appropriate charges. "Therefore I have brought him before you all, and especially before you, King Agrippa, so that, after we have examined him, I may have something to write. For it seems to me unreasonable, in sending a prisoner, not to indicate the charges against him."

Agrippa said to Paul, "You have permission to speak for yourself." Then Paul stretched out his hand and made his defense. He said he was fortunate to give his defense before Agrippa since the king was familiar with the customs and controversies of the Jews.

Paul pointed out that, being a Pharisee, he had lived according to the strictest party of the Jews. He said that he was on trial because he believed the promises God made to the Patriarchs. Then he asked, "Why is it thought incredible by any of you that God raises the dead?"

Then he told of the time where he, himself, was opposing the name of Jesus of Nazareth, including locking up followers of The Way and having them put to death. He even went to foreign cities to hunt them down.

When Paul told of his conversion and the vision that had occasioned it, Festus said "Paul, you are out of your mind; your great learning is driving you out of your mind." But Paul said, "I am not out of my mind, most excellent Festus, but I am speaking true and rational words. For the king knows about these things, and to him I speak boldly. For I am persuaded that none of these things has escaped his notice, for this has not been done in a corner." Speaking directly to Agrippa, he asked, "Do you believe the prophets? I know that you believe." Agrippa said to Paul, "In a short time would you persuade me to be a Christian?" And Paul said, "Whether short or long, I would to God that not only you but also all who hear me this day might become such as I am—except for these chains."

After this, we all departed. We agreed that this man had done nothing to deserve death, or even imprisonment. Agrippa told Festus "This man could have been set free if he had not appealed to Caesar." I believe Festus would have set Paul free but was afraid it would be an affront to Caesar. No one would dare chance that.

In time, Nero became emperor and Festus was replaced by Clodius Albinus who was succeeded by Gessius Florus as procurator of the Judea Province. The Jews, who were never happy with Roman dominion to start with, became more resentful as they were discriminated against in favor of those they considered foreigners. Resentment turned to rebellion when Florus raided the temple treasure for taxes. The Jews rioted and the Romans responded with crucifixions. I went up to Jerusalem myself to ask Florus to be merciful to the Jews. He refused. I was nearly killed in the uprisings.

Agrippa also spoke to the Jews, sympathizing with them and asking for their cooperation in ending the conflict. When they turned on us and burnt our palaces we fled to Galilee and later turned ourselves over to the Romans.

By now it was all out war. The Romans moved into Jerusalem with the twelfth legion. Nero then sent Vespasian to Jerusalem to put down the rebellion. He was joined by his son, Titus, and together with three legions of 60,000 soldiers they marched across Galilee and up to Jerusalem.

A long, bloody war ensued. It was during this time however that I met Titus and we began our relationship. When Vespasian was declared emperor, Titus was left in Judea to finish putting down the rebellion. Less than a year later, Jerusalem was sacked and her temple destroyed. Titus returned to Rome but I had to stay behind.

It was four years before we saw each other again. Agrippa and I went to Rome. Agrippa was given the rank of praetor, or magistrate. I moved in with Titus in the palace. The Romans do not like me any more than the Jews did. They say I am an immoral woman. Who are they to talk? I will have my revenge when I become empress.

Printed in the United States
By Bookmasters